PRAISE FOR KANG YOUNG-SOOK

"Young-Sook's perceptive stories provide an unwavering and honest gaze at human nature."—*Publishers Weekly*

"Much as the title of [*At Night He Lifts Weights*] evokes a kind of physical exertion, so too do the stories within hum with a visceral quality. Sometimes, that quality works to turn the bizarre into something familiar; at others, it magnifies the extraordinary and often disconcerting experiences of these stories' protagonists."
—Tobias Carroll, Words Without Borders

"Perceptive and subversive, the stories in *At Night He Lifts Weights* vary in tone and genre, but each is singularly captivating, swirling around themes of loss — ecological destruction, loneliness, and death. Each has a subtle illusion of calm that conceals what lies below in the unnerving depths."
—Pierce Alquist, *Book Riot*

"The way in which the novel creates a family that accepts members from any nationality, sexual orientation, age, or gender has no precedent in Korean literature. Kang's unique style of writing is equally radical. Her imagery is bare yet powerful, almost discomfiting in its unfamiliarity, and certainly too innovative to categorize or name." --Kim Hyung-jung, *Hankook Ilbo*

OTHER BOOKS BY KANG YOUNG-SOOK

RINA

BY KANG YOUNG-SOOK

TRANSLATED BY BORAM CLAIRE KIM
AFTERWORD BY SO YOUNG HYUN

Curated by Janet Hong for the 2024 Translator Triptych

OPEN LETTER
LITERARY TRANSLATIONS FROM THE UNIVERSITY OF ROCHESTER

Originally published in Korean in 2011 by Random House Korea
Copyright © Kang Young-sook, 2011
Translation copyright © Boram Claire Kim, 2024
Afterword copyright © So Young Hyun, 2015

Published by arrangement with Dalkey Archive Press

First edition published by Dalkey Archive Press, 2015
First Open Letter edition, 2024

Library of Congress Cataloging-in-Publication Data: Available
ISBN (pb): 978-1-960385-08-6 | ISBN (ebook): 978-1-960385-04-8

Cover design by Eric Wilder

Printed on acid-free paper in the United States

Open Letter Books is the University of Rochester's literary translation press:
www.openletterbooks.org

RINA

Rina has two moons.
One of the moons may be bleeding
but the other one has so many spectra
that it is impossible to fathom.

TABLE OF CONTENTS

1

THE SOLDIERS SLOWLY APPROACHED THE TWENTY-TWO ESCAPEES, guns leveled. One of the escapees, a teenage girl who had been licking her lips with a parched tongue, jumped up and opened her mouth to say something.

"We told you not to move!" the soldiers yelled. The girl got back down on her knees and watched the soldiers. Although they were carrying guns, they too had hunger written all over their faces.

The girl's name was Rina[1]. She was short and had a thin face with yellow pimples on her forehead. Rina was sixteen years old, and her parents had been coalminers back home. Rina used to go to the youth vocational training center after school and assemble machine parts late into the night. Whenever she got sleepy or bored, she would pick up a screw, hold it up to her face, yell "Die, die!" at it, and toss it to the floor.

One of the soldiers approached the kneeling cluster of escapees. The worn rubber sole of his boot flapped open like the mouth of an angry toad every time he took a step. He crouched down in front of a little boy who sat crying and sniffling next to Rina, and tapped

---

1 The name derives from the Chinese characters *li* (俐), meaning clever, and *na* (娜), meaning beautiful, pretty, slender, or supple.

the boy's head with his finger. Rina could feel the boy trembling against her arm.

"Hey, kid, sing us a song. Come on, you must know some. Sing something you learned at school. I'm bored out of my mind here."

"I don't go to school," the boy answered, and burst into a louder refrain of sobs. His father, who sat a few paces away, made a face as he tried to comfort his son, but it was no use. The little boy's sobs echoed across the darkened border as if they were in a cave. There were rumors that little boys captured while fleeing the country were sold abroad and forced to work 36-hour days with no rest, while girls were circulated from one red-light district to the next and only released when they were diseased or dying. These stories mystified Rina. It was hard to decide which was worse: spending the rest of her life in a cramped house in a mining town pockmarked with graying sheets drying on laundry lines, or becoming a whore, if it meant getting a taste of life abroad.

"I'm a pretty good singer," Rina volunteered, but her offer was drowned out by the two toddlers of the group—a one-year-old and a three-year-old—who began wailing. Their hungry sobs dragged on piteously, but all their anxious mothers could do was pull out their breasts and shove them at the babies, like milk machines.

They said the border was a couple kilometers away. Rina had dreamt of it every night since the day her father had told her about their plans to escape. Every night, the border was flush with the sounds of wind, gunfire, and exploding columns of flames. Escapees captured while trying to cross over were stripped, lined up, executed by firing squad, and finally burned to black ash, all under the sullen gaze of the watchful owls.

Still, Rina had no doubt that the border, which hovered before her like a vast blue levee, would open itself up for her. The blue levee would flow toward her like a colossal wave and open up like a stairway to heaven. She believed that an invisible hand would gather up the escapees safely in a net and magically usher them across the border.

The group of twenty-two escapees was made up of three families and a group of young people who worked at a sewing factory. They were all from a region near the border where they had lived their whole lives. When Rina's father had first told her in a low voice that he had found some people to escape with, Rina hadn't believed him. Her father was incapable of even dreaming of crossing a border into a new world. His decision had reminded Rina of something she'd once been told by an ancient auntie who had died a few years back in a famine: "Everyone, even the biggest idiot, will face three challenges in her lifetime for which she will stake her life. When those three challenges are over, so is your life." It had been hard to understand the old lady's toothless mumblings, but that was the essence of her lesson.

The soldiers paced back and forth among the trembling escapees. All of them were still armed and many were smoking. All of a sudden, Rina's eye caught a round, white light approaching from far away. It looked small at first, but got bigger and bigger as it turned a brilliant blue.

"A light!" Rina yelled, in spite of herself. It turned out to be a small truck carrying food from the border checkpoint. The women clung to each other tearfully, fearing that this was the end. A man got out of the passenger seat, and was followed shortly by the driver. Together, they walked into the checkpoint watchhouse.

"Isn't that him?" the men whispered nervously to each other.

They could see the soldiers smoking through the lit windows of the watchhouse. A few minutes later, the man from the passenger seat of the truck came outside and assembled the fathers of each of the families. After a minute's quiet discussion, the fathers dispersed clumsily; their legs had fallen asleep. Turning their backs to each other, they pulled out wads of cash that had been secreted away in bundles or in undisclosed locations on their bodies. The man collected their money, licking his fingers to count the bills, and walked over into the watchhouse.

"Those sonsofbitches," the sewing factory workers fumed, trembling with rage. For a minute, it looked as though they were about to march into the watchhouse. Instead, they got back on their knees. While the men in the watchhouse enjoyed their feast, all the escapees could do was feed off the sounds of their own mouths watering.

After a long while, the man came out of the watchhouse. He wore tight-fitting pants, a jacket, and a hat that covered the contours of his face so that the subtleties of his features were obscured. Since it was impossible to escape directly to the country of P, their final destination, he was the first of several guides who would lead the escapees to a third-party nation, a number of which they would have to pass through to get to P. Their fates depended on this guide. When Rina saw his tanned face with its defined features, she felt a jolt of elation; she was sure she'd found the man she was destined to love.

Without a single gunshot fired, the twenty-two escapees crossed the border. The border wasn't on a wide levee stretched out like a blue band, nor was it on a river sparkling with the reflections of silvery lights from a pier. It was merely a part of a hilly path blocked off from an escape route. The moment she crossed the border, Rina felt like she could breathe again, as if a piece of candy that had been stuck in her throat had slipped down into her stomach.

Past the border, the road turned slightly downhill. The twenty-two—including the babies on their mothers' backs—quickened their pace, waddling like they had just jumped off a pot of burning coals. By now, it was so dark that the silhouette of the road was barely distinguishable, and the occasional pale flash of a sleeve or bundle were the only signs of human activity. The guide went first, quickly and quietly. It wasn't long before the elderly escapees ran out of breath and began to cough, and the babies let out scattered cries. With each step she took, Rina's toes burrowed so deeply into the ground that it felt like her feet were planted in the soil, and her ankles tingled, forcing her to stop and rest at intervals. Walking downhill was far more painful than trudging uphill.

Rina was sure that her father had purposely neglected to tell her the exact date and time of their escape. There was no way he would have left her younger brother behind, and since it would be hard for him to get remarried, he would have to take his wife along. Rina was sure that she was the only member of her family whose abduction or death by firing squad wouldn't break her father's heart. Even if Rina had known the exact date of their departure, it was doubtful she would have found a more appropriate pair of shoes for the journey. The only two pairs of shoes she owned had long since deteriorated into an unwearable state, and at this very moment, Rina couldn't help but think of all of the shoes she'd seen her friends wear to school. *If only dad had told me sooner, I would've stolen a pair of those comfortable-looking white sneakers with the thick soles.*

None of them knew how many borders they would have to cross to get to the country of P, but at any rate, they soon arrived at the mouth of the river leading into the first third-party nation. The guide took his shoes off, rolled up his pants to his knees, and waded into the river. They plodded in after him. The river was low after a drought, barely reaching Rina's waist. As they stepped into the water, the people turned around to face the border they had just crossed and bowed, rubbing their palms together. Rina had to be carried across on the back of one of the men from the sewing factory. It made her so nervous that she clenched her buttocks the whole way.

The river was crawling with processions of people fleeing the country. No one spoke, no one asked what route you had taken to cross the border, or what your reasons were for fleeing. The night was filled with shadows and the sound of legs slicing through water.

The processions of escapees spread out across the riverbank. Just under the riverbank was a pathway that led through to rice fields, and it was only once they got to that path that they fell back apart into their initial groups. After several minutes of walking, they were back to the original twenty-two. The twenty adults and two infants filed down the narrow path. The guide walked at the head of the line. Rina's father brought up the rear, and Rina was in front of him. Every so often, Rina had to calm herself by groping in the darkness to feel the back of the person walking in front of her.

"Let's take a break," the guide said. At his words, the twenty-two collapsed to the ground in a row, like magpies on a wire. The elderly were wracked by dry coughs. The babies started whining again, and their mothers stood up to suckle them, murmuring apologies for what was hardly their fault. Not wanting to be stuck in the back, Rina was walking up to the head of the line when she tumbled into a ditch. It was deeper than she had expected, and the guide had to help her out. Her mother, who had been sitting near the front of the line clutching Rina's brother in her arms, scolded her.

"If you don't stop acting so reckless, we'll leave you behind in this strange country!"

"You're the one who's reckless! Maybe they'll leave *you* behind."

The others snickered at this, and Rina's mother glared fiercely at her. She'd had Rina when she was nineteen years old. She would always remind her daughter of this whenever Rina did something wrong, and when Rina lashed out, her mother would laugh and say, "That means you'll be having a baby in three or four years, just like me, you smartass." Rina could never tell whether this was meant as a blessing or a curse. She resented her mother for carrying her little brother close in her arms wherever they went, and she hated her little brother, and this hatred was all she had right now to help her endure her hunger. The babies' cries grew louder. The guide took a handful of candy out of his jacket pocket, gave one to each of the mothers, and told them to keep their babies quiet.

The incline grew steeper until eventually they reached a low, naked mountain. Clearly, the shortage of firewood on this side of the border was just as bad as it was back home. In the spring, forest fires would break out on the slopes and rage until there was nothing left to burn.

They had climbed over the bare mountain and nearly reached level ground when they heard an explosion in the distance. To them it sounded like a hi-tech tank tearing through a jungle, but it turned out to be a single motorcycle. Even so, they all ran and hid deep in the forest, completely ignoring the guide's instructions. Rina wondered for a second where her family was, but she was too afraid of being discovered by the white spotlight to get up and look around. So, she lay face down, expecting to be clubbed on the head at any moment and dragged away. Only the smell of the damp dirt on her nose calmed her fear.

The motorcycle flashed its headlight blindly, then disappeared without a trace. The escapees began to grow restless; the babies cried and the adults sighed heavily, pale from what they felt had been a brush with death. They got up and started walking again. No one knew how much time had passed, or what lay ahead. Rina's eyelids grew heavy, and she kept tripping over her old sneakers, constantly twisting her ankles.

Rina dozed as she walked. Orange lights flared up before her eyes. Bathed in the orange light, cozy blankets and cotton stuffing breathed gently. Small, floury, white balloons grew and grew until they puffed up into warm loaves of bread and embraced her. Wherever she stuck her tongue out, sweet bread filled her mouth. But the next minute, she found herself wearing a pair of elastic pants, walking a tightrope. She felt dizzy and off-balance, like she couldn't move her feet. All she wanted was for the sun to come up so she could see what was in front of her. She wanted something to lean on so that she could fall sleep.

It was dawn when they reached the edge of the plains and saw glowing lights. The guide led them to a run-down shack. He opened the wooden door, and there was a dirt floor with two beds up against one wall, and a table in the middle. On the table was a bowl with strands of old noodles stuck to it. In one of the beds lay an old woman with a tuft of hair on her head, still as a painting. Another woman, perhaps the old one's daughter or daughter-in-law, sat at the table, sewing. The guide went through the cabinet, taking things out and putting them back, as though he owned the place. The old woman on the bed, the woman at the table, and the twenty-two escapees stared at each other as if trying to figure out who was worse off.

The twenty-two sat in a circle on the dirt floor and looked around, waiting for someone to offer them something to eat. Every now and then, you caught the eye of the person sitting across from you, and you glared at each other for a bit. Some people began to nod off. Rina took her sneakers off and shook the dirt out of them. The insoles were worn and floppy and caked with dirt from her tumble into the ditch.

The guide handed out packets of sleeping pills to the mothers.

"We have a long walk ahead of us. The pills are for the babies, so they won't cry. Hurry up and feed them, so we can get on our way again," he instructed.

Rina began to wonder what other riches might be found in this guide's pockets, which had already yielded such wonders as candies and sleeping pills. The mothers dissolved the pills in bowls of sugar water, which they fed bit by bit to the tired babies. The babies found the sweet liquid an improvement over their thumbs. The adults gathered round and glared at them.

"Shit, don't *we* get anything to eat?" one of the men finally exploded.

"You'll have to learn to curb your temper if you're to get to where you want to go. This is only the beginning. You only crossed the border a few hours ago," the guide reminded him.

Rina wanted to applaud him for his resoluteness, but held back. The safety of the twenty-two was in his hands, so no one dared talk back after that. The chilly dawn air skimmed their shoulders. Once in a while, the heavy mist shifted to reveal a corner of a roof or the front door of a house. A dog barked for a while, then eventually faded away. Rina hugged herself as the dawn mist seeped into her sneakers and up her whole body.

They walked for some time down a winding road bordered by small clusters of white birch trees. The mist was slowly thinning. They came upon a clearing, and the mist drew back for a moment like a curtain to reveal a brightly colored bus. The guide and the driver spoke for a long time in a language the others didn't understand. They all sat down by the road, glancing back and forth between the guide and the driver as they talked.

Again, the guide rounded up the fathers. Again, they dug through their bundles and the deepest layers of their clothing and handed over wads of cash. The guide counted the bills, gave some to the bus driver, and pocketed the rest. One of the men pounced on the guide and grabbed him by the collar.

"Damn you, you already got our money at the border checkpoint. What's this for?" he yelled. The guide easily extracted himself from the man's grasp and spat onto the ground through his teeth.

"That was for getting you across the border, and this is for bringing you all the way here and getting you on the bus. I've done my part, and I'm leaving now. Remember: if you get caught, they may kill you first, but they'll kill me, too."

"You can't leave us here in a country where we don't even understand the language. You bastard, you have to take us somewhere safe!" the man yelled.

"And where would it be safe for you?"

No one had anything to say to that. Rina stared after the guide, who was already walking briskly down the misty road away from the bus. She ran after him, feeling like she had an important confession to make, but when he turned around to look at her, she was at a loss for words. She shuffled awkwardly, looking down at the ground. The guide stared at her for a moment, then reached out and touched a strand of hair stuck to her forehead. Finally, Rina managed to open her mouth.

"Can I have some of those sleeping pills?"

The guide reached into his bulging jacket pocket, took out a few white packets, and handed them to her.

"Too many of these at once, and they'll kill you."

Rina stared at the guide as he walked away from her. He seemed fated to a life of traveling back and forth across borders. Eventually, he disappeared into the mist. The enraged fathers fell upon the foreign driver, even though he didn't speak their language, and begged him to find another guide for them. The driver ignored them and started the car. He gestured for them to go relieve themselves before the long drive, pointing first to his own fly and then to the rice field, making sure to look each of them in the eye as he did so. "As if we've been eating and drinking enough to piss," they grumbled as they headed down the fields. Rina tumbled down the steep embankment and joined one of the older girls from the sewing factory who was squatting with her bare buttocks exposed. Both of the girls were pitifully bony, but neither was ashamed. Rina pinched the girl's butt cheek and they both giggled. As she shook herself off after peeing, a blade of grass grazed Rina down below. It felt like the tickling of raindrops on her face, and a shiver coursed through her entire body.

The twenty-two members of the group barely managed to fit into the small bus with its colorful coat of paint peeling off in curls. The driver gave each of the men a cigarette and talked at them loudly.

The bus chugged along an endlessly winding road. They all fell asleep—the men who had smoked the foreign cigarettes, the women who had inhaled the secondhand smoke of those cigarettes, and the babies who had taken the sleeping pills—and the bus moved along.

Rina was awakened by the blinding sunlight pouring in through the window. The bus had stopped in front of a little marketplace. The driver was gone, and a smoky odor, along with the smell of meat, wafted up into the bus. Others around here were also waking up and looking around as they stretched their limbs. There were people near the market entrance sitting in twos and threes, gambling or eating noodles. They were wearing not-quite-white button-down shirts, their unwashed hair sticking out in every direction. Here, babies were strapped to their mothers' backs with their legs stretched out straight, like some form of punishment.

"I don't want to keep going. We don't even know if the country of P will let us in," the girl from the sewing factory said, leaning on Rina's shoulder.

"You're a big whiner, aren't you?" Rina leaned over and tickled the girl's armpits, damp with sweat. The girl didn't laugh.

The driver returned, looking like he'd had something to eat; his nose and forehead were slick with grease, and he had changed into a short-sleeved shirt.

"Don't we get anything to eat?" someone asked.

The driver, of course, didn't understand the question. One of the men made the gesture of spooning food into his mouth. The driver pointed to the bus door, crossed his wrists, and pretended to be handcuffed and dragged away. No one could argue against this skillful pantomime, so they all stared stonily out the windows.

The bus started up again. It rocked so heavily as it passed through a high, narrow mountain pass, that Rina was hardly able to sit still in her seat. On one side of the pass was a steep precipice. It was an unpeopled landscape; only herds of black cows and old sheep with bells hanging from their necks sometimes blocked the road.

On its way down, the bus abruptly stopped and the driver got out. They all clambered to the front to see what was going on. A landslide was blocking their way. The driver came back and pulled several men out. The men cleared away the dirt and rocks while the driver sat and smoked. When the road was clear, the bus started up again. The men who had been forced into sudden labor passed out, exhausted. A small triangle of brown river appeared between the mountains. The triangle got bigger and wider until it was cut off by an enormous cement dam. The river wasn't wide, but its yellowish waters wound around the high mountains like a giant serpent.

"This is no place for people. It's no better than where we came from," somebody remarked, breaking the silence. The river grew muddier. Rina pressed her face against the window. *Even if all twenty-two of us fell into the river and died, that water wouldn't bat an eyelash. The river swallows everything without leaving a trace. No one would even know we were here. It's like we're floating in the air.*

2

IT WAS ONLY AS THE SUN WAS SETTING THAT THE BUS TURNED ONTO a road teeming with traffic. They had been stacked and layered on top of each other for so long that they had lost feeling in their legs and buttocks. As the bus rolled into the heart of the city—where cars, bicycles, and exhaust curled into one big bundle and lurched forward—the twenty-two pairs of eyes shifted their collective gaze onto the splendid city night draped in lights. The whole place seemed to be suspended above a layer of gray air. Steeped in dust and fatigue, the squalid foreigners clambered off the bus, stood in a circle, and looked around.

Their second guide was a tall woman with a long, aged face. The bus driver spoke with her briefly, handed out another conciliatory round of cigarettes to the men, then exited smoothly through a bustling alley. Famished, the twenty-two congregated in front of a hamburger joint and stared through the window at the food on the tabletops. Although it was hard to tell where the guide was from, she spoke Rina's language well.

"We don't have much time here. You all have to get on the night train."

"We're starving. We can't move until we've had something to eat. If you make us go now, we'll tear apart the train and eat it."

The fathers gathered around the new guide, their eyes gleaming hopefully. Rina looked at the colossal city unfurling toward infinity with lights and skyscrapers, cars honking and people bustling. She saw people leaving shops with happy faces and hands full of merchandise. Rina found herself gravitating toward a row of street stalls selling headbands, little dolls, and shoes. She approached the shoe stall and reached out a hand to touch a pair of high-heeled boots trimmed with white fur. The fur was so soft that a cry of joy escaped her lips. Her hands that caressed the white fur were rough as bark and her nails were caked with yellowish dirt. *They say that the country of P, where we're all going, is even richer than this country. One day, I'll wear jeans and high heels like all of these women. I wonder if I'll get to go to college. At the very least, I'll be able to eat until I feel like I'm bursting open.* Rina laughed giddily to herself.

"Rina, what are you doing here? Mom is looking for you."

Rina invited her younger brother to touch the white fur boots. As he reached over, the stall-keeper approached them waving his hands, and smacked the little boy on the head. Rina kicked the stall and ran away down an alley, ignoring her brother's calls. The alley was lined with small storefronts. In one, a man lay on his stomach while a woman in a long blue dress massaged his feet. The woman had a slender face and a porcelain complexion, but the hands that kneaded away at the man's feet were thick and gnarled. A woman in a red skirt looked up and furrowed her arched eyebrows at Rina. When Rina didn't move away, the woman made a face and gestured at Rina to beat it. Rina slipped out of the alley.

The sun had set on the city, now deepened into an ashy gray, and dull gray air—whether it was fog or smoke, it was impossible to tell—hung so low above their heads that it was difficult to breathe. The streets were so crowded that it was easy to lose their guide in a moment of carelessness.

The main plaza of the darkened train station was all abustle. Policemen patrolled the area, but no one asked them to show identification, or where they were from. No one paid them any attention. They went to a waiting room on the second floor, where the guide handed out train tickets to the men of each family. All of the seats were taken, and the air inside was stifling. The floor of the waiting room was littered with garbage and cigarette butts. The train wasn't departing for another two hours, but the people of this country apparently showed up hours beforehand to wait. It wasn't just the trains—buses, boats, even planes were notorious for not leaving on time. The guide opened a bag she'd been carrying, took out several plastic bags filled with white dumplings, and handed one to each family.

"You only get two each," the adults warned.

Rina was so hungry that she didn't give a second thought to the people around her. She shoved the dumplings into her mouth without bothering to dip them in soy sauce or pause for a drink of water. The women sitting across from her stared at her dumplings. "I've never had such amazing dumplings," someone marveled aloud. When the dumplings were gone, they all turned expectantly to the guide, wondering what she would give them next. She pulled out a bunch of curious-looking tropical fruit and handed one to every other person. Split in half, the fruit revealed translucent, ruby-red kernels.

A group of Westerners in brightly colored clothes captured the landscape of the waiting room with their cameras. Rina wondered what it was they saw, but she was even more fascinated by the strange odor coming from their bodies. At that moment, a loud clanging of bells rang out from the turnstiles. Even though the train wasn't due for another hour, everyone rushed over to stand in a line that quickly spilled out of the waiting room and into the stairway leading down to the first level. The people stood and waited dumbly for another hour. When the turnstiles opened, the bodies flowed forth and up and down the stairs like a muddy brown river. The twenty-two huddled around their guide and proceeded in hurried steps, struggling to stay close.

The train was dark green and looked as if it had slogged through a swamp. Uniformed conductors tried to organize the passengers into a line with wooden batons, but they were soon engulfed by the throngs that had descended onto the platform, and eventually gave up and vanished.

Rina's family gathered in a car with sleeping berths. Her father and mother took the bottom bunk. The coquettish voice of a woman singing an upbeat tune came flowing out of the speakers. The guide went from car to car to make sure that everyone had made it on board. The terrified escapees shut themselves in their cabins and didn't dream of venturing outside.

"When they come to check your tickets, don't say anything; just give them your tickets. Don't speak. Also, you may want to use the bathroom to freshen up. Don't do it. It increases the chances of your getting into some sort of trouble with the locals, and that could be a huge pain in the ass for all of us."

The guide closed the door behind her as she left, but that didn't shut out the noises from the hallway—car doors being opened and slammed shut, people conversing loudly in the aisles, the singing from the speakers. Rina's mother dozed in her seat until she eventually drooped into her berth and fell fast asleep to the rhythmic rocking of the train. By now, Rina's father looked just like any other local, his hair slick with grease. He had pulled his money out from its hiding place on his body and was now thumbing through it. Rina took out her pocket mirror and examined her tanned face.

She climbed down off her berth, cracked opened the cabin door, and peered out. Some people were perched on window ledges, smoking. Others tossed fruit peels out into the corridor from their cabins, and still others were dipping their hands into yellow bags of sunflower seeds. As they spat out the hulls, they commented on the betting games that were also going on in the corridor. The children slept in their beds, and the adults were too busy to care what the children were doing.

By the time the train let out a long whistle and eased out of the station, it was so dark that Rina couldn't see what was outside the window. She lay on her stomach, staring through the narrow gap of the curtains, trying to catch a last glimpse of the biggest city she had ever seen as it disappeared into the distance. She dozed off, but jumped at every small noise. When she did manage to fall asleep, she was plagued by her dreams. Dressed in layer upon layer of ill-fitting rags, she walked through unknown lands. Attendants dressed in white ceremonial robes with cotton cords tied around their waists walked toward her, their faces covered in white masks. Then, she fell into a vat of white sugar. At first, she eagerly lapped up the sweet, fine-grained sugar, but eventually it filled her up to her throat, her feet slipped, and she drowned to death. The next thing she knew, she was walking barefoot because her shoes had fallen apart. Eventually, the bare soles of her feet became so embedded with pebbles that she was forced to walk on her hands in circles.

The train stopped moving in her dream. When Rina opened her eyes, she realized the train had actually stopped on the tracks. She drew back the curtains. It was pitch black. All of a sudden, the lights came on in the corridor outside, and she heard voices. Cabin doors were being violently flung open. Rina hopped down to the bottom berth and pinched her father's arm. He got dressed in the blink of an eye and was sitting stiffly with an anxious look on his face when they came in.

Of the twenty-two, Rina's family, an elderly couple, and a family of four with a newborn were dragged off the train. There were also a few locals who had not paid their fare and were jabbering away in confusion. By now, all of the escapees had grown accustomed to kneeling on the ground and putting their hands above their heads, and they did so without being told. Rina's body kept on tilting to one side because the ground was uneven and bumpy underneath her. Two armed policemen poked at their bundles with guns. The guide was talking to an unarmed policeman. Every time the newborn whimpered or the old man coughed, the others' hearts leapt into their mouths for fear that the irritated policemen would order the train to leave without them. It was colder outside than expected, and the train windows were frosted over. The guide approached the men of the group.

"It's the same deal as anywhere. They want money."

Stumped, the fathers blew their noses into the empty air.

"Those thieves! What money do they expect us to have? And how do we know they won't just take our money and let the train go on without us?"

"They won't. The train isn't stopped because of you, it's because there was a power outage. These people are quick to notice things, and we just got unlucky."

The fathers deliberately took their time reaching yet again into the deepest recesses of their pockets. When they had collected the money and handed it over, the policemen grinned and gave each man a cigarette. The ten of them clambered back on the train and the furious men finished their cigarettes in the corridor.

The twenty-two survived the fifty-hour train ride on the dumplings and crackers that the guide handed out occasionally. The country seemed to spread itself out viciously, so that no matter how far southwest they traveled, there was no end to it. They got so bored that they visited each other, switched cabins for fun, used the bathrooms like they were their own, and even chatted with some of the locals.

It was warm and drizzly on the day they reached their final destination, a city on the southwestern-most tip of the country. The locals who had traveled with them had had plenty to eat on the train, but it seemed like they still had a lot left; with giant bundles in both hands and hoisted onto their heads, they walked out into the station plaza, where all manner of vehicles awaited, from taxis and minivans to horse-drawn carriages, bicycles, and motorcycles.

The air that now caressed the tip of Rina's nose was different from anything she'd felt so far. The sun rose early here and there was no chill in the breeze. Rina let out a sigh of relief—with her sneakers, it was a good thing it was so warm. The twenty-two piled into two carriages drawn by slick-looking horses wrapped in red and blue cloth. Now, they were going even further southwest, and no one knew what might happen on their way to cross the border into yet another third-party nation. Rina stared at the horse's waddling haunches. She and her fellow escapees, numbed by the train ride, stared blankly out at the foreign landscape.

The road was lined on each side with onion fields. Fieldworkers slouched together, eating lunch out of large cans. It was so warm that the front doors of the roadside houses were wide open to view. Women followed bare-bottomed toddlers around with bowls of food, feeding them as they played. Old men sat in front of their houses, staring blankly into the distance. At a mineral processing factory, they saw stones being carved and shaped into flowers. They saw a man cutting black meat into long strips and hanging it on a line to dry. Black cows slowly wandered around houses, behind which stretched fields and paddies.

How far had they gone? When Rina's bottom had become so numb that it no longer seemed to be attached to the rest of her body, the clip-clopping of the horseshoes slowed down, and the carriage stopped. Passing through the gates of an ancient citadel, they were met on either side with a long row of shops as far as the eye could see. The streets were lined with fresh poplar trees. Old men with their lips clamped around hookah pipes stared so hard at the twenty-two foreigners that their eyes seemed to turn red from the exertion.

The guide took them to a run-down noodle shop in an alleyway. It didn't have a separate kitchen, just a shelf out on the street with containers of seasonings, and some folding chairs and tables. There wasn't enough room for everyone, so they spilled over into the noodle shop next door. The townspeople gathered to watch the pathetic, grimy travelers.

They were all so famished, from the elderly to the infants, that they inhaled the noodles without giving a second thought to how greasy the broth was.

"The brown berry you see there is often used for its narcotic effect. They put it in the noodles, too," the guide told them.

No one gave a second thought to the berries; they were all too ravenous. The alley was silent save for the sound of slurping, and scowling faces were beginning to soften. The owner of the noodle shop offered the men cigarettes, and those who had finished eating blew smoke up into the air while the women sat around and chatted lazily, something they hadn't been able to do in a long time.

After the feast, they were led to a residential estate that had once housed a powerful ruling-class tribe, back when the nation had been powerful and prosperous. The property had once belonged to the highest orders of the establishment; now, it was used as government welfare housing for the poor. Most of the units were empty, draped in cobwebs, and falling apart.

The twenty-two walked into a square-shaped two-story structure with a central courtyard. Rina climbed up a flight of stairs pale with dust. The second floor was separated into a number of rooms furnished with elegant beds, armchairs, and clocks that stood just as they had a century ago. It was so warm that most of the people preferred to sit outside in the courtyard. Someone found a mat rolled up in a corner and set it out. The babies, who had been tied to their mothers' backs all day, crawled eagerly onto it. While the women unpacked and reorganized their bundles, the men gathered around the entrance of the building to admire the ornate windowpanes and paintings.

"We'll take a break here and get on the bus at night. There's going to be a lot of walking after the bus ride, so you should get some rest now."

The guide had barely finished speaking when one of the men from the sewing factory jumped up and scurried to the bathroom. Minutes later, a few others followed him outside. It was an epidemic of diarrhea. The infants, happily oblivious to their mothers' anxiety of running out of diapers, emptied their bowels and licked the diarrhea off their own fingers. Eventually, the people became too frantic to wait in line for the bathrooms and pulled their pants down, using the great outdoors as their outhouse. Rina found a small shrine within the residential complex. She knew she should wait her turn for the toilet, but she simply couldn't hold it in. Her stomach puttered a drumbeat, and no matter how hard she clenched her sphincter, she couldn't control herself. Only their guide remained unaffected.

"What happened? My butthole is all torn up. Those noodles I just ate came pouring out the other end!"

"The rich broth must have irritated your stomach, especially since you'd been starved for days. I'll go get some medicine."

The guide left, and the people, weakened and doubled over, stood in the warm sun, ready to run to a toilet nearby at the slightest signal from their bowels. And so they waited, silent and propped up against doors or pillars until the guide returned with medicine. Rina was leaning against a pair of wooden doors when she heard a crack behind her, as if the hinges were coming undone. Turning around, she saw carvings and paintings of creatures half-human and half-beast, locked in a deep sleep in the wooden doorframe.

That night, the twenty-two climbed onto a bus with sleeping berths. When they took off their shoes to climb into the beds, the stink of feet was nauseating. Their faces were haggard and their collective will seemed to have been quashed. The few people who still had diarrhea went to a field behind the bus station instead of paying to use the public bathrooms. They were so hungry and tired that all they could do was to lie quietly, clutching their stomachs. The departure time came and went, but the bus did not budge.

Rina sat behind the guide and watched the people outside. Some sat on tiny wooden stools and bet on games of marbles. The locals seemed to have no problem with the delay—no one protested, and in fact, some were peacefully snoring away. Their bus had been blocked off by another bus whose driver had parked and disappeared. It was a ridiculous situation for the twenty-two who risked their lives with every move they made, but nothing could be done.

The bus left two hours behind schedule. By now, the lights of the city had faded away, making it look like a model of an ancient city inside a smoky glass box. The mothers sat in the bottom berths at the back, getting up every so often to breastfeed their babies. Aside from stopping once for gas, the bus drove without any interruptions.

The bus arrived two hours later than planned, at eight in morning, in the country's southernmost city. The locals didn't wake up. When the guide began waking the escapees in a low voice, the city was already slowly sending up the sun upon a vast fleet of commuting bicycles. The twenty-two sat together in the street in front of the bus station and ate sweet potatoes for breakfast.

They boarded a new bus now, which they filled up in a matter of seconds. A group of women who were of the country's ethnic minority boarded after them. The women's black hair was neatly pushed under triangular black hats, they wore long-sleeved gowns that looked like black judo robes, and carried giant bundles on their heads. The only ornamentation on their black robes were three blue stripes embroidered on the sleeves. Since there were no more seats, they sat neatly in a row on the floor at the center of the bus, and the bus began its ascent.

The sun was prickly and hot, but the breeze that blew in through the open window and caressed Rina's arm and neck was not unpleasant. Rina looked at the narrow paths that led up into the high, wide mountains. It eventually became so warm that the babies were disencumbered of their thick sweaters. They toddled around with their skinny little arms showing through their thin underclothes, occasionally bursting into giggles. When Rina also took off her thick sweater for the first time since leaving home, her back, which had been slouched and contracted, seemed to straighten of its own accord.

"I don't know that we made the right choice. You think we'll make it safely?" some of the men wondered aloud. No one answered. The car grew quiet, and the minority women furtively shifted their freckled faces this way and that to steal glances at the escapees.

The twenty-two got off the bus at a farm village. It was only then that the minority women turned to look at them. Rina waved, but the women looked away. The guide took the group to what appeared to be a farming commune, with a central well and playground. The twenty-two sat in a lot next to the well, and rested peacefully.

"The southern border of this country is an eight-hour walk from here. But you have babies and you're hungry, and to get across the border to the church run by missionaries from the country P who are going to help us, eight hours is a very optimistic estimate. If we make a wrong turn, it could take days. Once you get there, though, you can have hot food. The missionaries are there to help escapees, and they'll give you passports and help you safely enter P. Of course, that will be by plane."

No one could resist breaking out into a wide grin at the sound of that word, *plane*. They drew water from the well and washed their faces and feet. Rina grumbled about how women couldn't comfortably wash themselves in public, and satisfied herself with splashing some water on her feet. Some people tried to lighten their loads for the long trek ahead by sorting out clothes and whatever belongings were not immediately necessary, and leaving them by the well. Rina circled the well in search of some tough blades of grass, which she used to tie up the mid-sole of her sneakers. Then she took out her pocket mirror, wiped the dirt off her face, and carefully examined her reflection.

3

THE SUN WAS JUST DROPPING BEHIND THE RIDGE OF THE HILL AS they set off on a newly elevated road toward the southern border. The farms under the mountain were quickly engulfed in darkness. The higher the road climbed, the lower the atmospheric pressure dropped, and the harder it became to breathe. Even as they were headed forward, their footsteps seemed to be dragging them back. After a while, the guide crossed the road, and they followed her. Beneath them stretched out a landscape they had never seen before.

"These terraced farms were built over the course of a thousand, two thousand years by the ethnic minorities that live nearby. Apparently, tourists come from all over the world to see them."

The farms were scattered in a giddy whirl along the mountain slope like a child's playful painting, but they somehow fit naturally into their surroundings, and the farmhouses that studded the hillside looked as small as fingernails. The twenty-two stood single file along the road and looked down on a thousand years of time past, as if they were the tourists from some nation so fabulously prosperous that they had traveled abroad to assuage the boredom of their wealth. The sun, which had been gradually waning, now vanished all of a sudden in a flash of white light. At that moment, they heard the sound of a flute. Next to the road was a small shack with a thatched roof. Inside were two indigenous women dressed all in white, with pink vests. They were pretty, with their black hair combed back and pulled up, and their eyes shyly lowered. As the people gathered around to enjoy the music, the younger woman came out and boldly held out her hand. When no one offered her payment, the other woman stopped playing.

On their right, they spotted an uphill road leading from the newly constructed road to the mountain path. The guide and the men led the way, and the women followed. Their footsteps were muffled by the dirt road, and even the faraway barking of dogs was instantly erased by the rustling of the wind in the leaves. As the mountain grew steeper, they reached a dense forest of thick, towering trees. The women had to be pulled forward by the men to make it through. Rina could see her dad walking ahead of her. She wondered what had prompted her thirty-nine-year-old father, born in the mines and destined to die there like his father before him, to flee. But they weren't close enough for her to ask him such things. She also wanted to ask him who had chosen the name Rina for her . . .

The mountain was so steep that the more they climbed, the harder it became to see the path ahead. At that point in the year, the leaves were crispy and dry, and they crackled every time a body brushed by, causing birds to fly up from their perches in a frenzy and tiny animals to flee. This made the babies wail and their mothers would plop down, grumbling, until the guide chided them: "Do you know what happens if they catch us here? You saw those huge terraced farms back there, right? Do you want to get stuck farming those horrors for the rest of your lives? It doesn't matter whether you're a kid or an adult; all they see in you is manpower. The government here has a one-child policy for people in the cities, and it's two in the countryside, but they break the law all the time 'cause they need all the help they can get out here, on the farms. They don't even register their births. If they found you, you can bet they'd jump for joy. You even look sort of like them. And we're so far from any government offices here . . ."

The younger children clambered onto their parents' backs. The mothers hummed and murmured as they walked, trying to pacify their babies. One of the three-year-olds fretted constantly, but his newborn sibling never made a sound. The grass became damp, and the moisture seeped into Rina's feet. By now, she was forced to clear the path with her hands and feet as she advanced. Here and there came the dull thuds of people getting their feet caught in the grass and tripping. Some of the younger men from the sewing factory split the heavier loads among themselves. They were all feeling rather bleak when the mother of the one-year-old began to scream.

"Oh god, look here!"

The guide got there first and shined her flashlight in the baby's tiny face, which drooped listlessly away from its mother's chest. The baby's father plucked open her eyelids and peered in at them. The infant's eyes were incrusted with a yellowish substance.

"I only just gave birth to you, you can't die on me," the mother wailed. Rina stared at the woman, who was in her early twenties at most.

"People don't die that easily. Shut your mouth," scolded her husband. There was nothing to be done, so they decided to keep moving forward.

It looked like it was going to be a hard night's trek over the mountain. Everyone was exhausted, and the gaps in their procession grew wider. Rina's sneakers slowed her down so that she lagged far behind even the oldest of them. She looked through the branches up at the sky, which was turning blue above the black forest. Under the moonlight, the forest had deepened into yet a darker shade of black.

After a while, Rina's mother collapsed. Her father was carrying their bundle on his back, so Rina had to carry her brother.

"Rina, I-I keep on having to go p—poop." Her eleven-year-old brother had never stuttered before, but now he could hardly get a word out. He felt as light as a feather on her back. Her mother had always boasted that whatever they could find to eat, she fed her youngest son, but now Rina grumbled to herself that her mother must have been eating it all herself. She dozed as she walked, but kept her fingers tightly interlocked for fear of dropping her brother. Whenever she opened her eyes, they were still in thick vegetation; there was no way out.

Then, she caught a whiff of something into the air. Her father came running back toward them, calling her name. Gratified to hear his voice, Rina answered him, but he simply took her brother in his arms and walked away. Someone had caught a few wild pheasants and was roasting them. They were so deep in the woods that no one worried about getting caught. The grass was splattered with blood and a few stray pheasant feathers were still floating about. The people tore up the pheasant flesh into little pieces, skewered it onto branches, and put the skewers on heated stones. As soon as the meat had cooked, each person took a bite, starting with the elderly. The woman with the sick baby had her back toward everyone else; she was massaging her nipples in an attempt to breastfeed her child. Rina looked back over her shoulder at the silent and uncomplaining woman.

"I'd give her some water if there was any. Do you think I should at least have her drink some urine?" the woman asked, looking up at Rina. In her eyes, Rina could see she knew that something was terribly wrong with her baby. Rina approached the people gathered around the flickering fire.

"Does anyone have any water?"

"And who would have water in the middle of the forest?" one of the men retorted sullenly. He turned to the boy sitting next to him. "Hey, go take a leak and give it to the baby," he said, without looking back at the young mother.

"Where's *my* meat?" Rina asked. No one answered. She stuck her hand into the mass of blinking embers, grabbed at whatever was left, and stuffed it in her mouth, but it turned out to be a charred piece of bark or maybe a lump of dirt. The people threw more wood onto the fire and dozed in small groups, hugging their knees with their arms. Rina wove her way close to the fire and sat down among them, hugging her shoulders.

It got colder. Rina was awakened by the sound of crying. Everyone seemed to be asleep. She looked around. Again, the whimper of a stifled sob echoed throughout the woods. Eventually, Rina noticed a three-year-old boy standing alone. She ran over and held him close to her. The terrified boy turned around and covered his eyes with his hands.

At dawn, the twenty-two hastened on their way. Their lips and fingertips were covered in black soot and some even had blood on their faces. Oblivious to the fate of the twenty-two travelers, the woods were being reborn, shedding nighttime layers of darkness one by one. The young leaves looked dewy and fresh, and the green moss and the moist ground were bursting with life.

The people had changed. They were too weak to talk, but their eyes were set with a forceful steeliness. Nerves and irritability were at their most sensitive. The men found thick branches that they used to beat down everything in their path. The sewing factory workers were the first to begin eating pieces of bark they had peeled off branches. Some people climbed trees and tried to catch birds by throwing rocks at them. The three-year-old sucked his thumb like his life depended on it, while everyone scattered throughout the forest in search of food. That's when the sick baby's mother let out a sharp shriek. The baby was dead. Her skin had turned black and blue like a frog, and her eyes were so tightly shut that they couldn't be pried open. The mother unwrapped the baby from her breast and felt her hands and feet, but every bit of her was blue and dead. She fainted, the baby sling still hanging from her chest.

"I'm so sorry. Maybe I should have tried some flu medicine," the guide said.

Speechless, the baby's father bowed his head in grief. A while later, he jumped up and roughly untied the sling from his wife. Rina noticed that a button from the mother's sweater had left a distinct round imprint on the baby's forehead. It looked like one of those crop circles that people believed had been left by spaceships.

The father wrapped the dead baby in the sling and walked into the woods. As soon as he was gone, the remaining people started to whisper.

"That poor mother. This might just kill her, too."

"I don't know. I mean, I'm so hungry I just don't know. I sure wish that baby had been a dog or a deer. Who knew it would be so hard to find something to eat in the woods?"

The father returned a while later, burned a white cotton kerchief he held in his hand, and set it afloat above the trees. And so the twenty-two became twenty-one.

The mother lay with her head on her husband's knees. They waited for her to come to. Her eyes were closed, but her hand remained on her belly. Then, suddenly, she opened her eyes and began to hit her son, who had been staring blankly off into space. Afterward—Rina couldn't help wondering where she got the strength to do it—she turned to her diminutive husband and slapped him, over and over again.

When no one was watching, Rina ran down the path to retrace the father's steps. Even though she walked quite a ways, there was no sign of the baby's corpse. After a while, she realized her brother was following her. She looked up and saw the blue sky leaning over her, hugging the forest. She was beginning to feel faint, and there was still no sign of the baby. She turned and ran, and noticed a single baby's sock on a large rock.

"R-R-Rina, look, a tiger must have taken the baby," her brother said. She looked around but still found no trace of the body. Rina put the sock in her pocket.

"There are no tigers here, stupid. And stop stuttering."

In the afternoon, the older people picked though each other's hair and ate the lice they found, while the men dug through the dirt and looked under rocks for bugs to roast. There weren't enough to go around. Some of the braver women tried the roasted bugs, but couldn't keep them down. They sucked on some of the pine cones to calm their stomachs and vomited again. The guide told them that the people of this country ate anything with legs as long as it was alive, and someone caught a dragonfly passing by. Rina ate two dragonflies herself, and one bug that looked like a scorpion. Had there been more, she would have gladly devoured them. Afterward, she felt the dragonflies flapping around in her chest, trying to unfold their wings and get out. Her intestines were crammed so chock-full of scorpions that it became hard to breathe.

Night came again, and so did the pale moonlight. They all huddled close to the fire. Some of them bit into the flesh of their own arms, while others scratched their armpits and ate whatever fell out. Still others ate their own toe jam. A long-haired newlywed woman chewed on strands of her own hair. The people and the night air grew warmer.

When all of the sparks had been put out, they started, at the guide's behest, walking again. They were on the verge of dropping dead when they reached the edge of the forest, but they were too weary to be excited. Behind them lay the dense vegetation they had just crawled through and spread out before them was a plateau that rose up and then dipped smoothly back down. Short yellow flowers like dandelions were sprinkled all over the highlands. The escapees gathered their strength and walked briskly so that they were soon looking down at a path that unfurled below their feet. The couple that had lost their baby hovered around the outskirts of the woods like animals with unfinished business.

The guide, who had been walking ahead along the downhill path, suddenly ducked, and gestured to the group to do the same and hide themselves. One by one, they fell to the ground. An unidentifiable sound, like a gust of wind, blew through the forest and over the highlands. Rina's curiosity got the better of her, and she raised herself and craned her body forward to see what was happening below. The deep black plateau stretched out abysmally before her. In front of her, the guide and the men from the sewing factory were huddled alongside some of the younger men and women of the group. Rina's parents and brother were directly behind them. Just as Rina was about to duck back down, the guide and all the others in front jumped up and began running to the right side of the road. Those who were quick enough followed them. Those who were too far away to take orders sat like deer in headlights. It was too late, and Rina knew it. A group of men dressed in rags and armed with pickaxes and shovels had traversed the hillside and were bounding like squirrels toward the remaining fugitives. One of the escapees who spoke the language of this country—she had been an administrative worker back at home—approached the men and said something. One of the men brought his pickaxe down onto her shoulder.

The newlywed woman, the female administration worker, Rina, and the old man were dragged to the edge of the dark plateau, closely followed by the men with pickaxes. At the end of the plateau was a colossal building, a shade darker than its dark surroundings. Shaped like an overturned soup bowl, it had no outer walls or windows, just two large cylindrical smokestacks. The men with the pickaxes each grabbed a fugitive by the neck and shoved them inside.

4

It was a chemical manufacturing plant that emitted nauseating toxic fumes. Every inch of its high ceilings were crammed with thick, corroded gray pipes. In the center was a row of frighteningly large horizontal cylindrical tanks. At the center of the cylindrical tanks, just above the sharp screws and propeller blades enfolded in each tank, like the heart of it all, shone a row of evenly spaced red calibrators. The walls and floors were lined with containers of all sizes containing unknowable substances that could have been dyes or pesticides.

"I'm a newlywed. Please, please, let me go."

"I'm just an old man. Please help me out here, son. I have an old wife. She'll die without me."

"We have to get to the country of P."

"Please let me go back to my mom and dad."

The four captives begged, but the men with the pickaxes simply exchanged imperturbable looks among each other. A door to their right opened, and the prisoners were dragged outside and up a hill.

They had to hold their noses when they stepped into the damp log cabin. Fifty or so workers were sleeping in layers on the heated floor. Some looked like giant bugs, others like bundles that had been carelessly dumped on the ground. They were caked with a mixture of grime and sweat. There were a few blankets steeped in filth and urine that barely covered the knees of those who were lucky enough to have them. The ceilings and walls were covered in rat piss and mold, and the bathroom was separated from the main room by a single grimy drape. The four captives collectively agreed that it looked just like the homeland they'd chosen to flee.

Yelling, one of the armed men shook a worker who had been sleeping in the doorway, and like dominoes, they all began to rise. Soon enough, a space was made in the midst of the fifty bodies which then closed in on the four newcomers, who were too afraid to turn around to look behind them, and too afraid to look up; they just stared down at the floor. There were people who wore socks that had burst open at the toes. There was a person whose foot had been amputated.

"Don't these people all belong in an insane asylum?" the women wondered aloud, then began to cry when they realized what they had done. The old man tried to calm the workers down, insisting that they hadn't meant insult, but he received a shower of pickaxes and shovels for his troubles. Even though he was robust for his age, the old man fell to the ground crying, legs flailing. It was only then that Rina realized what they were in for.

The mornings began when the boiler that spat out large quantities of water vapor started up with an odd whirring sound. The pulverizer pulverized fiercely and far too loudly and far too close to them. Plugging their ears with their fingers, the women helped with the morning gruel. It was made of dry millet that was not quite yellow and not quite blue. The storage containers in the main room were filled with cornmeal and plain millet, but no rice. The millet was half pebbles, half millet, and it took them forever to filter it with a bamboo sieve. Rina picked up the pebbles one by one, muttered "Die, *die*," at them, and threw them at her feet. The old man swept the front of the factory and collected trash in a pile. Within a day or two, death had come into full bloom on his face. When he wasn't working, he sat under the eaves of the factory building and stared off at the faraway mountains.

Even when the grains of millet were fully macerated, the porridge was watery and smelled strange. Stirring it with a wooden spoon, Rina impulsively spat into the porridge. A man looking in through the kitchen door saw her. He was the factory manager and had a pair of wide, frightened-looking eyes in a neatly square face.

Every day, chemicals from a large barrel were poured into an even larger barrel and stirred around, then solidified to the texture of pudding. The solidified chemicals were mixed with dozens of additives, moved around between various kinds of equipment, blasted with hot air and cold air, packed up and piled up in front of the factory, then shipped away on trucks.

Behind the factory was a valley. The waste was expelled from the factory without any filtering process, so the stream that flowed through the valley was milky white. Wherever the water flowed, the hills and fields were utterly devoid of vegetation or any form of life, be it a bird or a single fly.

The gruel was cooked in the morning and doled out to the workers twice a day. They sat single file at a gray table to one side of the factory and ate it with coarse salt. Rina couldn't tell which of these men had captured them on the plateau. As the women served breakfast, Rina noticed a youthful boy staring up at her, his head hanging low. The hollows under his eyes were stained dark, and his face was dappled with dry white patches. He wasn't slight, but he was as skinny as a stick, and his bare feet looked like claws. Rina stuck out her tongue, and their gazes met. The boy quickly looked down.

All of sudden, the neatly square man grabbed one of the workers by the scruff and dragged him into the factory. He gestured to the worker and the worker took off his shirt and lifted both of his arms, trembling. The neatly square man picked up a bucket next to him filled with watered-down chemicals and flung the milky liquid over the man's body. Then he whipped the man so that everyone could hear the leather against the flesh.

It was with this single whip that the neatly square man ruled over the fifty factory workers.

"Can somebody please tell us in our own language what the hell this place is, please?!" Every time there was a beating, the women covered their eyes and wept. At the drop of a hat, the neatly square man would drag the male workers one by one to a corner of the factory and beat the living daylights out of them. Afterward, the beaten men bounced like rubber balls back up the ladders to resume working as if nothing had happened. At any hint of rebellion, they were force-fed feces that the neatly square man collected in a rubber pail. On those days, the odors of excrement and chemicals were married and chemically distorted, and gave Rina horrible migraines. But as time went by, they all became inured to the sight of the beatings and abuse, and eventually no one cried, not even Rina.

The neatly square man stopped taking his black jeep home in the evenings as he usually did. Instead, he would go into the small side room of the factory where the women sat together, holding hands. He would take the two married women outside, one by one. The women would return with a bag of crackers, which they would eat trembling, and fall into a deep sleep once they were done. When this started happening, the married women fell into a quandary. The newlywed was the most tortured.

"If our husbands find about this, they'll never forgive us once we're reunited with them in the country of P. We have to keep this our secret," the women whispered to each other. Rina cocked her head.

"I can keep a secret. But the old man said yesterday in the yard that you were floozies and tramps. And we're the only women here."

"Really? You mean that old geezer knows everything that's been going on in that bastard's room? No, no, no! What should we do?"

"Couldn't we do something about that square-faced pig, if we acted together?"

Nobody answered. The next morning, as usual, the women made gruel and the old man swept the front yard. During the day, the neatly square man beat a few innocent workers and carefully washed his hands afterward. He dozed with his legs perched on a chair, and when the chair broke with a loud crack, he started up and beat the workers again.

When night fell, the women sat with their knees bent and stared down at the tops of their feet. Rina didn't really know what it was to pray, but she put her palms together and tried. As if in answer to her prayers, the door opened and the neatly square man's face appeared in the doorway. This time, he grabbed Rina by the wrist.

"Come on, she's still young!" the married women protested. But the man held his grip on Rina's wrist, and Rina regretted her prayer. It had been her first.

The man's room was next to the engine room, and had a window with a thick curtain over it. The neatly square man sat on the edge of his bed, took off his shirt, put a thick, stubby cigarette in his mouth, and lit it. His neck was red and his stomach was fleshy. His armpit hairs stuck out from under his arms toward his chest like black blades, making him look like a mountain bandit. The man cocked his index finger at Rina and beckoned her toward him, and she approached sideways, like a crab. He grabbed her and pulled her between his legs. Murmuring something, he touched Rina's hair and the nape of her neck. Petrified, Rina stared at a pair of bull's horns that decorated the wall next to the bed.

The man repeatedly murmured a two-syllable word into Rina's ear. His bed was damp and an incandescent light bulb hung so low from a wire that it threatened to shatter if she bumped into it. The man continued to murmur the same word while he undressed Rina. He unbuckled his belt and took off his pants. Lying on the bed, Rina looked up at the ceiling. Her eyes traveled from one corner to the other. When the man finally undid his wristwatch, Rina's body was rigid with terror down to her tightly clenched toes.

She hadn't taken a bath since crossing the border, and she hardly recognized her own body and the strange smell it gave off. Undaunted by the flakes of diarrhea that had dried around her anus, the man rubbed his lips against Rina's labia for a long time. Then, murmuring the same word through his neatly square lips, he climbed on top of Rina, crushing her with his weight. Rina jumped up, pulled the horns off the wall, and flung them at him. She was jumping up and down on the bed like a possessed shaman when he caught her. She kicked him, threw pillows, and pinched him. She struggled, even though the man was so strong it was like an elephant playing with a kitten. Still murmuring the same word, he climbed on top of her and pinioned her. Then, when his red eyes were bulging to the point of exploding, he spilled a liquid onto Rina's stomach and flopped back down onto the bed. It was a long time before the creaking of the bed and his panting subsided. When things had quieted down, Rina dipped a finger into the liquid and held it up to the lamplight. It was a chemical substance that stank enough to make her insides heave. She drew back the curtains and put her hand on the windowpane, then stepped back in surprise. Outside, the window was crawling with ash-colored moths.

Rina waited for the truck that came once every four days to pick up the chemicals. Every time the truck came, she imagined climbing onto it and escaping to the country of P. No, she imagined the other escapees from whom they'd been separated coming to find her, so that they could all escape together. The chemical plant was a place of exile, and there was nothing to do there aside from the daily labor.

The chemicals continued to be manufactured, and it was impossible to distinguish seasons at the plant. The stunted flowers that had taken root in the black dirt were always in bloom, and at times white, salt-like grains of sand blew in from high up on the plateau. The flowers of the plateau were always yellow, and they neither grew nor withered.

The women continued to make gruel and launder the workers' uniforms and wash the dishes. Thanks to their labor, the workers and the factory became a little cleaner. The old man continued to sweep the yard. Instead of muttering "floozies and tramps," he now denounced the "loose young slut." The newlywed woman took a pair of rusty scissors from the kitchen and cut her beautiful, long black hair off in three fell swoops. The woman who had held a high-ranking administrative position recited political doctrines from back home under her breath.

Rina and the women sometimes went to the village in the neatly square man's car to work in the fields. The villagers assumed that the women, who were dressed in the same uniforms as the factory workers, were mute. After work, the women were given a bowl of rice so meager that the grains would have blown away at the slightest puff of air, and a cup of tea with a bitter aftertaste. Once in a while, they were gifted old clothes, shoes that were ready to be thrown out, or handfuls of dried narcotic herbs to smoke.

When the neatly square man left the factory for the day, which wasn't often, the chemical plant workers would sit out in the yard and play. They would have fun taking turns singing and clapping. One of them would stand up and mimic the neatly square man. He would pretend to beat the others, then someone would pull his pants down and they would all laugh. The old man would watch them with a wretched look on his face and click his tongue, muttering, "pathetic bastards," as Rina and the women, now part of the family of workers, laughed along with the others.

5

One clear morning, the neatly square man took Rina by the wrist and put her into his black jeep.

"Where are you taking her? Take us, too, or leave her here, you bastard!" The two other women and the old man clung to the jeep, but the man ignored them and started the car. As they drove away from the chemical plant, the man took out a pair of glasses with dark lenses, and turned up the music. The wind felt cool on the bridge of Rina's nose, so she pressed her face up against the window and looked out without saying anything. The simple, quick rhythm of the music radiated throughout the woods. The neatly square man talked without stopping, once in a while looking over at Rina, as if he were telling her stories of the best times of his life.

The song played over and over again. The sun got hotter and pricklier. Rina's eyelids trembled, and she leaned back into her seat. The neatly square man opened a compartment, took something out, and put it in Rina's palm. The flat, hard thing was chocolate. The sweetness that touched her tongue and spread throughout her mouth filled her head with scattered thoughts. She missed being lost in the woods. She wondered if the seventeen others had safely entered the country of P, and what had happened to the sewing factory girl, and to her parents. She missed all that. She looked down at her shoes for a long time. Soon, a cement factory came into sight, and after driving down a narrow road for some time, she saw a small village nestled at the foot of a low hill.

They got out of the car and were walking toward the village when they ran into a group of men standing around and handing out drinks. They refused to let anyone enter the village without taking a drink first. The neatly square man gulped down a large bowlful of liquor, and made Rina drink some, too. When they were done, they were each given a round, red rice cake, a stack of which had been neatly lined up on a wooden bench. The man told Rina to go help the village women, who were slicing up rice cakes and moving trays of fruit. They sang and laughed as they worked. When she was among them, no one would have guessed that Rina was a foreigner not yet sixteen years old.

Both the men and women of this village wore elaborate headdresses; and long skirts dyed red, blue, or yellow, and layered with a band of white cloth. The children were in charge of filling up and carrying buckets of water to the men, who scrubbed their horses and bulls clean down to every nook and cranny, even inside their ears and around their anuses. Water dripping onto dry ground, the clip-clop of contented horses trotting about among the people, kids chortling until they were out of breath—Rina hadn't heard such peaceful sounds in a long time. She stood quietly for a moment and enjoyed them.

In the afternoon, they all gathered in an open lot. The women had draped blue cloth over their white dresses and stuck red flowers all over themselves. The men were wearing flower wreaths around their necks. The meticulously cleaned horses and bulls also had flowers around their heads, and they trotted to and fro happily among the people, while the drunk people ran among the horses and cows like little children. The neatly square man took Rina over to one of the women, who put some makeup on her face. The women smiled at their reflections in mirrors that had been brought outside. Rina couldn't remember what she had looked like back in the sleeping car, or reflected in the water of the well. From a certain angle, she felt like she looked like a certain old auntie who was now dead; from another angle, like some man she didn't know.

Someone started to pound on a drum, and five men with naked torsos stepped out into the center of the lot, shaking their long black hair. The quick and regular rhythm of the drums worked them into a frenzy and they spun around with their swords. All of a sudden, the swords came down on the necks of the horses and bulls. The bodies of the decapitated beasts writhed in the grass, and the men collected the blood spurting from the animals' throats and smeared it all over their white clothes. Then, the women who were decorated with flowers, and others who had adorned their necks and limbs with brass rings began to sing and spin around in circles. The men smeared blood on the members of the audience as well. On this day, the white clothes of all who were present were to be covered with blood.

At the center of the lot were masks painted red, yellow, and blue, on a candle-lit altar. A priest dressed in red and wearing a mask with large ears and red lips stepped out and embraced the bloody corpses of the dead livestock. He put them in large white sacks beautifully embroidered and adorned with flowers, slung the sacks over his shoulders, and dragged them away. The villagers bowed with as much reverence to the dead beasts as they would have paid to their ancestors.

Everyone stayed up and chatted the night away. Rina found out that each brass ring represented a momentous and often perilous event in the lives of the women who wore them. Once the rings were secured, they never came off. It was a strange fate. When it got late, the people broke up and congregated at a few houses, where they played marbles or cards for money. The neatly square man gambled, too. Even though it seemed like an opportune time to escape, Rina couldn't quite shake off the man's persistent glances in her direction.

When night came, the neatly square man undressed Rina yet again, murmuring the same two-syllable word she couldn't understand.

"What the hell are you saying, you bastard?" she demanded. The man opened his eyes and repeated the word, as if in answer to her question. In the beginning, Rina had been paralyzed with fear from the moment the man unbuckled his belt and took off his pants up to the moment he unfastened his wristwatch. She was no longer afraid. She lifted her legs when the man told her to, and put them down again when he told her to. She rolled over onto her stomach when told, and lifted up her ass up when told. That night, she realized that her sixteenth birthday was probably coming up soon.

A group of villagers had gathered around a house. The lights were ablaze all throughout the house, and everyone was peering in. The woman had a small, dark face, and a giant belly. She lit a fire and heated some water, which she then poured into a white porcelain basin on the floor. She did this all herself, waddling around the house, stopping when the labor pains hit her, then straightening back up when they had passed. She took off all her clothes and lay on the floor with just a white cloth draped over her belly. An old woman with white hair came in, stuck her head in between the pregnant woman's legs, and uttered an incantation. As her contractions came more and more frequently, the pregnant woman put a mysterious looking berry in her mouth and chewed on it. Rina found herself eagerly pressed against the front door without even realizing it. While the two women waited for the baby to come, the husband and his friends waited outside, smoking dried herbs.

When the baby didn't come right away, the old woman started to doze off. The woman in labor was drenched in sweat, and she looked like she had passed out. Then, her five children came in, looking as though they had just gotten out of bed, and each planted a kiss on her heaving belly. Perhaps that was what did it; the woman let out a violent scream, at which the old woman started awake and began to utter a very powerfully intoned incantation, spitting into the pregnant woman's crotch in her agitation. Rina found herself breathing heavily along with the woman in labor. Just then, the black mound of the woman's pubic hair split open, revealing the top of the baby's head. For a while, the baby seemed unsure whether or not it should come out. But by some force, the tiny black head gradually made its way out. The old woman took the baby's head in her hands, shifted it from side to side, and the head slipped out, followed by the shoulders. It was over, and both Rina and the young mother exhaled loudly. The baby made no sound. The baby's father and friends came in and wrapped the infant up in white cloth, then strangled it on the spot. All children born on the day of this festival were bad omens, and were not allowed to live. The men took the dead baby away, and the old woman sat on the young mother's stomach until her placenta spilled out. No one wept—not the people who had been watching, and not even the woman who had just given birth, but Rina felt a sharp pain in her lower belly.

Rina walked to the entrance of the village and looked down at the road leading away toward the hill. She wanted to call out for her mother, but she didn't. She thought that if life meant looking at the neatly square man her whole life, listening to his two-syllable word her whole life, having a baby on a festival day and killing it with her own hands, she might just be able to spend the rest of her life here. She stared at the valley as it prepared for the rising sun. Something that looked like white snow fell onto her head and face, so she cupped her hands and caught some. Grains of sand.

On the drive back, the neatly square man drove the jeep in loops and veers, perhaps because he was drunk. They got back to the factory around dawn.

6

It was cloudy for several days. The skies were overcast all day long and only the center of the heights, where it was still a bit humid, blossomed with yellow flowers. The slender-faced boy who cleared the table after lunch looked over at Rina and grinned. The neatly square man saw Rina stick her tongue out and flirt with the boy. The man dragged the boy into the factory, stripped his shirt, threw cold water on him, and began to beat him mercilessly. Rina ran after them.

"Why don't you pick on someone your own size instead of a kid, you mean son of a bitch. You're a rotten, crazy bastard, you fat rodent!" she yelled.

The man slapped Rina across the face and she fell to the floor. The boy who had been beaten half to death was called "Pii."

Like a madman, the neatly square man beat every one of the workers, all fifty of them. Perhaps it was the weather. The sound of the whip gave everyone goose bumps. The old man sat clutching the brown notebook that he took everywhere with him, his expression like that of a philosopher confronted with a moment of utmost gravity. The newlywed woman clipped her nails with a pair of scissors, not caring one way or the other, and the woman who had held the high-ranking administrative post yelled out her political doctrines louder than ever. They were all mad. Rina hoped this was all a dream. She sat up in the corner where she had fallen on the floor and snickered like a crazy person.

In the afternoon, all they had to do was reheat the gruel that had been served for breakfast and ladle it out into fifty dishes. Rina took three of the sleeping pills she'd been given by the first guide and crushed them in the bowl she planned to serve up to the neatly square man. When she had served everyone else, she picked a chipped bowl and added two pills into the gruel and mixed it well. She first served the neatly square man. He had just woken up and he downed the gruel. The face of the old man as he ate his gruel from the chipped bowl seemed sad, somehow.

That night, a rough wind blew over the heights. The neatly square man lay on his stomach on his damp bed in a deep sleep. Rina pinched his cheek and twisted it. She grabbed the cord of the incandescent lamp and shook it. She pinched his limbs. Nothing; he had surely passed out. Rina went outside where the women were waiting, and called them in. There was no way they could move his body on their own.

Rina ran to the log cabin in search of the boy. Another man had rolled over the boy in his sleep, so she couldn't see his face, but when she called out his name, he sat up. Rina took the boy by the hand and led him to the room of the neatly square man. Even with the boy's help, it was impossible to move the sleeping man. The boy went to the log cabin and brought back a stretcher. It took all of their strength to roll the man onto it.

They dragged the man up to the factory and stopped in front of a giant container shaped like a drum can. Raising their arms as high as they could, they brought the corner of the stretcher up to the edge of the container and slid the neatly square man's body into the gelatinous white chemical substance. Then, they all collapsed. The neatly square man never made a sound as his body spiraled softly around in the container.

RINA

Next, it was the old man's turn. He had been sleeping among the other workers, and was light and easy to move, even without the stretcher. There was a brief disagreement about what should be done with him.

"He's done nothing wrong. It's all our fault. And how sad his old wife would be if she was left all alone."

"What are you talking about? If he opens his mouth, we're screwed."

"No, it might be better. If our husbands leave us we can get remarried to men in the country of P. Think of how nice that would be. I bet you the men of P would be really good to us."

Ultimately, the women decided that the most important thing was to guard their reputations as chaste women. In went the old man. The darkened factory lit up; they had activated the centrifugal extractor. The screws inside the container began to rotate slowly, followed by the drum, and gradually, everything sped up. After a minute, the separation was over and the white liquid began to boil like a blast furnace. The women stood under the giant container rubbing their palms together and mumbling their apologies to the old man. They also talked about the neatly square man.

"He's huge and takes a really long time to come. It was tough for me, but God knows, it really must have hurt for you," the women said, looking thoughtfully at Rina.

Later, the three women walked to the valley behind the factory and watched the waste come pouring out of the factory. The neatly square man's belt buckle, shreds of his black pants, pieces of his black wallet, bits of the old man's striped clothes, and the cover of his brown notebook all came floating down. But surprisingly, not a trace of blood. Rina licked her lips nervously, terrified that the two men might suddenly show up alive and well. Feeling like heroes, the women ran up to the log cabin to wake up the sleeping workers.

"You're all free now. Get up! Get out of here!"

But the workers paid no attention to them; they simply hunched over even more tightly in their sleep. Rina grabbed the boy's hand and they started to run, along with the other women. Soon after, her right sneaker broke in half, so Rina took off her other shoe and used the shoelace to bind together the split halves. She then strapped the contraption on her shoulder.

The three women and the boy passed over the dark heights and walked toward what they thought to be south. The exhilaration of escaping the plant soon faded, and was replaced with the suspicion that they were going in circles. They would find themselves under the hill covered in white flowers that they had just passed, or by a pair of very familiar looking large trees. But like soldiers leaving a battleground, they continued doggedly in silence. No one mentioned the chemical plant.

The sun was the master of this place; it heated the earth and sky. The air at the height of day seemed to boil yellow and the earth, scorched from the sun and drought, was laced with a network of fine fissures. There was not a creature in sight, not a single bird flying through the air. It seemed that anything, plant or animal, would burn to a crisp in the sun. After what seemed like hours, the dizzyingly high mountains gave way to plains of waist-high wild grass. There, they encountered a lone tree. It had branches like open arms, and was burned black as coal.

The ground was uneven and sunken, like earth after the rain that had been trampled by a herd of bulls. What had happened to this path? Rina bent down to touch the dirt. It was sand, like coarse grains of salt, browned by the sun. No matter where she looked, no matter where she turned her gaze, there was no avoiding this road that stretched resolutely across the plain, covered in yellowing grass. Rina christened this road the field of salt. The earth was dried and full of protrusions sharp as knives. After just a few steps, the remaining sole of Rina's shoe was completely torn up. She was forced to take that shoe off as well, tie it up with her other shoe, and sling them both over her shoulders. This meant she had to walk gingerly, hopping from one foot to the other. Every time she took a step, a pain in exact proportion to the weight of her body pierced through her foot and made its way up to her heart. In the beginning, she screamed with each step, but eventually, lost the energy even to scream; her mind became fuzzy, and she felt cool and unburdened to the top of her scalp. Her mind was consumed by the pain under her feet from the field of salt, and she forgot all about the arduous process of crossing the border. The pain she experienced on the field of salt lived on like a raw thing in her; for a long time to come, it would manifest itself in her blood vessels as an unexpected palpitation.

The salt field ended abruptly, as if it had never existed, and was replaced with a desert of dizzying sand swirls. Here, the wind blew incessantly, filling their mouths and ears. It was impossible to figure out which way to turn your face to avoid the tiny grains of sand. They all reflexively covered their faces with their clothing. Night came and the temperature dropped, chilling their exposed flesh. The high-ranking administrator put her hands on her hips and made an executive decision to stop for the night. The two women crawled into a hole in the sand first and lay down, clinging to each other. The sun had heated the sand, and the hole was warm, like under the sheets of a recently vacated bed. Rina and Pii climbed in after them and lay down on their sides. All they had to rely on were each other's fevered, starving bodies. They all cried in their sleep that night, calling out the names of their pets back at home, the names of people they'd met while fulfilling their patriotic duties. During the night, roused by a noise, Rina sat up and saw an orange column of fire shoot up at the edge of the desert.

Rina was afraid of the desert, so she held tightly onto Pii and filled her eyes with his face. She gently wiped the sand off of him, but it kept blowing in and quickly filled their ears again. The gunshots they'd heard near the border, the mother sobbing as she held her dead baby, the chirping of birds in a faraway sky hidden by a complex of large branches—sounds, all of these sounds poured into Rina's ears like the sand and she couldn't keep them out. Pii gripped Rina's shoulders and mumbled in his sleep. At dawn, the sky had turned an inky blue and Rina thought she heard something. She sat up and saw a giant headed toward them, carrying the blue sky on its head. The giant had long black hair and its silhouette moved as one with the sky. Rina shook the others awake. They followed the giant, walking in its soft footsteps and mimicking its ponderous movements. Strangely enough, the pain in Rina's feet had disappeared, and her body felt light. As the desert gave way once more to plains sprinkled with yellow flowers, Rina looked back and watched the giant, now just a dot on the horizon, head back toward the desert.

By the afternoon, they were almost out of the desert. The grass was shorter, the ground softer. They saw a river, bordered by tall grass burnt yellow at the tips. As soon as they saw the water, all four of them tore their clothes off and waded in. None of them had taken a proper bath since crossing the border, and now they doggy-paddled around awkwardly in the lukewarm water. It was heavy, murky, and smelled fishy—unlike the clear, running water Rina was used to. Her limbs loosened as soon as they hit the water. Rina had always been a good swimmer, but now she barely had the energy to paddle her arms; it was difficult to even keep her head above water. When she let her face drop under the surface, her body floated up so that it was parallel to the floor of the river, making her forget her own weight. The water was so murky with floating particles that it was impossible to gauge its depth. The river extended south and grew wider downstream.

Rina lay naked on the riverbank and dried herself. The moisture soon evaporated, leaving her body nice and toasty; the only trace of wetness left was in her hair. Her eyes seemed to be enveloped in a milky layer of drowsiness. She sat up to force herself to stay awake, which made her dizzy, so she curled her spine forward like a bow, and straightened it out again. Just as fish swim passively with the current while they're in their element but flop around out of the water, Rina flopped about on the ground, twisting her body this way and that. She looked down at her feet. They were swollen from blisters that had popped and reformed. She couldn't remember what her feet used to look like. It seemed impossible that they would ever go back to not being covered in scars.

They walked along the river. At one point, the river became visibly narrow and sluggish. Soon, they were no longer able to walk alongside it because there were too many sharp stones. They were trying to decide what to do when a large basket-shaped boat made of woven bamboo glided by. It looked like a hot air balloon Rina had once seen in a book as a little girl, and she was overjoyed for a moment at the thought becoming a scientist and flying off into space in this hot air balloon. It was hard for all of them to climb into the small, woven boat; it kept on tilting over from one side to another, and they had to sit very still to stay balanced. Eventually, it got caught on a branch that had fallen into the river and refused to budge no matter how hard they struggled with the oars. They all cursed vehemently, grumbling that they should have stayed back at the plant, living comfortably off gruel. As the river tapered even further and the marsh gave way to dry land, they all stopped rowing. At that moment, the bamboo basket boat broke apart with a loud ripping noise. They all burst out laughing despite their exhaustion, and the rush of energy helped them to swim out of the river. They dried off quickly, but the lukewarm weight of the river stayed with them through the marshy grass that stuck to their backs, and drained them of their strength.

Their pace slowed to a crawl. Rina wished that when she blinked once, she would be in the middle of a city. Of course this didn't happen, no matter how many times she blinked. They plodded along the river. The sun set in a flash and night came, but they went on. We can't just do whatever we want to the rivers, the desert, or the trees! Rina thought to herself. And then, they started to hear—faintly, at first—the quick and easy beat of a song, coming from somewhere in the dark. In the distance, they saw cars crossing a bridge that extended over a dried-up riverbed, bringing the din of a city with them.

7

HOLDING PII'S HAND, RINA HAD LANDED IN THE HEART OF A CITY
on the southwestern tip of the continent, best known for its
narcotics tourism. They had to hitch rides with six separate cars
to get to the center of the city. A few times, they were picked up by
fruit trucks and got to eat bananas and other tropical fruit that the
drivers tossed back to them. One time, a man in a suit, who had
picked them up without asking any questions, kept stopping at gas
stations and making phone calls instead of filling up his truck. They
eventually caught on to him, and when the man left for a moment
at a deserted gas station, they rifled through the truck and ran
away. All there was to steal were some cigarettes, some candy, and
a half-eaten bag of cookies.

In the mornings, they found themselves being buffeted in
all directions by the crowds in the streets. The city was near a
national border and acted as a sort of narcotic triangle through
which drugs entered the country and were circulated. The main
industry was drugs. Here, all of the buildings were painted
white. There were no brick buildings stained with rain, no wood
buildings baked by the sun. There were no faded, timeworn,
weathered colors. All of the buildings had front yards filled with
small, brightly colored flowers. Flower-lined paths led to upscale

boutiques, whose clientele consisted of extraordinarily tall or big tourists with blue eyes.

Rina would sit on a street bench or lean against a wall and dumbly watch the people go by. This city was different from the many places she had passed through; here, the people's faces showed no wrinkles or wounds that spoke of sorrow. After a while, she learned to hold out her hand whenever a tourist shoved a camera in her face to take her photograph. Some tourists unabashedly took the fruit they had been eating and placed it in front of the beggars, as if giving leftovers to a dog. Still, the fruit peels they gave had plenty of juice to suck up. Rina and her friends would swoop in like eagles and snatch away unfinished bottles of soda from outdoor cafes before the waiters came out to clear the tables. Once, they picked up a half-empty bottle of liquor and drank it without realizing. Rina's insides swelled up and she rolled around on the ground in pain. But it was the only way for them to get enough to drink.

At night, the face of the city changed completely. Minibuses filled with tourists milled about the streets, and oversized neon signs sparkled precariously in the air. People exited their cars in small clusters and went to upscale restaurants where they ordered tons of food that they never finished. Rina once saw an overworked and tired waiter get slapped by a woman, who then proceeded to giggle and chatter away as if she had short-term memory loss. The waiter left the restaurant through the back door and cried for a bit next to a giant pile of disposed of food, then made a phone call. When he went back inside, Rina and the others dug through the restaurant dumpster. They found some shriveled up sausages that had gone bad, and a cake speckled with mold. By now, even rotten food failed to give them diarrhea.

Once the crowds returned to their clean homes in the suburbs, the homeless took over the city. They slept in dead zones of the road, next to phone booths, pretty much anywhere on the street. They never made a fuss. Rina often slept under trees or near some of the bigger municipal buildings, and sometimes, although it was dangerous, on a wood plank under a truck at the truck depot.

Once in a while, gunshots broke through the order of the city and paralyzed the traffic. Sometimes, lovers came from faraway countries to commit suicide together, and sometimes, people would stagger along the central lane divider, then dive into the oncoming headlights. Once, when Rina was sleeping under the newly repaired awning of a temple, the night air was filled with several minutes of gunshots. Police sirens followed shortly, and an ambulance. Several men in white shirts were sprawled out on the road, bathed in blood. A couple of cars had smashed into a row of storefronts, and a few others had driven over onto the curb. The city was back to normal by the next morning, but several homeless people who had been sleeping out in the streets were killed and their bodies were taken to the morgue.

Rina had also been to the morgue, once. She had been sleeping in front of a building and woke up on a hard bed with her arms and legs tied to the bedposts. The building hummed with activity. They had mistaken her for a corpse and taken her there. In a panic, Rina called out for her mother. She managed to slip out of her restraints and into the basement without being seen, and took advantage of the opportunity to explore. Rows of boxes containing corpses were lined up along the walls, and a man carrying a steel-ring binder would pull out the drawers, examine the faces of the dead for a moment, then slide them back in.

After a ruckus in the night, there would usually be a crackdown, even if it was just a formality, and the city would fall silent for a while. Restaurants that had been bustling the day before would see a sharp drop in customers and leftover food. The best option at such times was to get official handouts from relief organizations. But, as always, those places were overcrowded.

One evening, while the two other women went looking for food, Rina and Pii sat under the awning of a house boat, gripping their empty stomachs and looking out at the city that spread out before their eyes. The house boats were fastened to a stake, and they swayed a little along with the current. The night air was gummy and all the mosquitos made it impossible to sleep. Rina regretted not walking into town with the women, but she lacked the energy. The flamboyant nightscape sparkled under the dark sky. The lights that shot up to the skies like cannons were blinding. Pii, who had staggered up to go pee over the ledge of the narrow balcony, turned his head and looked into the window of the house. He zipped up his pants and beckoned for Rina to come join him. There were three men inside the house sitting around a cardboard box filled with bills. The men were taking the bills out one by one and holding them up to a machine that shone a pale blue light on the paper. Suddenly, one of the men turned to the window and pulled a knife out of his pocket, and the two other men followed suit. Rina and Pii took off and ran to the center of the city in record time.

About three weeks after their arrival in the city, they chanced upon a full-length mirror outside a public restroom and were able to admire the state they were in. The two married women were now as slender as they'd been when they were single. They all commented on how much Pii had grown since his days back at the plant, and measured themselves against him. Rina pounded and pinched at her thighs, which had become as solid as rock. The four of them put their grimy black faces together and took a photo without a camera.

The fantasies of the country of P that had filled their heads were gradually fading away. Rina became very ill with a high fever. Sitting out in the sun made her body feel mushy, like it was giving way. Rina crawled into a trashcan and began waving her arms deliriously in the air.

"You're our leader, you can't be like this. If you don't stop, I'll put you in an insane asylum or take you back to the factory," the newlywed woman said. The women snickered at this, since she had been the one acting crazy back at the plant. But Rina got weaker and weaker. She couldn't stay awake.

One day, they were sitting in front of a municipal building picking bugs out of a bag of crackers, when two good-natured-looking men walked up to them.

"Hello, it's so nice to meet you. We're missionaries from the country of P. We know how hard it must have been for you to get all the way here. We want to help you get to P safely. God bless you all," one of the men said, with a big smile. These men seemed much taller and gentler than the people of P that Rina had seen on television.

"Such handsome men," the women whispered to each other. Yet none of them could quite believe what was happening.

The missionaries had rice crackers, bottles of water, and a first-aid kit in their car. One of the men put his hand against Rina's forehead and fed her an aspirin. After she had chewed the aspirin and swallowed it, Rina covered herself in a quilt and fell asleep in the backseat of their car, clutching her sneakers.

They were taken to a white church building with a courtyard filled with flowering trees. The missionaries took them to the back where, like paradise at the end of a nightmare, the trees made everything seem unreal with their fragrance. The place was full of people who had fled their homes to get to P. There were people washing their clothes by a water pump, people covered in blue nylon cloth as they got their hair cut, people mending clothes, people picking at their ears while they chatted, people singing and playing pipes. People who all looked peaceful in that moment. Even so, their bodies seemed weighed down by the weariness of their respective journeys—journeys that had layered themselves onto the people's bodies and at times dragged their expressions to dark and incomprehensible places.

The missionaries took the four of them through the yard and into the annex where there was a box full of clothes. Rina got a monochrome sweat suit and the women got floral print dresses, which they put on and admired, smiling shyly at their reflections in a mirror. The clothes were nice, but truth be told, it was the slow and steady smell of food that stirred them. They went into the cafeteria and were served soup and rice on a tray. The missionaries warned them that they'd often seen people die from eating too much too quickly in one sitting after having starved for a long time. They delivered a rambling prayer that abbreviated in an orderly fashion their journey from escape to present day, and also included their aspirations for the future. The four of them looked down at the soup and white rice, not knowing whether to cry or laugh. They were all deeply moved. They started eating quietly at first, but their spoons began to move faster and faster.

From the cafeteria, they could see out the open door into the backyard. Other escapees strolled among the white flower petals that fluttered down from the trees and fell onto their heads. That's when Rina saw three people leaning against a white wall with their backs to the large pillar of the main building: her father, her mother, and her brother. Rina's tongue went stiff and she was unable to speak for a moment. Finally, she managed to whisper under her breath, "I see you're getting along well, just as you always used to." She interlaced her fingers and looked down at them without moving for a very long time. She wanted to go back to her family. But she was too frustrated with the world. Her temper was too foul to return to them without making a fuss. Rina looked from her family up to the white petals fluttering onto their heads.

Two men came running in. The two women who had been eating looked up and ran toward them—their husbands—who were still waiting to get into P. They embraced. The women began sobbing and sighing with relief into their husbands' arms. Rina flashed them a V-sign with her fingers. Moments later, the wife of the old man who had met his tragic end at the chemical plant came running in in her bare feet.

"Where's my old man? Wasn't he with you?"

Everyone who had contributed to the old man's death looked away uncomfortably, and the disappointed old woman collapsed to the floor, shaking. They were told that the seventeen remaining members of the group had split up into three groups. Rina wondered what had happened to the sewing factory girl, but she didn't ask about her, or anyone else. She put down her spoon and stood up quietly. The men turned to their wives.

"Isn't that the kid who escaped with us? Her parents are over there," Rina heard the husbands say, but she pretended not to hear them.

Rina took Pii's hand and together they walked out into the street. There were several stalls stocked with piles of fresh tropical fruit. The tourists sat outside under parasols, reading. A pair of pointy-toed shoes covered in pink beads and sequins caught Rina's eye. She imagined herself in a thin, airy dress and those shoes, walking under a hot sun. She'd never owned a pair of shoes that weren't sneakers. The first thing she wanted to buy, in great abundance, when she got to the country of P, were shoes. Rina turned and looked for Pii, who usually stuck by her like a shadow.

"Pii, hey, Pii, look at these. Look at these shoes."

She heard no answer, but couldn't look away from the shoes.

"Pii, Pii! Look at these shoes."

She turned around, but Pii was gone. Rina hesitated, wondering whether she should take the shoes and run while the stall owner was busy with a customer. The whole time, she kept looking around for Pii. Ultimately, the shoes were sold around sunset to a tall blonde woman who picked them up and exclaimed *Beautiful!* several times before buying them. Rina stared at the empty space where the shoes had been. Then, she jumped up and headed toward an alley swarming with tourists. The sun had set, and Pii was nowhere in sight.

Rina searched for Pii for days. The city had been preparing for a long festival for months, and there were rainbow-colored cloths tied to branches and the tops of buildings. Rina followed a procession of men dressed in white cotton loincloths, their faces covered in a white powder meant to ward off evil. There was a sewer pipe that protruded slightly above the sidewalk running from the market to the river. It was where the pipe met the river, where the sewage poured out into open water without being properly filtered, that she found Pii lying on top of a cement covering, like a tired old dog. As the sewage spewed out into the river, the house boats, anchored by a single stake, drifted slowly downstream, then back up, pushed back bit by bit by the sewage.

8

THE MEN STOOD UNDER THE WAXING MOON IN A CIRCLE AROUND the singer's white tent, which glowed in the lamplight like an egg about to hatch. They smoked cigarettes that they held between two fingers in a leisurely manner. As the night deepened, the babies clung to their mothers' chests, and the women in turn rested their chins on the crowns of their babies' heads and looked up at the sky. Rina and Pii had followed the procession of men with white powdered faces throughout the ten-day festival. The men didn't wash themselves for a whole month, and danced wherever they went. Rina and Pii had followed the men because there was nowhere else to go. Now, they had come to a plain high up in the hills, populated with clusters of white tents like a refugee camp. It was dark now, but during the day, you could see the horizon beyond the low tents.

The woman who sat in front of a cracked oval mirror framed with floral gilt was called "the singer of eternal life." She struggled to raise her eyelids, heavy under the weight of her false lashes, and stared into her own bloodshot eyes. Thick, dark brows trembled above the reddened rims of her eyes. The singer stared at her reflection as if it was the only place where she could see herself. Her eyes grew increasingly bloodshot from the intensity of her gaze. A boy came into the tent and loosened the silk shoes that had been wrapped tightly around the woman's ankles. He grinned when he saw the old woman's toes wriggle. With one hand, the singer took the glass of cold water that the boy passed her, and with the other, she pulled off the heavy wig pressing down on her skull and placed it in front of the mirror. It was only when the giant wig came off that her slight shoulders and collarbones were exposed. With her right hand, the singer slapped her own neck, killing a mosquito that had been chasing the light. The squished mosquito was matted with its own blood on the woman's palm.

The drums sounded, signaling the opening of the performance. As the singer came out with her head held high and piled with black hair, she ran into Pii and Rina, looking like a pair of wretched beggars. The singer wore a blue silk dress cinched at the waist with a wide silk belt. Her face was as cold as a piece of finely polished lead. When she saw Rina lurking about the tent, she coughed as though she had a fish bone caught in her throat, then finally got a word out. Rina had a pair of worn sneakers hanging around her neck, and holding one in each hand, she bowed to the singer, as she was wont to do. At that moment, Rina had no idea that in the very near future, she would be wearing the older woman's clothes and performing as the most famous singer in the region.

The singer didn't use any special instruments on stage. The audience was filled with child-sized seats. A group of adults who had been conversing loudly suddenly tipped back in their chairs, making everyone laugh. The singer slowly walked up on stage and sat down, picked up her only instrument—a small drum—and slipped it onto her feet. When she moved her feet up and down, the wooden planks clicked together, and the performance began.

Eooo, ng ng ng ng, ahhhhhh, eeeh-heeheeheehee.

The first sounds to come out of the singer's throat were short and staccato, like wood being chopped. Her voice was low, and she kept the tempo at a moderate pace. Once in a while, a gust of wind would join in and hit the flap of the tent. The people gradually got excited and stood up. Someone lit a stick of incense and placed it in front of the singer, and someone else played an erratic song on a two-stringed homemade instrument. A woman got up and wandered around the audience, waving her hands in the air. The singer's voice fluctuated with the audience's reactions. Her voice was as unsteady as the wind that wandered across the plains, and at times, it seemed like her throat might start to bleed. As the fluctuations in her voice became greater, the white makeup on her singer's face became splotchy with sweat. The atmosphere in the tent ripened. A man with a crew cut came out and clasped the singer's knees and wept. Others followed suit, murmuring about all of the unjust things that had happened to them. As the singer's voice rose, the people began to sway aimlessly or droop to the ground, clinging to their neighbors' sleeves. *I thought I'd buried my love deep in my heart and forgotten about it, but it's all coming back to me as if it happened yesterday. Love goes on.* Rina later found out that these were the lyrics to the song. The babies strapped to their mothers' backs kicked and gurgled happily. The people clung to the feet of the singer of eternal life, muttering and rolling their eyes back in their heads. That's when Rina realized that perhaps she was in a very strange country.

There was a five-minute intermission in the performance. Rina loosened the strings around her ankle and wriggled her toes, which had been tightly wrapped in silk, one by one. Pii came in and spooned some fruit juice into her mouth and massaged her shoulders. Rina would always reach back to grab a hold of Pii's wrists, and only then did she feel at ease. By then the intermission was already half over, and for the rest of the time, Rina slept all the sleep she would get that day. All the while, horses loped around the plains outside. One of them, born with a short leg, spent its days galloping up to the horizon then back, over and over again.

KANG YOUNG-SOOK

Rina's performance as a singer was rather silly. The songs that the singer before her—who was now ill—sang had settled into the very flesh of the people of the region from hundreds of years back, when faraway western maritime powers had frequented the country. They couldn't be taught or learned. Rina had tailored with her own hands the old costume that was too big for her, and she sat onstage and said whatever she felt like. At first, this embarrassed her, so she would imitate bits and pieces of rap songs she had furtively learned from her friends at school, or perform drawn-out versions of the songs she used to sing while playing jump rope.

"You don't have to be a good singer to do it for a living. You can pretty much say whatever you want, just in a song. No one's going to understand, anyways. And we need to eat," she told Pii, and demonstrated what she meant. Pii had tilted his head in a confused way.

The audience stirred when Rina stepped on stage. The older audience members that had worshipped the original singer like a goddess were no longer in attendance; they had been replaced by teenage boys and men young enough to hold jobs. These people, who lived with the horizon in their hearts, found Rina as fascinating as a fairy from the heavens. This was mainly because the strict regulation of births per family made girls of Rina's age a rarity in the region. Such young girls were often treated with leniency, even if they were frauds. Acutely aware of this was the region's only so-called talent manager, Producer Kim, who at this moment stood at the back of the tent, picking at his ear. Rina closed her eyes, furrowed her brow, and began to babble away.

> Today's story is the story of a girl who crossed a border
> into your country and is now twenty-four.
> The lower part of the globe is filled with poor
> women. You say there are poor women everywhere?

RINA

Hold on, even if you have something to say. Right now, it's my turn to speak.

This eighteen-year-old is always cheating others, always being cheated, but there's nothing she doesn't know. She knows where to touch men so they like it, she knows where to touch women so they like it, she knows it all. When my dad, who spent his days loafing around anyways, suddenly died of an illness one day, the broker who always used to stare at me came to see me the next day. If he hadn't brought that bread filled with white cream, I might have stayed home. Every piece of bread filled with white cream took me farther and farther away from home.

As soon as we crossed the border, the broker sold me. He sold me for a sum of money that wouldn't even buy a crumpled up shell of a car. The man who bought me told me I would be in trouble if I ran away, and he took me to bed every night. I escaped one night in my underwear. Then I met a good-natured-looking woman. She sold me, too. I wonder how much money she got. I was sold to someone in a city that was more than a ten-hour drive away. I don't even remember what I did there. You know, ten of you probably couldn't amount to the price of a girl like me. That's what the man who guarded us used to say. I got weak and skinny, and they sold me again.

I went to the countryside, the real countryside, with nothing but fields and paddies. A skinny man with a small face welcomed me with a purple bellflower. He needed a woman to help with the farm work. He didn't beat me, and he didn't starve me. During the day I had to work on the farm, and at night he worked on me, so I was dozing off all the time, even when

I walked. Then I had a baby. When the baby turned three, this is what it started to say:

Damn it, my mom's a foreigner. Is your mom a foreigner? My mom crossed the border to make money to pay for her older brother's tuition, and she met my dad. Then she had me. I'm a lucky kid with an adventurous mother. My mom's papers are fake. But we're proud of who we are, us farmers. But my mom wanted to go to another country. My dad said, why don't you go out and make some money. So mom went to a city where there's an airport and tall buildings. I'm going to get out of this backwater town someday, too.

People from the city ask me, Where are you from, ma'am? Then I say, I'm only twenty-four, how dare you call me ma'am, really. Then they ask me again, Where are you from? Why is your accent so odd? Then I answer them, shyly, the border.

When Rina was done with her bit, the producer, who had been standing in the back with his arms crossed, slowly walked up to the stage. He gave a short, crude translation of Rina's words, then instigated applause. It was impossible to hold a performance if it rained, or if the producer was passed out from too much drinking. Pii stood in front of the tent and collected admission. Some people brought unplucked chicken carcasses as payment, or sheets they said had been part of their dowries, and that now smelled of mothballs. Pii noted down every person's face, and kept his notes carefully. Over the next few days, he would have to go from house to house, collecting unpaid fees.

9

Rina and Pii came out of the tent and walked a long way. When they arrived at the village, which constituted several houses sprinkled cunningly over a low hill, they headed to their house and lit the lamp by the front door. They went inside, rolled up the shabby lace covering above the bedposts, and carefully inspected the face and body of the former singer who lay breathing heavily. If it had been impossible to figure out her age while she was on stage, she was now an obviously old woman without her thick makeup and her costume. Rina lifted the old woman's hips and patted the sheets underneath.

"Let's see if you peed the bed today, Granny. There were so many people in the audience tonight."

With a moistened towel, Rina wet the parched lips of the former singer, and fed her some water. After a moment, the water that the old woman couldn't swallow came dribbling out from between her twisted lips. Now that she had lost her job, the former singer spent most of her days in her bed, with its yellowing, worn lace trim. Perhaps she had yelled too loudly; one day, one side of the singer's body suddenly curled up and froze. The audience rushed the stage and squeezed her body, attempting to straighten it out, but the contortion, which had happened around her left shoulder and arm, refused to loosen up despite their best efforts and incantations. Sometimes, when she was tired of lying in bed, the former singer would walk painstakingly over to an armchair that was by the window, and sit there, stroking the scruff of a neighborhood cat that had crawled in through the window. When she tired of that, she went back to bed. These little journeys were like long marches for her.

It was Rina who fed her and took her to the bathroom. Rina had nowhere to go, and the former singer had no one to take care of her. At first, the village women took turns helping out, but they had to work all day in the tobacco fields, and stopped coming by. It was perhaps very good luck that Rina had naturally inherited the role of the singer, in this region where the only available work was the tedium of working in paddies or fields. In return for cleaning the singer's stinking waste, the old woman handed over her old jewelry and trinkets to Rina. A pair of wooden shoes with toes that curved up like a bow, silk dresses speckled with jade-colored mold on the seams of the sleeves and waistline, several small vials containing the musk from a cat's anal glands, some rusted earrings that were so heavy Rina couldn't wear them—all these now belonged to Rina.

Pii prepared dinner in the kitchen. Rina sat in an armchair that was so worn down that the stuffing leaked out like guts, and watched Pii cook. He'd grown so that none of his pants reached below his ankles. His shirts were tight around the shoulder, short in the sleeve, and his hair was long. The floor was littered with objects around which Pii had to carefully navigate as he cooked. He started by pouring some oil into a black pan and threw in some diced potatoes and water parsley. When the greens had wilted, he made a little space at the center of the pan, added noodles and spicy peppers, and sautéed it all for a few more minutes. He also added a spice that the locals added to all their dishes. He ladled some onto a large dish and took it, along with a glass of watered down liquor, to Rina in her armchair. Draped in her long dress, Rina stretched her legs out and ate the noodles, while Pii painstakingly fed the old woman. It was usually Rina's job, but Pii knew how tired Rina must be after a day of performing. Back at home, men who were too considerate of their women were considered fools. Afterwards, Pii took his seat in the lone armchair in the house and ate his noodles. Rina sat with her chin in her hand and asked him questions.

"How old are you?"

"Euh," Pii would say, laughing, or "Nauh," his mouth full of noodles.

"Dummy. I asked, how old are you?"

Still, Pii would repeat "Euh" or "Nauh," and keep eating his noodles.

"Where are my noodles? I haven't had my dinner yet, you brats."

Producer Kim came striding in just as Rina was ladling a second helping of noodles onto Pii's plate. He had approached Rina, telling her that his job was to evolve underrated local singers who were past their prime into international stars. He was from the same country as Rina, and technically had once also been an escapee. He said he was from an inland city with strong educational and cultural public policies, and he wore a cross around his neck that he often chewed on.

The producer also worked in a tent about an hour's drive away from Rina's house. Rina could never quite figure out how he transformed singers past their prime into rising stars; the tent itself was rather strange. In the morning, the man would drop off a carful of women at the tent, and take them away again at night. The tent was on a slightly raised plain and filled with several heavily made-up women sitting in wooden chairs. The women spent their days fixing their makeup, filing their nails, and getting into fights. They ate there and pissed there. They sat in a row under the tent, looking out toward the plains with their painted eyes, picking fights with the passing wind or throwing stones at passersby, accusing them of indifference. They would get irritated when their hair, which they had pulled back high on their heads, whipped against their faces in the wind; they would have to angrily puff on some cigarettes to calm themselves. When they got really bored, they would yell at the top of their lungs. When they got tired of that, they would crouch on the edge of the hill, not even realizing that they were flashing the entire prairie, and doze with their heads in their arms. No one knew where these women came from, but one thing was certain, they were going to be sold off by Producer Kim.

"Do you want to live here? You want to get to the country of P like everyone else, don't you? I'll tell you one thing though, the economy in P isn't so good these days. They don't give you much resettlement money. Don't you think it would be better to go to another country and make lots of money? I can sell you at a high price. It would be a good opportunity to get a job in a classy restaurant in a city."

On her way to get the money she'd put away in a ceramic pot, Rina nearly tripped over the household objects strewn all over the floor. The smoke from the producer's cigarette wafted above his grimy hair. Embarrassed, Rina nudged the knickknacks out of the way with her feet. The producer spent his days gambling with other loafers in the village. When the time came for Rina's performance, he headed over to her tent to promote the show. He extracted money from Rina in exchange for telling everyone in the village that she was a great singer. She trusted him because they were from the same country, and more than anything, it was a relief to be able to talk to him in her language. But even so, Rina wasn't always entirely at ease with him. For his troubles, he accepted neither gratitude nor the chickens and pigs that wandered around her yard, only cold, hard cash.

"Thanks. Generous as usual, I see. How old are you, anyways? Want me to guess? Sometimes, I could swear you're over thirty," he asked, as he counted the bills.

"Why do you care how old I am? Don't worry about me, just worry about your women in the tent."

"I gotta know how old you are to get a good price for you when I sell you. What are you going to do with this old hag? You're not going live with her till she dies, are you?" The man gestured toward the bed.

"Why? You want to sell her off, too?"

It was Pii, rather than Rina, who seemed more on edge around the producer. Ever since the producer had walked in, Pii hovered around the front gate, pacing back and forth with an anxious look on his face. Rina turned on the radio as if she didn't care whether the producer was there or not. The former singer called out to Rina in a strange voice. Rina went to see her, and came back out.

"Granny wants you to leave. She wants you to forget about selling me. She wants to know if you can make her better and save her."

Rina pretended to be calm as she waited for the producer to leave. The truth was, Rina was so terrified of him that she hardly even knew what she was saying. The producer was looking into a mirror hanging by the door and stroking his face.

Ever since Rina had crossed the border, she couldn't shake off the feeling that someone was following her. The suspicion that no matter who they were, they were conspiring to ruin her life, followed her wherever she went. Man or woman, old or young, it was all the same to Rina. They were always watching her, prepared to argue over the price of her body for collateral.

The producer left and the house became quiet again. The houses on the hill were all built without walls or fences against the horizon. From the house at the top of the hill, you could see the house at the bottom, but from the house at the bottom, you could only see the house directly above. The roofs were all shaped like shiitake mushroom heads, like they'd all been built by the same person, and there was an opening, rather like a terrace, about halfway through each roof. The residents often winnow grain in these terraces. They woke up early to work in the fields and paddies, then returned in the evenings, ate dinner, and went to bed early. Going to see the singer perform in the tent was all there was to do in their free time.

A woman sang wanly on the radio. Pii tried to explain to Rina what the song was about. He covered his eyes with both hands, squinted his eyes, and pretended to cry.

"Weeping lady? I'm right, aren't I?" Rina burst out laughing, and Pii waved his hands no.

"Then what is it? Try again."

Pii put his hands over his eyes and gently brushed his hands down over them.

"Oh, I get it. Close your eyes!" Pii clapped and laughed. Rina and Pii laughed and horsed around like fools in the cramped, messy house. Time passed very slowly.

There was a knock at the front gate, and the old woman's lover came to visit. He was pale from having rushed over so quickly. He opened a plastic bag and pulled out some pomegranates he'd brought over as a gift. He split one in half and handed one piece to Rina, the other to Pii. No one knew exactly what their relationship had been like when the former singer was at the height of her career, but now, he was her only visitor. When she saw the old man with his round little hat, the mobile side of the old woman's face crinkled up into a smile. With the help of her suitor, the old woman walked very slowly to the bed and lay down. The old man lowered all the curtains from the bedpost and sat where he could best see the old woman's face. The old couple giggled the hours away behind the curtains.

Rina had been trying to maintain a distance from Pii. Every time she heard the old woman purring, a part of her body stiffened and her buttocks clenched so hard that they lifted slightly off the armchair. At first, she thought the old woman was in pain, and that she must save her from the old man. But she soon found out that it wasn't pain. Pii was lying on the bare floor, where he often fell asleep. She could hear the old man chuckling, and the old woman's purring got louder. Even though she was weak, her purring carried a sort of energy in it. Whenever she heard it, Rina would look over at Pii's body, which clanked gently whenever he touched the dishes or the table on the floor near him. Angular shoulders and slender wrists, hands that were too big to be a boy's, long feet attached to emaciated ankles. Rina suddenly felt that Pii's body might rise up out of its ragged integuments and walk up to her. At that moment, the excited tones of the former singer escaped her contorted lips and shot through the mushroom-shaped roof up to the sky. Rina sat with her arms wrapped tightly around her knees and tried to keep her gaze down. Eventually, she was no longer able to help herself, and looked over at Pii. Their eyes met. Something was sticking out down there, under Pii's tattered pants, making a tent. Rina quickly looked away. Producer Kim was watching everything from his spot by the window. Drunk, he leaned against the glass. Rina looked at Pii's pyramid reaching up to the sky, and then at the producer's face floating in the window. It was so windy that they hadn't heard the dog barking outside.

10

THEY SAID THE WIND BLOWING IN FROM THE SEA WOULD BRING a violent storm. The clouds in the sky travelled ceaselessly above the horizon. From the highest point to the lowest, it took a long time for the wind to change direction and create the airflow that would bring rain with it. The people knew in their bodies what was happening above their heads, and they were afraid.

Just a few days after it started to rain, a 400-year-old marble bridge broke. It had been the pride of the village, with nine arches and intricate lotus flower patterns engraved carefully into all the ledges. The men of the village instinctively grabbed their shovels and ran to the river, but the swollen riverbed had swallowed the center deck and sent it cascading off downstream. As the old men clicked their tongues in agitation, the second deck, and then the last, were slowly and deliberately swept away, and eventually all traces of the bridge disappeared.

The rain travelled as if purposefully following the people wherever they went. Some of the concerned people gathered to light mugwort-scented incense. They drew roads and houses and trees on some paper, and wrote in pencil how many houses, cows, and pigs had been swept away by the flood. They drew it all because they couldn't hear each other above the rain.

At night, the horses turned wild with fear. The people tried to calm them by holding their heads tightly and whispering into their ears. When the rain came down on the houses on the hill, no one could go out. The water that flowed down the hill ate away at the soil so that the houses were on the verge of toppling over.

About ten days after it had first started to rain, they received word that a tunnel in a neighboring town had been completely demolished. As the tunnel collapsed, it brought down the steep hill from which it had been dug out, blocking off the whole road. The single radio station continued to play its old-fashioned songs about respecting elders.

When there was no more food left in your own house, you would ask your next-door neighbor for some food, and when even that ran out, you would eat raw grains drenched in moisture. It was impossible to fall asleep on an empty stomach with your waterlogged cotton blankets, and, if for some reason you were able to nod off, your ducks that were sleeping right outside your front door would be swept downstream. So, the people took to locking all of their livestock behind their gates. Even the mice figured it out, and joined everyone indoors, creeping silently across the walls with their spines arched and tails alert.

The rain showed no sign of stopping, and some of the village children that had been suffering from fever and diarrhea died. The women dressed their dead children in their prettiest clothes and hats and shoes, sat them in the buckets used for collecting rainwater, placed them in the center of the room, and talked to them every day.

The monsoon peaked when an old shrine about a kilometer away from the village was destroyed. The peaked spires of the shrine had inspired awe from miles away. The shrine had been built to immortalize the country's founding ideology. It was built on a hill, with dozens of rooms running from the base of the hill to the top. It had looked down on the vast plains and the horizon, surrounded by towering trees. When the people woke up that morning, it took them a while to figure out why the landscape seemed less cluttered. Then they realized that the shrine was now nothing but a lone roof on a heap of sand.

After nearly a month, the seasonal wind blew itself out. The sun warmed up the tubs of water that the villagers had left outside their doors. Before they realized it, the air was full of seed fluff and heat waves. The house was moldy and humid from the monsoon, but even worse were the bedsores that had appeared on the old woman's hips and buttocks.

They lugged the bathtub out into the yard and filled it with the sun-heated water. The old woman was much lighter than they had expected, and Pii was able to carry her easily on his back. The milky rainwater was full of cloudy debris. The old lady sat in the warm water and soaked her crooked body for the first time in ages. Pii lugged all of the household items and furniture outside, beginning with the old woman's bed. All of the families on the hill brought out their household wares and laid them on the roof, the windowsills, and in their small yards to dry.

Those who were intent on preserving the past worried that the shrine, which had preserved the spiritual strength of the village, had been destroyed. But the pragmatists were glad that the rainfall would make for an abundant harvest.

11

THE FIRST PERSON TO VISIT RINA AFTER THE MONSOON WAS MISSION-ary Jang. He was from the country of P, but unlike all the other transparent missionaries, who intimidated escapees by boasting of their country's democratic political system and dazzling night life, he would say, "Your country's crazy, and *my* country's rotten." He would tell the escapees that the country they had left was an insane asylum, and that the country of P was floating on bubbles. In his zeal to criticize the country of P, he often forgot his duty to guide the escapees there. Despite his keen anger, which he kept sheathed like a sword, he looked just as hungry as everyone else.

When Jang spoke, he always looked you straight in the eye with his head slightly cocked and his short, thick neck tensed. He urged Rina to go to a third-party nation with a fervor that was impossible to distrust.

"I'll help you. This is big country, but the people in it are unhappy."

"I have no money. I can't go anywhere."

"Do you know what the people here spend their money on? It used to be to that old woman, and now it's to you. If you can just scrape together what you have, I'll figure something out. You can always come back if you don't like it there. I'll help you."

Like everyone else, the first thing he demanded was money. It wasn't enough that their minds and bodies wanted it; if escapees wanted to get to P, they needed money. Jang came to Rina's performances every day and prayed without moving all throughout the performances, and even afterward. Seeing this made Rina trust him even more. Everyone trusted his reliable looks and lively gestures.

Even though she planned on leaving soon, Rina had to keep performing. Besides, she wasn't making a lot of money because of the bad weather. She needed more money because she didn't know what would happen to her in the future. All of the escape stories she had made up were similar, and getting old.

Rina's concerns eventually materialized in a very specific way. About an hour's drive away, a group of foreign women from the northwestern region of the continent had started their own performances. She finally understood why her tent had been so empty lately. The foreigners' performance venue had a wide cement stage built high up on a platform, and the indoor seats were so comfortable that you could watch the show without any distractions. The women didn't sing. They wore bikinis covered in sequins, and tossed their hair to the beat of the music, opening their mouths once in a while to moan. The people in the crowd wanted their bodies to intersect with these women's bodies, their legs, their squishy, quivering breasts, and their eyes that distilled all those body parts into a single shade of blue. What was even more surprising was that these women spoke the local language. Rina and Pii were speechless on the bus ride back after watching one of these performances, but everyone else was so busy expressing their rapture that they missed their stops. When Rina got off, she stood in front of her house and tried to imitate the women who shook their breasts with outspread arms, but it only made her burst out laughing.

There was only one audience member at Rina's last performance the next day. She had replaced the tent, which had been swept away by the flood, with a makeshift canopy, but no one came. Rina waited for the drum that announced the beginning of the performance, but instead, Pii came running backstage, a single finger lifted to tell her *one*. There was no interpreter, only rows upon rows of empty seats. But it was a beautiful night, with a bright moon and a gentle breeze. Rina bowed to the one woman who had come. The woman stared sullenly at Rina, and kept her hands buried in the folds of the apron tied around her waist, as if she had to go to the bathroom. Rina wanted to do well on her last performance. She had always wanted to tell her own story. Now was the time.

Today's story is the story of a girl who crossed the border when she was sixteen. Now, she's eighteen.

Twenty-two people crossed the border. There was a man who helped them. Everyone else went to the country of P, where they hoped to eat well and live well, but I followed that man. I fell in love with him at first sight, you see. My mother told me that if followed him, I would no longer be her daughter, so I wrote on her arm a contract breaking the bond I had with my parents and signed it with my spit. The first place this man took me to was a public bathhouse in the center of the city. I scrubbed myself for two whole hours. Then he took me to a store. He bought me a skirt and a pretty blouse and took me to a restaurant. He fed me rice and meat and took me to a fancy bar on top of a castle in the center of the city. I don't know what I had to drink, but I remember seeing some women dancing and singing amid a group of policemen. When I opened my eyes I was lying in front of a human trafficker. He asked me, how did you end up here? Can you tell me? That's the only way I can set you free. He said he liked fairy tales. So I told him stories every night. Stories of crossing the border, of splitting my shoes open. He enjoyed them. I asked him to let me see that man. I said, I hadn't even spent the night with him. And then he said, if you tell me lots of good stories, I'll let you see him. And so, I lied every day. So I could get my first night with the man I loved.

For the sake of a clean ending, she left out the part about killing a few people in a chemical barrel. The woman in the audience had dozed off, exhausted from a hard day's work in the fields. At that moment, Missionary Jang walked in. The woman got up and walked out without batting an eyelash. Jang sat Rina down and they went over the process for a safe escape. Jang asked for his payment upfront.

"Tomorrow morning, a car will stop in front of your house. Don't worry, no one will hurt you. You must have faith at all times that God loves you."

Rina handed the bundle of money over to the missionary. As soon as the money changed hands, Jang stood up, a bit hastily, it seemed.

It was time to cook one last meal for the old woman. While Pii made dinner, Rina packed her bags quietly, so the old woman wouldn't notice. She packed her sneakers, the things the old woman had gifted her, and one of her performance outfits, for memory's sake. When Pii had finished in the kitchen, they ladled the food onto a plate and took it to the old woman in her bed. The old woman drooled through her twisted lips as she ate her noodles, then suddenly reached out her good hand and caressed Rina's cheek.

"I'm sorry, Grandma," Rina said in a small voice. Pii poured some liquor into a glass and poured some into the old woman's mouth. Rina took a sip, too, and Pii finished off the rest.

After dinner, the old woman's lover came by. The old woman smiled through her contorted lips. The old man opened the plastic bag he'd brought with him and pulled out a bouquet of flowers tied together with a nylon string. For a second, the old woman's face showed a hint of the keen coldness it used to bear back in her days onstage, but it soon returned to its usual contorted state. Rina offered the old man her chair and straightened out the lace covering of the bed.

Late that night, Pii sewed up the armchair that had burst open, its yellow foam stuffing sticking out like guts. Rina knew nothing about where she was going, but she didn't want to feel anxious about it. She lay down on the spot on the floor where Pii usually lay. The sounds around the house grew deeper with the night—hammering against a windowpane, someone pulling a door into its frame, the old lover whispering sweet nothings into the old woman's private parts.

Rina lay with her ear to the floor and her arms around her shoulders, and fell asleep. When she woke up, she could no longer hear the hammering or the creaking. She saw Pii's face as he lay on the floor, an arm's length away from her. Rina rolled over twice and approached him. She firmly put her lips on the lips of that helpless boy from another country, that boy who couldn't speak properly, who was always being smacked for messing up his work. As the two lay there, holding hands, their lips on each other's, Rina remembered a word she'd heard a long time ago back at the chemical plant. At that moment, Pii whispered into Rina's ear that very word she'd wanted to understand. That word was "pretty," and as soon as Pii said it, Rina knew exactly what it meant.

Producer Kim was staring down at them with utter contempt, his hands in his pocket. Rina sat up with a start, and looked over toward the old couple. Fortunately, they were still sound asleep, arm in arm. The old woman still clutched the bouquet of flowers in her good hand. The producer sat in the armchair, crossed his legs, and lit a cigarette.

KANG YOUNG-SOOK

"You're leaving tomorrow, aren't you? I have to say, I'm a little sad that you'd leave without telling me. It's kind of rude, considering we're compatriots and all."

He flicked his ashes into the narrow space between the wall and the chair and smiled, showing all of his teeth.

"You will always be followed. Just one look at you two, and anyone can tell. They'll steal your heart from you, even steal the underwear off you. They're ready to strip you of everything you own. Be careful."

"Is that what you came here to tell me? I'm kind of disappointed, considering we're compatriots and all. Thanks a lot."

The man stood up, went over to look at the old woman in her bed, then came back and handed Rina a white envelope.

"This is a recommendation letter to give to the owner of the restaurant where you'll work when you first arrive. The owner is also from our country. Give it to him when you get there."

The man's black pants and white striped shirt were as shabby as always. Legs still crossed, the man beckoned for Pii to approach him, and Pii did, glaring. The man unbuttoned his shirt and puffed up his chest as if to show him the scar that lay diagonally across it. Then he took a small knife out of his pocket and suddenly stabbed Pii in the chest with it. Rina ran toward them, and the man pulled the blade out of Pii's chest. He stood up and wiped the blood off the blade.

"Sometimes, I have to do stuff like this to keep from getting too bored," he announced, then grabbed Pii by the neck and put the blade up to his throat. "You, you're just a kid. Give me all the money you've got. Otherwise I'll kill this retard," he said, looking over at Rina. Rina ran to get her jar, brought it back, and emptied its contents at the man's feet.

Early the next morning, Rina moved quietly so as to not wake the old woman. She heard singing outside, and gently pushed the door open to go see what it was. It was a wedding procession; the newlywed couple and their groomsmen and bridesmaids were singing as they passed over a hill. The procession was flanked by rows of slender horses. Pii joined her, rubbing his eyes, and the two began to move their bags.

"Isn't it a little early for a wedding?" demanded Rina, pouting.

A minibus approached the house. Missionary Jang, who had joined them at the house, gave Rina a hug and a pat on the shoulders, and helped her load her bags onto the back of the bus. The front of the bus was already filled with the brightly made-up women who worked in Producer Kim's tents. There was barely enough room for Rina and Pii. It occurred to Rina that something was odd, so she opened the envelope that the producer had given to her the night before.

"This girl is eighteen years old. She escaped from her country when she was sixteen, and is a chronic liar. Do not trust her."

The driver passed out a round of cigarettes to all of his passengers and started the car, chatting loudly. One of the girls insisted on smoking out the open window on an empty stomach while the others caught up on their sleep. They passed the mushroom-shaped roofs and shallow hills and the tent where Rina used to sing night after night. As the bus chugged up a hill, Rina felt her lips go dry and her blood run upside down. The act of escaping was beginning to feel like a plastic pouch full of blood that she had to carry around with her and keep filtering in order to stay alive. One of the girls began to sniffle and cry. They were driving past the open tent where the girls had used to spend their time. The driver looked back at them in his rearview mirror and yelled, but the sniffling and weeping didn't stop.

The car drove on, the next day and the next. On their way, they picked up a woman who had several swaddled babies placed in a bag. Through the open zipper of the bag, the babies' pink faces slumbered peacefully under the influence of sleeping pills. The woman calmly informed them that she was on her way to sell these babies; their parents had abandoned them. The girls from the tent began to get into hair-pulling fights over the cramped space. The driver had to stop the car and smack them on their heads to break them up. When they got bored, they sang. Their voices were sweet, and harmonized beautifully with the line of the horizon that extended in the far distance. That's when Rina knew: not everyone was meant to be a singer.

On the sixth day, the minibus passed over the southern border into another country, and the women were sold off in small groups.

12

EACH MORNING, THE FIRST THINGS TO MATERIALIZE ABOVE THE surface of the water were three pairs of cement pillars. They were the remnants of a bridge that had been abandoned before the deck was constructed; on foggy days, the columns remained invisible, and on clear days, they appeared above the surface of the water. On foggy days, even the steep mountains on the other side of the river seemed to fall halfway into the river. The river split off into so many branches that the eye couldn't follow them all, and the water lapped against the shore like a bright blue chemical substance in a flat dish. The riverbank was free of iron rails and lifeboats, as if inviting you to fall in and drown.

Adults and children alike living in the tiny village overlooking the wide spread of the river called the place "Shi-ling," but that was not its official name. From the outside, Shi-ling looked like a modest and quiet village, but it was locally known for being a red-light village, so to speak. Behind the houses of Shi-ling rose a low hill with a perfect vantage point onto the riverscape. The hill was dotted with a few mansions built for wealthy tourists. The empty houses stayed lit every night, waiting for owners that visited them a couple times a year.

Some mornings, when all the women of Shi-ling were asleep, the sound of helicopter propellers resonated from the hangar they said was somewhere across the river. About an hour later, the farmers living near Shi-ling gathered for the local market, where they sold produce, and carpets and fabric they had woven themselves. They also sold small mirrors and cotton handkerchiefs, mosquito repellent and cigarettes, seasoned bracken and wild aster, and other homemade dishes. Women came on bicycles with their children tied to their backs and bought as many pounds of tomatoes, peppers, millet, and red beans as they could carry back with them. When the market closed and the farmers cleaned the roads and returned home, Shi-ling became silent once again.

It was said that there were a lot of whores in Shi-ling because of the train. At the beginning of the twentieth century, when this country's national railway was being constructed, many of the laborers shipped out to work on the tracks stayed out there or were unable to return home. One of the reasons was because the mountain terrain leading to the northern region of the continent was so rugged that many of the workers died in accidents. They said the second reason was because the river was so beautiful that many people didn't want to return home. The river ran almost level with the ground, but had never flooded, and while the rest of the continent was flooded with earth-shattering deluges, the river of Shi-ling, it was said, had never once run over. The third reason was said to be the drugs, which you chewed like gum, and which were cheap and high-quality. Women came to Shi-ling in search of their husbands who had disappeared for one reason or another and banded together while they searched. Time passed, the women got old, and their daughters grew like weeds.

From the day Rina arrived in Shi-ling, she was sick. The air around the river was always heavy and the humidity seeped into her bones. Strangely enough, the heavy humidity reminded Rina of the former singer's bed. Rina thought the old woman might already be dead, or that she might die soon. Rina prayed the old woman would shake everything off and become the immortal singer she had once been. Once she started praying, her thoughts naturally turned to the missionary with his head cocked to one side. Right before Rina had left, when the door of the minibus had opened and she saw all the strange women from the tent inside, she had realized that the missionary and producer were in on it together.

As all the women here in Shi-ling did, Rina got dressed in a thin, translucent, floor-length silk gown, and combed her hair up. She awkwardly lit incense and washed some wine glasses as she waited for the men from the city. The first thing Rina was told when she arrived at Shi-ling was, "No one cries in Shi-ling." She was sitting in the room of the woman they called the pimp's wife, who shook a black fan at Rina's nose as she explained how things operated in Shi-ling. Rina was used to bowing from the waist up when introduced to people who were older than her, and everyone in this foreign country thought that this was a special greeting. The woman told Rina to sit, and Rina, by now used to the language of this country, was not afraid of the woman. The woman's fleshy stomach quivered whenever she spoke. She grabbed a large pair of scissors from a basket and approached Rina. Terrified, Rina begged the woman to stop. The woman stood in front of Rina, grabbed a fistful of hair from the crown of Rina's head and snipped it off mercilessly. Then she shoved a mirror in front of Rina's face. Rina's new bangs brought out her bone structure so that the angles of her face looked much more prominent. It also made her look much older. The woman offered Rina a cigarette, and Rina almost tucked it behind her ear out of habit, but she caught herself and put it in her mouth. The woman lit her own cigarette, then Rina's. She inhaled deeply and let out a long puff of smoke. At that moment, Rina felt way down in her lower stomach, no, even lower than that, something moving, something beating inside her. She thought the cigarette was a cure to wake up her sleeping uterus. After the cigarette, she felt fresh again.

The women here opened their homes only after the river, agitated by the helicopter returning west, had quieted down again.

Pii followed the long-bearded pimp around and helped him carry his purchases and fix up houses. After work, he kicked a ball around with the neighborhood children.

Children in a town full of whores. If there was one area in which Shi-ling was different from other red-light districts, it was that it was full of children playing, everywhere. Their shouts and laughter filled the riverbanks. The kids who didn't play ball did their homework while their mothers worked in the next room, and they learned to read and write ancient hieroglyphs from the old men of Shi-ling.

The men who came to Shi-ling would pick out a piece of colored paper from a basket. They would then roam the streets until they found the house with the same color paper attached to it. Three hours away from Shi-ling was a city full of factories and tall buildings. They said it was pretty big. The men came to Shi-ling from the city in buses or small cars that looked like water beetles, or sometimes in silly-looking motorcycles with the paint peeling. Even when they came at night, they kept their sunglasses on except to check their pieces of paper. The pimp explained the rules to the men:

"In Shi-ling we never serve more than one glass of alcohol per person. You're not allowed to bring drugs in. You're not allowed to hit the women. If you break any of these rules, we will cut off both your ankles."

A man with a dark gray jumper stood at Rina's door. Pii went out to check the color of his paper and let the man in. The man stood in the center of the house and looked around, blinking. His big, dark toadish hands and the metallic scent wafting from his body hinted at what he did for a living. While Rina was with her customer, Pii locked the door to the room next door and darned a hole in his sock while eating sunflower seeds.

The man asked Rina for tea. Rina served him some brown tea that smelled of rice sheaves dried in the shade, and the man sat cross-legged and chatted about this and that as he drank: about his work at the factory, or about gambling with his colleagues after work. His accent was so thick that Rina couldn't understand what he was saying, but she nodded as if she did. The man radiated a strong sense of repression, as if he was gripping a rough hunk of metal and trying his hardest to hold onto it. Before the man left, he turned to Rina.

"Who's that boy?" He spoke so clearly this time that she couldn't pretend that she hadn't understood.

"He's my son."

The man left and Pii came out of his room. Pii showed Rina a piece of paper on which he'd sketched everything the man had talked about. Skyscrapers lined the streets of the bustling city and cars drove by in front of them. Listening to Pii's explanation of the drawing, Rina detected a faint metallic odor on her body. They chatted and horsed around until someone knocked at the front door again, and Pii took the ticket and left, saying he was going out to have fun. Shi-ling was a beautiful place, but it was, after all, a town full of whores.

Rina lay on her stomach in bed and listened to the kids playing soccer by the river. Once in a while she also heard the pimp's wife. She imagined the woman's fat figure hovering in front of the hot fire as she made snacks for the children. The pimp's wife was a truly fascinating woman, even from the perspective of another woman. Even after Rina had come to Shi-ling, new children continued to arrive every so often, and they were assigned to live with the whores. At first, Rina thought they were being bought and raised to be sold for other reasons, or used as whores in the village. But the children acquired by the pimp's wife were usually severely disabled or orphaned. Except for those who were unable to walk alone, all of the children went to a nearby school. The pimp's wife did not make them do hard work, nor did she hit them. In this, their childhoods were different from the typical children of this country, who were made to work hard from a very young age. According to Pii, most of the kids who found their way to Shi-ling were either severely disabled, girls born to families that wanted sons, or from poor families. They had led tragic, nomadic lives before ending up at Shi-ling. Every evening, the pimp's wife cooked rice in a giant cast iron pot and fried meat and vegetables and boiled tea for the children. All of the children began to look happier and chubbier after a short time in Shi-ling. The children playing by the river were healthier than any of the other children Rina had seen in this country. The number of children increased each day.

Stories of what went on in Shi-ling spread, perhaps on the wind, perhaps through the stories of the men who visited the village. Once in a while, women would show up who said they had changed trains a countless number of times going from the other tip of the continent to find their lost daughters. The women usually arrived in the morning, looked around the river, then lingered on the empty roads of Shi-ling waiting for a passerby, or even a stray dog.

It was here in Shi-ling that one woman finally found her little girl, who had been cast out by her father. Soon after the news got out, other parents with lost children and government officials began to visit the village. The pimp and his wife asked for nothing for returning the children. The children's reactions, however, were often surprising.

"I'd rather become a whore in Shi-ling than go back home and starve and not be able to go to school and have to work with my hands in dirty water," one of the girls announced. Her mother had to drag her back home, kicking and screaming. Several days later, the mother returned to give the pimp a small bottle of honey as a gift. Either way, such stories spread to the nearby city, and Shi-ling became very famous. It was said that the town was run so hygienically that no one contracted any sexually transmitted diseases there, and nothing scandalous ever happened.

Indifferent to all of this, the river lapped at Rina's feet like blue water in a dish. When she dipped her hand in it, a chill coursed in from somewhere deep and far away. One day, Rina was staring at the water when she ran into the house as if she had suddenly remembered something. She got out all of the money she had collected, and without bothering to count it, she tied it up into two bunches and went to the pimp. She told him that she wanted to bring the old woman to Shi-ling.

"That old woman is going to die soon. You should spend your money on the future, rather than bring someone from far away who's going to die soon. Let's bring more suffering kids." Still, Rina insisted, and after three days, the pimp conceded.

The early morning fog around the river cleared as the morning market was wrapping up. By the time the river had returned to its pure blue self in the afternoon, Rina was awake. As she looked out toward the river through her open gate, a blue-tailed bird flew over her head. The white clouds hanging in the sky were flying up and away from the river. Rina hunched her shoulders as the chilly air caressed her nose. The pimp and his wife and a few men sat by the river, talking intently. The men looked like officials who had come from the local government to inspect the whore-town.

Rina had been feeling dull and heavy, so she stayed in bed late into the day. As she peered into the mirror hanging above her bed, Rina saw an unfamiliar woman who seemed to be aging rapidly. There were dark circles around her eyes, and a set of long, deep, vertical wrinkles framed her mouth. Rina washed her face and rubbed and caressed it for a long time. When she looked in the mirror again, the impressions of age were still visible. Irked, Rina went outside to get some fresh air.

A young couple was sitting by the river, eating ice cream and dangling their feet in the water. Rina approached them quietly, her arms crossed. She watched them. It was the girl who noticed her first and turned around.

"It's your mom," she said.

When he turned around seconds later, Pii's face was beet red. Rina remembered the face of the woman she had seen in the mirror just moments ago, and bit her lip. Pii looked up at Rina.

"Do you want some ice cream, mom?" he asked.

Rina felt the blood rush to her cheeks, and her heart quavered. She had to walk away. Pii's ice cream was as gray as if it had been made of ground rock and had melted. Rina turned around and spat onto the surface of the water.

When Pii came back home, his face was drenched in sweat. He gulped down a glass of water without looking at Rina, who sat at her dressing table. She picked up a perfume bottle and threw it at Pii. When it hit his back, Pii sank silently to the floor with his head bowed. Rina collapsed with her legs splayed out in front of her and sobbed. Pii sidled up next to her, put his arm around her shoulders, and tried to look her in the eye, but Rina avoided his gaze. She didn't know why, but she couldn't manage looking directly at him. She stared at his unwieldy feet, put her face up against them, and embraced them. She felt the dust from the riverbanks on her lips. Rina sucked the dust.

13

THE UNMARRIED GIRLS OF SHI-LING GATHERED AROUND THE riverbank, chattering loudly. They wore heavy headdresses made of silver and were prettily made-up. Today was the day that the unmarried girls were allowed to propose to any man they wanted. According to the customs of the region, this was the one event in which even the whores, who were usually busy working indoors, could participate.

Mothers were up at the break of dawn, neglecting their fieldwork so they could nag their daughters to get themselves done up as nicely as possible. The mothers hoped their daughters would be able to lead lives that were the opposite of their own messed-up ones. They hoped that their daughters would sever ties with their kind of life by finding husbands who were better than their fathers.

The pimp and several of the elderly men of the town stood in a line along the riverbank and puffed on their pipes made from water buffalo horns. At the entrance to town, people played large instruments made of bamboo. Children, young girls, and old women all gathered by the riverbanks in anticipation. The mothers of the single women were dressed in navy blue or red. They eyed the crowds determinedly, bent on finding a good son-in-law. The young women themselves looked rather thin and wan, perhaps from the weight of their heavy headdresses.

It took all of Rina's energy to drag her heavy, tired body out of bed. She looked at herself in the mirror. There were dark circles under her eyes and her skin looked rough. She couldn't bring herself to eat anything. When she opened her eyes that morning, she had felt her mother's words pierce through her heavy body. *I had you when I was nineteen. That means you'll be having a baby in three or four years, just like me.* The mocking tone rang in her ears all morning.

By the time most of the population of Shi-ling had gathered by the river, it looked like a river of color was flowing next to the river itself. One girl in particular caught Rina's eye. It was hard to know all eighty prostitutes by name. Rina wrapped herself in a green shawl she'd knit herself and slowly walked down to the river. The smells of food and heat wafted up and clung to her the closer she got to the crowd. Rina walked up to the girl she'd noticed earlier; she was dressed in a red silk traditional costume.

"Hey, don't you know me? It's me, Rina. We escaped together," she said, quietly.

The girl turned around. She stared silently at Rina. It was the girl from the sewing factory. The girl from the sewing factory who didn't laugh, no matter how hard Rina had tickled her. The two women said nothing. They just held each other for a long time.

The beautifully adorned girls began to dance. They couldn't dance very vigorously because of their heavy accessories, but they opened up their arms and chests as if they were welcoming everything in the world. The tunes of the pipes spread farther and farther, with the interjections of whooping and encouraging yells adding to the vitality of the music. The children adopted by the pimp's wife were adorned just as prettily as the young girls, and they writhed happily to the music. Things got heated when the hopeful young men began to dance in circles behind the women. The whores of Shi-ling were eager to forget that they were whores. The mothers danced alongside the young men and women, their bodies expressing the feverish hope that their daughters find good husbands tonight.

In the afternoon, the river became choppy. The people ate rice cakes and pork, drank liquor, and frolicked. By then, Rina was in the room of the girl from the sewing factory. They caught up on the past few months, but they'd been through such similar events that there wasn't much to talk about. Rina suggested that they wait for the right time to run away, and the girl agreed. The girl opened Rina's shirt, and with a feather quill, drew a small butterfly above her left breast. Under it, she wrote "Rina." The two girls looked at each other and laughed quietly.

Rina went back outside in search of Pii. She found him far upstream, smoking a cigarette and dangling his feet in the water. His face was covered in dry patches and he looked thin. He was no longer a boy. Rina stared at his feet in the water, then dipped her hand in the water, and washed his face. She smoothed his hair back and straightened his clothes.

"Son, you must also find a bride to spend the rest of your life with," she told him. And she dragged the unwilling boy to where everyone was gathered.

The pimp's wife was in charge of running the biggest event of the region. When the time came, she shifted her big belly importantly, and fanned herself as she gave her solemn orders:

"Now you may all pick your husbands." The girls pulled out their most precious keepsakes—small combs, pretty necklaces—from the recesses of their dresses, and approached the boys they wanted. When she saw the young, unmarried girls shyly offering up their gifts, Rina's heart dropped. She'd imagined herself in this situation so many times, offering a flower to a boy. She felt like her body was full of flowers to give, but that she had no one to give them to. And that's when she saw it: the girl who had been eating ice cream with Pii by the river handing him a little doll. Rina turned and spat into the river.

The girls who had chosen their husbands looked overjoyed. They ate and chattered loudly. Their happy parents sang, played music, and munched on some mildly narcotic herbs. But the girls who hadn't found husbands went back home, angry. Their mothers sat by the river all night and wept while their husbands puffed angrily on their hookahs, chastising their sullen wives.

"It's your fault we didn't raise her well!"

"Well if you don't see the both of us tomorrow morning, just assume we went and drowned ourselves in the river, you good for nothing!" The festival that came once a year ripened into a bedlam of laughter and resentment. Some of the drunk men fell into the river, but nobody bothered to jump in after them.

The more the positive rumors about Shi-ling got around, the rougher the customers who came to Shi-ling. Some came furious; others were wealthy and vigorous young men from faraway cities who came out of defiance toward their parents. It was a whore-town nonetheless, and it ate away at the whores little by little to soften these rough men.

A few days later, the former immortal singer arrived at Shi-ling. She was lying in the car buried among her little bundles. Rina was surprised to see the old lover pop out from under the piles of blankets and clothes. Producer Kim, the trafficker of humans, stepped out of the driver's seat, still wearing the same old black pants and striped shirt. Rina helped the old woman in and congratulated the old man on safely making the trip.

"See, what'd I tell you? I was right to sell you here. It's a good place to live. Where else could you enjoy such a magnificent river? You should be thanking me for helping you to live near such a great river." While the producer was putting on airs, Rina patted the old woman's face and shoulders.

"That old geezer, he left everything to his wife—his house and his kids—to elope with the love of his declining years. Crazy old bastard," the producer told Rina.

The old man wanted to see the river as soon as he got out of the car; this was his first time away from home. He told Rina that the house he'd left his wife was a broken-down hovel not even worth the price of a cow, and that his life had been full of good fortune since he'd met his mistress.

"Look, I brought the old folks all the way here, I think deserve a token of gratitude," the producer interjected.

Rina had already paid him through the pimp, but she handed him a few extra bills. He smoothed his greasy hair back and gave Rina an odd look.

"What about something else, hm? Why don't you give me a shot? You are a whore, after all."

Rina snorted. "In your dreams, old man. Now scram." The producer lingered around the neighborhood for a while. The old couple was invited to dinner at the pimp's house. Afterward, they took a walk by the river to enjoy the moon, and Rina took a customer who worked as a train conductor in the big city nearby. If not for the drunk producer yelling and swimming by himself in the river, it was a serene and beautiful night just like any other.

The Shi-ling River was enveloped in fog on the day that one of the newer whores was beaten to death by a visiting technician. Early that evening, they heard screaming coming from the girl's house, and everyone rushed over. The girl was naked from the waist down, her neck was twisted, and her body was jammed into the mattress. A child was locked in in the next room, scratching at the doorframe with his fingernails. The pimp went inside and covered the body with a blanket. He dragged the technician, who had his head buried in his hands, outside. The pimp's wife went to the room next door and held the child in her arms, and gave him some candy.

The pimp and four other men took the technician to the riverbank. In the milky opaque fog punctuated by small campfires, it looked like a stage. The pimp's wife gathered the children and fed them snacks, making sure to keep them from wandering down to the river. The men went around politely asking all the clients to leave, and posted a "Closed for business" sign at the entrance of the village.

In a blink of an eye, the four men had tied the murderer to a tree trunk. The man was still spirited at this point, yelling out that the girl had tried to kill him first, and that he had acted in self-defense. The pimp recited the vow that all clients made before entering the village of Shi-ling. The man nodded grudgingly when he heard this, but then started to yell again. He said that hurting him over the death of a stupid whore would endanger the town, that this was all some asshole's fault, and other things that no one could understand. The pimp stroked his beard and the four men brought out a knife. The man started to rave when he saw the knife. He rubbed his feet against the ground in terror. All of the whores that had gathered around trembled with fear, their mouths covered. The pimp stripped the man from the waist down, just as the man had done to the whore. Then he ordered the four men to beat him. The four men resolutely beat the man who had murdered one of the whores of Shi-ling. The man passed out after a few blows, and they waited for him to regain consciousness. When the man finally came to with a shiver, the pimp asked him if he had any last words.

"Workers unite!" the man yelled. The pimp sliced the man's ankles off like a man in a martial arts movie. The four men untied the footless man before he had time to fight back or scream, and tossed him, along with his two feet, into the river. Then, together, they pushed the man's car into the river. The river bubbled for a bit, then went quiet.

When it was all over, the kids came spilling out of the house, yelling and kicking their soccer ball around as if they'd been waiting for ages. Rina listened to the peaceful sounds of their play while she sat on her bed, looking into a mirror. She imagined their nimble movements.

They'll run after the ball as fast as they can to keep it from falling into the river. The kid with one arm will probably forget he only has one arm, and he'll run at the ball with everything he's got. The kid from a battered family will have a huge smile, at least while he's near the river. The kid with the congenital disease, the short one with the thick neck, is the best soccer player in Shi-ling, at least for today! Their faces will be sweaty. There's the sound of a girl washing her face in the water! The water will be cold and blue. Tonight, the people will fall asleep to the sound of the kids playing soccer, and they'll forget the troubles and disturbances from earlier in the day. The kids' shouts drag all of Shi-ling's problems into the river.

Rina was lying on top of the old woman's unpacked bundles when she heard the front doorbell ring. It was a customer. It was Pii. He gave Rina a green ticket from his pocket just as the other men did. Rina took the ticket, put it in her porcelain vase, and took Pii by the hand into her bedroom. Pii took off Rina's socks and massaged her feet as he used to do when she sang in the tent. He took off his shirt and pants and covered his chest with his hands. There was a cluster of particularly bony vertebrae in the center of Pii's spinal column, which Rina now pressed down on with her fingers. She took off the green shawl she always wore, and unraveled the drooping silk that covered her body. When she put her hand on Pii's groin, his body gravitated toward her. As their bodies touched, Rina loosened her ponytail, and her hair spread out across the pillow. Pii took Rina's face in one hand and pulled her close to him. That part of him that was now hot, he pushed inside her. A smile escaped Rina's lips as she saw Pii's face floating above hers, that stupid boy who could never defend himself. With his lips and his fingers, Pii drew all over Rina's body the things he had wanted to tell her but didn't know how to in her language. Through her body, Rina heard his story, from his birth to how he ended up at the chemical plant, and she understood. It became light inside her head and the cramped walls of the room fell away so that the blue border stretched out at the other end of the sky rushed up toward her. When that blue levee rushed toward Rina like a tidal wave, her pelvis opened up infinitely and a strange voice that she'd never heard came spilling out of Pii's mouth. They held each other tightly and lay still until their breathing had become slow and measured again.

When Rina opened her eyes around dawn, Pii was sitting on the edge of the bed. The butterfly that had been drawn on the young whore's breast had rubbed off. The whore took the faded butterfly from her breast, moved it onto her finger, and placed it on the stomach of the young man sitting on the bed. Pii spread Rina's legs open and warmed her down there with his breath. It made Rina's rigid body turn languid.

"Will you tell me I'm pretty?" Pii held Rina and told her she was pretty, then covered his mouth and came silently. That's when Rina noticed the butterfly had landed on Pii's buttock.

Before morning, Rina went over the next room, where the old woman was snoring away. She took the woman's good hand, which was dangling limply off the bed, and put it gently on her stomach. Moments later, her hand still on Rina's stomach, the old woman began to cough as though she had a fish bone caught in her throat. She sat up slowly and began to sing in a low voice, and Rina remembered what a marvelous singer she'd once been. Every time the old woman worked her throat, Rina felt a strange energy push its way out of her stomach. It was magic. Her sunken stomach puffed up. Rina sat very still, neither crying nor laughing. She caressed her puffed up stomach and murmured, "This is my moon."

14

Three days after the worker from the city had been thrown into the river, five government officials came to Shi-ling with cameras around their necks and stood by the river, their hands clasped behind their backs. The pimp and his wife looked anxious and made a bigger fuss than usual. The officials skipped stones and admired the river and the mountains as if they were on an outing. Occasionally, they would look over at the pimp and his wife. One of them suddenly pointed to the depths of the river and called his colleagues over, and they all gathered around to stare into the water together. The pimp and his wife practically turned purple with fear. Luckily, neither body nor car door materialized on the surface of the water. On that day there were in fact several large, orange carp swimming about the deep cold water. The pimp's wife blinked her large eyes at them.

"You ate him all up, right? Yes, we know you ate him all up, oh you sweet little darlings," she whispered. She and her husband looked at each other and winked.

The women of Shi-ling cooked for hours. They slow-roasted lamb, making sure to slice off the excess fat, and sautéed mushrooms and greens and set out beer. They spread out clean tablecloths and waited to serve the bureaucrats. The pimp and his wife had commanded them keep everyone happy, so they all moved about in a beautifully orderly fashion.

When the sun began to set, the kids of Shi-ling gathered by the river once again to play soccer, and the whore-town seemed to have gone back to normal. Although Rina insisted that it wasn't necessary, the old woman, sensing the delicacy of the whole situation and wanting to help tip the scales in their favor, insisted on offering up her musical talents at the feast. It was true that the banquet room's large windows and high ceilings made things feel a bit empty and chilly. So the former singer rouged her cheeks and sat on a small stool with her hands in her lap, waiting as shy as a young girl for the guests to finish eating. The guests were being difficult; they didn't seem particularly interested in the food, and spent the whole time asking direct and cutting questions about how the town was being run. But they had to loosen up when the smell of lamb roasting and the sound of food sizzling on the grill wafted into the room. The women poured them drinks and brought out the carefully prepared dishes. As the warm liquor trickled down their throats, the bureaucrats pulled out their cigarettes, took their jackets off, and began to joke around. The pimp and his wife seemed relieved, although they didn't let down their guard.

While the officials were filling their bellies, Rina the whore and the girl from the sewing factory got together with a pencil and pad to organize an escape plan. Rina wore a thin, translucent silk dress that came down to her feet and her hair was pulled back, making her look very fresh and young, but she couldn't have cared less. She was lying on her bed with her legs propped up against the wall, and she had rolled up the silk material of her dress and stuffed it between her legs. Her pencil was tucked behind her ear, and she was chattering away, wildly gesticulating. They had no clue how to plan an escape, and knew no one who could help them. Rina longed for someone like Producer Kim or the missionary. She missed them dearly.

RINA

"If we stay here much longer, who knows when that pimp and his posse will try to do away with us? They'll kill us. I'm telling you, they're just the kind of people to stuff all the whores into the river and pretend like nothing happened. Have you heard? They smuggle drugs, too! That's why they take in the orphans and take such good care of them. It's their way of making sure they stop bad rumors before they happen, so they can keep on doing this shit forever and ever. They pretend to be good, but oh, they're *good*— but in a different way. They're going to get us. Those kids don't even have papers or identities, who would care about them? And, and, I'm telling you, let's pretend for a second that these *are* good people. This is still a town full of whores, isn't it? I'm right, aren't I?"

Rina felt a little guilty even as she spoke, and wondered if she was being too harsh on the pimp's wife.

The sewing factory girl, who was sitting in front of her vanity counting money, looked like she was in a daze. Rina pounded her feet against the wall. They were like two girl soldiers, burning with the spirit of the fight. They discussed who they would have to bribe and how they would approach them, what transportation they would use, and when they would leave. That's when a disagreement arose.

"Well, of course. We have to bring the old man and the old woman, and Pii."

"Are you crazy? Do you even hear yourself? It's not like we're moving to the suburbs nearby."

"It never even occurred to me to leave them behind."

"You ran into your own family at that church, a one in a million chance, and you didn't follow them. Now you're talking about hauling along some old people and a dumb boy you met in a foreign country? You're not trying to take them all into P, are you?"

It wasn't that Rina didn't understand the sewing factory girl, and she knew that in a way, she was right. But her attitude rubbed her the wrong way. Rina swung her feet back and forth as she sat on the bed, her mouth set. She picked at the red flower pattern on the sheet.

"If that's how it's going to be, you can go with someone else. I don't want to get caught trying to get out of here with those people," the sewing factory girl told her.

"Oh, yeah? Then why don't you try to find someone else to escape with you. See if you can find someone else willing to get out of here. And you may not know it, but no one is as good at escaping as me. You don't know how I got here!"

The sewing factory girl opened the window and lit a foul-smelling cigarette as thick as a smoke stack. Rina started to feel nervous. *Who should really be the angry one here*, Rina muttered to herself. She saw the girl's shoulders heaving, but couldn't think of a way to console her. The irregular shouts of the kids playing soccer outside pushed their way in through the open window.

At that moment of quiet, Rina suddenly heard the boom boom boom of a drum coming from somewhere deep within her belly. It started off small, then got so loud that it echoed throughout her entire body. It lingered in her ears before gradually disappearing. With every beat of the drum, Rina's lips twitched with the desire to travel to a city in a foreign country, a hot desert, even back out to the border. The veins in her body stood at attention, and her limbs were already taking large steps forward, advancing out into the air. She felt like she had to open her mouth wide and sing at the top of her voice to keep her eardrums from bursting.

There was a knock on the door; it was a customer for the sewing factory girl. Rina hastily smoothed out her silk dress and left. On her way out, she stopped, turned around, and stuck her tongue out at the girl. She was still angry. "Who does that girl think she is, calling Pii a stupid boy? Really." But then, she stopped herself and chuckled, "Well, I guess he is pretty dumb."

The breeze from the river gave her chills when it brushed against her cheek. The kids were still playing soccer by the river, and from the pimp's house, all lit up at the end of the street, she could hear the government officials laughing. Rina walked slowly up the street to the pimp's house, stuck her head in the front door, and peered surreptitiously inside. The civil servants were stripped down to their undershirts and having a grand old time. They scratched at their shoulders and arms and stuffed their faces with liquor and food and blew smoke everywhere. The old woman slowly stood up and walked out in front of them, and began to sing. It was a dignified and plaintive song that she had often sung back when foreign forces invaded her country. But the officials were being very rude. It mortified Rina to see the old woman, in whom she had invested her hard-earned money, bowing to these rude bureaucrats. She rushed into the pimp's house.

"What do you think you're doing?" she demanded. As soon as she opened her mouth, she realized what a huge mistake she'd made, but it was too late for regrets. The hot air wafted up into her nose, and all of the men turned to stare at her.

"Well, what do you know? One of the whores graces us with her presence," one of them said.

The men's eyes swept over Rina's body. They fell silent, too busy admiring her figure to say anything, and it was finally quiet enough to hear the old woman's beautiful voice. The angry pimp marched in, his white goatee waving, and he pulled Rina outside by the wrist. He smacked her on the head.

"You don't understand how important tonight is, do you? How can you act like such a fool? We're all bound together here by a common fate," he fumed.

"I really hate your goatee," Rina grumbled as he walked away.

Rina waited outside of the pimp's house for the old woman. There was some lukewarm applause, then someone pushed open the door, and the old woman slowly walked out. She looked like she was about to faint. She seemed very pleased with her performance, saying it had gone over much better than expected, and she patted Rina on the back, assuring her everything was going to be all right.

They ran into a young man and woman leaning on a wall of the alleyway in front of their house, staring into each other's faces, reluctant to say goodbye for the night. It was Pii and the girl who had given Pii her doll on the day of the husband selections. Rina helped the old woman in first, then turned around and looked at them. They looked over at Rina and smiled awkwardly, and Rina slammed the door shut.

After laying the old woman down on a quilt, Rina perched on the vanity and stared at her reflection in the mirror. She still wasn't quite sure that what had happened with Pii on the night the whore-murderer had his ankles cut off. The rustling of silk on silk, the tight floral pattern wallpaper that had seemed to fall all over her face, the swelling of her stomach when it came into contact with the old woman's hand, all of those memories seemed to disappear, floating away through her fingertips. Her stomach, which had been puffed up and swollen that night, was now back to its usual hollow state.

The lower alley was filled with raucous noise; the bureaucrats were getting out of their party. Giggling, they sauntered down to the river, their faces drenched with satiety. There, by the light of a few lamps, the children were playing soccer as they always did. The trouble started when one of the bureaucrats, having gone down to the river to relieve himself, decided to join in on the game. He straightened out his shirt that was sticking out of his pants, and suddenly charged in among the kids. He tried his best to score a goal, but he couldn't even get near the ball. He yelled at his pals, who were all about to get into their car, to come back.

"Hey, let's play some ball. It's been a while."

The pimp, who had offered to drive them back, couldn't deny them, so he ran back to the kids.

"Kids, you have to give them this game tonight. Under no circumstances are you allowed to win."

And so started the soccer match between the bureaucrats and the children of the whore-town of Shi-ling. It became chilly enough that whenever the kids yelled out, their breath came spilling out in white clouds, and the bureaucrats, too, expelled their alcohol-soaked sour breath into the air.

It was decided that the kids would score in the left-side goal, and the bureaucrats in the right. The one-armed boy passed the ball quickly to his friend, a girl with short hair, who then passed it to a short boy near her. A bureaucrat that had been positioned between them tripped over his own feet trying to intercept the ball, and the girl scored a goal against the drunk goalkeeper. The adults rebuked each other for their poor defense, and the field by the river heated up with the competition.

The whores that didn't have customers that night brought out chairs to watch the game. The mountain that rose high above the village had become invisible in the dark, and the chilly night air slowly invaded the riverbank. The soccer field began to resemble an official game with real fans. The kids stayed keen and focused, even when they stopped to tie their shoelaces or pull up their pants. They watched the bureaucrats' every move like hawks.

One of the men finally succeeded in intercepting the ball. He kicked the ball to his right with a yelp, and his buddy dribbled it up to the goal. Everyone cheered; the whores, who had been cheering for the men just to be polite, began to yell in earnest. While the offense was fumbling, the goalkeeper, a boy with a limp, came running out, intercepted the ball, and kicked it to the far side of the field.

"That's my boy!" his mother screamed, and an awkward silence ensued.

One of the players asked for a break. The men emptied their full bladders into the river, and the boys washed the sweat off their faces. The bureaucrats, under pressure, gathered in a circle to discuss tactics, and the kids stretched and yelled out cheers. The pimp was the most anxious person present. He walked around the field, extracting promises from the kids that they would throw the game.

With a score of 1–0 in favor of the kids, the game resumed. The men were sobering up, and grew quicker on their feet, but they were still no match for the children. In any scuffle, they were bound to trip over themselves or slip for no reason. The fastest boy in Shiling gained control of the ball and rushed toward the opposite goal. He kicked with all his might, and the ball hit the goalkeeper's shoulder and bounced back. A small boy with a spinal defect caught the rebound and made another shot, and the score became 2–0.

The bureaucrats huffed and puffed with anger. They argued that it was unfair, since they had fewer players on their team, and asked for some extra players. The pimp himself picked out a few players to be switched over, and it was decided that these kids would play with one sleeve rolled up, to distinguish them from their former teammates. Now they were even in number. The men were just as excited as the kids, and they began to rush the other team. The physical scuffles became intense. One of the men approached the kids' goal using some fancy footwork, as if he'd been a pretty impressive soccer player back in the day. The women screamed even louder. But before he got to kick at the goal, the goalkeeper, who was the son of one of the whores, charged him. The man passed the ball to a boy next to him, who had his sleeve rolled up. The boy forgot for a second which team he was on, and dribbled the ball all the way back to the other side of the field and scored a goal, ignoring the goalkeeper yelling at him that he was going for the wrong side. With his mistake, the score became 3–0, and the men became much more cautious.

The pimp ran to the crowd and waved his arms around to encourage people to cheer for the bureaucrats. The women clapped and yelled. It was almost pitiful to see the fat pimp hopping around like a housefly, unable to sit still. It really was the last chance. One of the boys, a fast runner, purposely passed the ball to one of the civil servants, and the kids slowed down, the fire in them now dying down. The man quickly dribbled the ball across the field and no one tried to stop him. He scored a goal, then turned around and glared at the kids who were watching with their hands on their hips. He looked livid. Then he suddenly marched up to the one-armed boy, who had been standing next to him, kicked him, and kicked him again when he was down on the ground.

Anyone watching that dirty scene would have wanted to curse out loud, but they all held their tongues. The soccer match ended 3–1. The handicapped children of the whore-town had defeated the bureaucrats. The men got dressed and climbed into the pimp's car.

"Wiseass punks. Who the fuck do these retards think they are, *letting* us score a goal? This is humiliating," the men roared as they were driven off.

The kids washed their hands and faces in the river and dried themselves with their clothes. The little ones, who had come to watch their big brothers and sisters play, went back home, wrapped around their mothers' legs. The players that had led their team to victory went back to their whore-mothers, looking very proud of themselves.

15

EVER SINCE THE NIGHT SHE'D SUNG IN FRONT OF THE GOVERNMENT officials, the aging former singer had begun to waste away. She complained of being cold, no matter how many blankets they piled on her, then would sweat until her underclothes were drenched. After a few days, she lay catatonically staring up at the ceiling without moving. Gradually, things got worse. She had to be spoon-fed, and she reacted to nothing. She couldn't urinate by herself. She went back and forth between lucidity and unconsciousness, and eventually stayed unconscious. "If you were going to die, you really should have done it back in your town instead of waiting until you got to this foreign country," Rina snapped at the old woman's blithely vacant face.

It seemed like the old woman would be sick for quite some time, and it was hard work for Rina to clean up after her every day, so Rina spread out a large sheet of plastic over the old woman's mattress. It was easier to watch over her this way because the plastic made a raspy noise every time she moved. Laid out on the plastic sheet, the old woman's body looked like the carapace of an insect whose body had disintegrated, leaving only the outer shell. She no longer sweat; her skin was dry as paper, and her hair, which was like corn silk, fluttered even when there was no breeze. The old woman stayed in bed all day, staring up at the ceiling, looking as indifferent to the world as a baby.

It was the old man who was burning up with anxiety. He stuffed every nook and cranny with twisted bits of paper to make sure there were no drafts. He sat next to the old woman, murmuring what may have been prayers, but Rina couldn't understand him. He would fall asleep with the old woman's arm, skinny as a piece of dried fish, draped across his face.

Time passed, but the old woman showed no signs of improvement. The old man insisted that they couldn't sit back and let her die, but no one expected him to be able to save his lover. He was too old and too poor.

"I'll go and find something to save her—the elixir of life. Just you wait and see."

Armed with a small backpack and two fists clenched in resolution, the old man left Shi-ling. Less than two hours later, his limp body was brought back in a wagon by some of the kids. He had been hit by a car while walking on the road by a tea field. The kids had seen it happen on their way back from school, and they recounted how the old man's body flew into the air and fell into the tea leaves.

Pii carried the old man's body into Rina's room on his back. He had no external injuries, and he appeared to be asleep. They laid him down next to his lover, and together, they looked like a Lilliputian couple. The old woman stared up at the ceiling, ignorant of the old man's death.

Rina went to the pimp to ask for a funeral. If the old woman died within a day or two, she was thinking of holding a joint funeral. She thought the girl from the sewing factory would probably be happy to hear the news, but she never came by, which Rina thought was inconsiderate.

Rina and Pii had a hard time falling asleep that night. When she'd finally managed to drift off, Rina was awakened by what sounded like a buzzing housefly. When she got up to see what it was, she saw that the old woman had pissed all over the plastic on her mattress. She and the old man lay there, still as death. Rina found it hard to believe that the old couple was going to die together, and she kept on pinching her own thigh. And yet she couldn't forget the sweet nothings they'd whispered to each other every night back in the mushroom-shaped house. She found herself watching them; they would not be lonely when they died, for they could continue to whisper sweet nothings to each other well after death.

But the old woman didn't die so easily. The day before the old man's funeral, everyone gathered by the river to clean his corpse. The water was cold, but the sun was warm, and the wind gentle. They placed the corpse on a bed made of woven bamboo and took it down to the river to gather water and pour it on the old man. The old man's skin was sunburnt and smooth, but rigid. The people stood in a circle around the body, put their hands on him, and prayed.

After the cleansing ceremony, they danced in a circle around the body as a last goodbye. Men wearing sheaves of rice, which symbolized wealth and health in the next life, came out and danced solemnly in front of the old man's body. A few others blew cigarette smoke all over the body.

Pii wasn't a very good artist, but he worked all night on a portrait of the old man holding a black plastic bag. They removed a painting of a peach from its frame and used it for the old man's funeral portrait. They wrapped the old man's head in a white kerchief, dressed him in a clean gown, and put him in a blue coffin, where he lay by the river until his funeral the next day. Rina watched over the old woman and Pii guarded the old man's body by the river.

Early the next morning, they held the funeral by the riverbank. They set food and fruit out on tables and lit incense. Men stood with funeral streamers attached to bamboo poles. The bier was placed at the entrance of the village. It was covered in tattered red silk with a pattern of two pairs of animal horns reaching up to the sky. An old man who liked to tell everyone that he was close to a hundred years old was in charge of presiding over the funeral. Next to him sat Rina and Pii, dressed in hemp, their palms joined. The old man sprinkled water over the food for the dead and lit a cigarette. The dead man's skin was even darker than the day before. The master of ceremonies blended some red powder with water and applied the mixture generously along the dead man's lips. Someone began to sing high-pitched songs of ancestral rites and the men closed the coffin and moved the body to the bier.

The men with the streamers went first, followed by the coffin. They all left the town, marched through a nearby town, and returned to the river of Shi-ling. They pushed the coffin into the river, where it sank slowly and became food for the orange carp that would nibble on it for a long time to come.

Early the next morning, Rina woke with a start, where she'd been lying with her face buried in Pii's waist. The old woman was not where she should have been, stretched out on her plastic sheet like a corpse. Rina found her by the river, where it was cold, humid, and foggy. The old woman was sitting in the empty funeral bier.

"Granny, are you crazy? Get out of there!" Rina yelled, but the old woman refused to budge.

Instead, she began to sing a song from back in the day when she had been the singer of eternal life. A very long time ago, in the city where the old woman had once lived, there had flowed a river as beautiful as the one in Shi-ling. The people of that country were poor, but they prayed that their small, weak country would one day become rich and powerful. The song, which started off *allegro moderato*, developed a very simplistic melody as the fog thickened around it. *Why do the men around me die so early? Ay, my fate. Who knows how many it's been.*

When I die, who will put me into the water? It was a beautiful melody, but the lyrics were so apt that Rina couldn't help but comment somewhat flippantly, "Jesus Granny, you sure have lived a long time! I'll never believe you now if you tell me that you're going to die soon."

16

ONE DAY, THE SOUND OF HELICOPTERS RANG OUT OVER THE surface of the water for a particularly long time, and the Shi-ling morning market failed to take place. All of the women of Shi-ling were fast asleep. Rina went to the old woman's room to cover her with a blanket, then went to visit the sewing factory girl. She felt now was the time to escape, and she wanted to hurry. The surface of the water was all ashiver, and the fog was heavier than usual.

Rina was standing near the entrance of the village staring blankly at a point where the silhouette of the mountain that hugged the river connected to the flatlands. And then she saw a herd of colossal and strange-looking machines heading toward the village, toward her. An orange crane, the likes of which she'd only see in large cities, a crane with a soccer-ball-shaped iron sphere attached to its snout, and a group of heavy machines with claws that resembled a giant fork were lined up and rushing toward the village of Shi-ling. Rina rushed to the pimp's house and banged on the door until everyone came out, rubbing their eyes. They were all speechless when they saw the oncoming march of the machines.

First came the bureaucrats with cameras and notebooks. The pimp approached them, trying to stay calm. The clean morning air was soon clouded with the thick dust kicked up by the machines.

Sleepy children cried for their moms, while women in their underclothes who had come out to see what the fuss was about covered themselves and ran back inside. Rina ran back home to wake up Pii and changed out of her drooping clothes into a sweater and a comfortable pair of pants.

The vehicles came closer and closer to Shi-ling, widening their file. And as if it were the most natural thing in the world, they began their attack from each side of the village, where the houses began. The giant iron sphere and large claws started on the upper level of houses with their mushroom-shaped roofs, and began to tear down their walls, roofs, and flowerbeds. The houses closest to the river went first. Where the houses had stood, in a matter of seconds, there were just foundations, or sections of walls. One of the homes, with its furniture strewn everywhere, had a family still sleeping in it. The woman who lived there—she must have been a heavy sleeper—sat up as if in a dream, looked around blearily, hugged her pillow, and went back to sleep.

From kids' bicycles to the brass caldron that was usually set out by the river, everything was trashed in the blink of an eye and pushed out into the lot by the river, which had turned into the village dump. The government officials were watching everything with their arms crossed. The pimp had collapsed on his belly at their feet, his head bowed in defeat. The people of Shi-ling were too frightened to even scream; they could only tremble numbly as they watched their lives turned to ruins before their eyes.

Shi-ling was completely destroyed before the sun had set. It looked like a war zone. Dust continued to cloud all around the village, turning its skies into a yellow mess. Without any pillars to support them, cracked walls crumbled long after the machines had left. Babies cried and mice squeaked. The kids, with no school to go to, sat in a circle and stared down at the ground. They had been through so much misfortune already that rather than whine or cry, they remained composed, watching everything unfold.

Around sunset, the bureaucrats hung a sign at the entrance of the whore-town that read "Zone Closed-Off," and left. The two hundred residents of Shi-ling gathered by the river and wept. They couldn't even hold council because anyone who tried to speak was eventually hindered by her own tears or cursing. They spent that first night, having lost their homes and their livelihoods, out by the river, staring at each other's backs. It seemed like they would stay there forever.

The next morning, the bureaucrats returned to Shi-ling. The first thing they did was to sit with the pimp, his wife, and all the men, and deliver a rambling lecture. They kept the women and children away, but foul-tempered Rina and the sewing factory girl and a few other whores went down to the river anyways.

"The government has ordered us to close down Shi-ling. We're just following orders. If you want, we can help you find jobs in other whore-towns."

Rina felt a little bad for the pimp and his wife, who fell to the ground and wept, and she was also irritated by the officials' arrogant tone of voice.

"Why don't you tell us who it was that ordered you to tear up this place like this?" she couldn't help demanding. The civil servants chuckled, and one of them lit a cigarette. No one answered. Rina was afraid, but she continued: "I've never seen public officials like you, forcing people out into the streets like this. What the hell is your problem with Shi-ling? Were you embarrassed because you couldn't get it up with one of us whores?"

"You crazy bitch!" one of the bureaucrats yelled, finally losing his cool. "If I wasn't a government official, I'd—" But Rina's fire burned hotter than theirs. She ran at them like she was marching into a raging fire.

"Then what is it? Don't tell me our pimp is behind on his taxes. You all know what good people he and his wife are."

"We know, we know. Let's just call it a violation of public order, and leave it at that. It's best for everyone."

One of the bureaucrats looked Rina up and down with his large eyes. Rina felt that this was the last chance to speak her mind freely. The sewing factory girl grabbed her hand and pressed her palm as if to tell her to stop, but it was too late.

"Don't tell me you guys are doing this to get back at our kids for beating you at soccer. We all know men can go crazy over stupid little things like that."

The bureaucrats looked at each other and cackled gleefully, as if this was the craziest idea they had ever heard.

"Shi-ling is slated to be developed for tourism. You're all banned from here. Go wherever you want, we won't come after you."

The villagers flung themselves at the bureaucrats.

"You can't tell us to move after you've torn down our town. Who taught you to act like this? Do you think you'll go unpunished after something like this? We won't go. We *can't* go!"

The bureaucrats stood up, getting ready to leave. But the pimp was not one to let them go now. He approached them, followed by a few men, his face set. The men were holding sticks, and the pimp had nothing to lose. Some of the kids began to throw stones at the bureaucrats, who fled. All of the villagers wept and blamed the soccer match.

They gathered towels and scraps of cloth to sew together some semblance of a roof for the night. From far away, the patchwork was bright and colorful and fluttered beautifully in the river breeze. They went to their torn-down houses to collect household items, after which they set up camp under the patchwork tent and drew the water from the river to cook and do the dishes and wash up. The problem was the weather. Now that the sun had set, it was cold, and it was impossible to stay exposed to the elements for much longer.

The older people were the first to get sick, plagued by hacking coughs. At first, no one thought of leaving Shi-ling, but each morning, their numbers dwindled. The people without families were the first to go, and they left one by one for places where they thought they might be able to make a living.

One night, the kids of Shi-ling gathered solemnly near the tent in the lot. They were all there, except for the infants. The adults clucked their tongues, saying it was a pity that the kids weren't able to play soccer; they thought that the kids were bored and getting together to play a game of rock paper scissors. Instead, the kids had a long meeting that lasted well into the night, long after the adults had long since fallen asleep. As the adults groaned tiredly in their sleep, the children left the village with just the clothes on their backs and a stick in each of their hands. They walked away without looking back once, as if they were heading to school or out to play and were planning on returning. But of course, they weren't. The wild grass had grown as tall as the kids, and the stalks waved in the wind that blew in from the river. A long, slow singing bounced off the mountain walls in the river valley and found its way back to the lot. Pii left Shi-ling with the other kids.

A few days later, from a city three hours away, a worker who had been an occasional customer of Rina's came by. His face still gave off a metallic odor, his skin was darker than before, and his stomach bulged even more. As he calmly surveyed the ruined town, he told them that he'd nearly passed by without recognizing the village.

"Do you want to move to the city with me? It'll be better there, even though there's no beautiful river."

Rina stared at the man as he gazed down at the river. She thought she saw the face and the gestures of the producer and the missionary in this man's profile. Her heart shriveled up bit by bit with each pump, her ears drummed away, and she found herself packing her clothes.

She packed all night. The man's car was so small that it couldn't fit all the remaining people. He had to take out the passenger's seat and pile all of Rina's things in its spot. The biggest piece of baggage was undoubtedly the old woman. Rina found a large handcart and a small chair that had been left behind. She put the chair inside the handcart and wrapped it up with old clothes. She wrapped the old woman in thick sweaters, sat her in the chair, and stuffed the rest of the handcart with clothes and baggage. She had packed the old woman's costumes in case she would ever have to perform again, as well as clothes and shoes she'd need right away. As she was packing, she came across her old sneakers, now in tatters. She took them out of their plastic bag, and touched them. As she felt them against her fingers, her toes curled up in pain; the soles of her feet stung, just as they had when she was walking the field of salt. As she thought of how Pii had left without even saying goodbye, her lower stomach ached as if it were being torn into.

Some of the people who had been sleeping in the tent got up and watched Rina's group leave. Rina attached the two handcarts to the back of the car. The first one for the old woman, the second for Rina and the sewing factory girl. The man drove very slowly, and all of the passing cars stared at their makeshift caravan, but Rina didn't care. She was too busy thinking of Pii, whom she envisioned running toward her from the direction of Shi-ling. She clutched her muddy old sneakers to her chest.

The city was small and quiet, without the life or bustle promised by the man, who had described it as a place full of factories and skyscrapers. The man had told her that he was the patriarch of a happy family, with a canny housekeeper for a wife and a couple of bright children, and that he was planning on moving to an even bigger city to buy a house and open up a shop. It turned out that he lived by himself in a housing complex owned by the factory, and that he was a depressed, hopeless bachelor with a distended belly.

The leather factory where the man worked was filled with piles of empty plastic buckets, and far fewer people. The workers were busy looking down at their work as they washed the rough leather in hot water and held it over fire. There was no laughter or leisure in their faces as they worked. The man parked his car in front of the factory and took them to his apartment.

The living quarters were attached to the factories and consisted of a cluster of four-story buildings filled with tiny rooms. The man led them to his third-floor unit, which was the size of a closet. It was so small that it wasn't so much a room as a cement floor surrounded by a few windows. Each floor had only one bathroom and one shower room at the end of the main corridor. For some reason, there was also a large laundry tub installed in the center of the shower. None of the indoor lights worked properly, giving the place a bleak atmosphere at night, and the ceilings were covered in cobwebs. Gourd-shaped chamber pots stood like tiny guards in front of the doors to each unit and finger-sized mice tiptoed around them.

That night, the man took the money Rina gave him and went out and bought dumplings. There wasn't enough furniture to sit on, so they ate standing, looking out the window. From the window, they could see the backside of the factory district, filled with low buildings. On one side of a half-built building, a family of homeless people slept in a row on wooden planks, covered by blankets. Rina prayed it wouldn't rain, and ate her dumplings with gusto.

The next day, the sewing factory girl and Rina tore up two of their floral-patterned skirts and made curtains, which they hung up in a corner of the closet-sized room. They wandered all over the city until they found what was either a bed or a table in a trash heap, and carried it with great difficulty up the three flights of stairs. The table legs were tall enough that you might very well break something if you rolled off in your sleep. As they had nothing else to do, they decided to spend their time recreating Shi-ling. But as there was no one to publicize the arrival of the women in town, they had no customers.

After a while, they noticed that some of the men would gather in the showers every night to wash their work uniforms. From that day on, Rina and the sewing factory girl went to the showers every day, hiked their skirts up, and made money doing laundry. Rina always tried to avoid getting her hands wet by only using her feet, but her meticulous coworker would first soak the uniforms in water, work them with her feet, and then rub them good and clean with her hands. Their hands got cold, and the nauseating odor from the uniforms made them dizzy.

The old woman, who had monopolized the bed during the day and spent enough time in it to ruminate on her life several times over, eventually got bored, got out of bed, and shuffled painstakingly around the house to cook for the poor young kids who were working so hard. But more often than not, she would drop the plates they had worked so hard to obtain, or accidentally set a corner of the blanket on fire, so she was more trouble than help. While Rina didn't rust the sewing factory girl, she did trust the old woman, which is why she chose to hide her money, wrapped in a plastic bag, in the older woman's pillowcase.

At night, the three women slept in the same bed, entwined like a giant pretzel. The sewing factory girl was afflicted with a rash that she'd first gotten in her youth while working at a factory. Her skin was very dry and it soon became covered in red spots. She was up all night panting and scratching herself, her face crumpled up in pain. Rina sat up on her knees on the bed and lifted the girl's sweater. Her stomach and chest were covered in scratch marks from her fingernails, and she had scratched the underside of her belly button so much that there were small specks of crusted blood. Her face was fine, but her body was a mess. Rina was suddenly gripped by a curiosity see what it looked like under her pants, so she pulled the girl's pants down. They stared at each other, both equally startled.

"Hmmm, your hair's really dark down here," said Rina, and she began to rub the girl's pubic hair with the back of her hand. The girl's pained moaning gave way to a different kind of moaning. With a finger, Rina pushed back the mound of pubic hair, and the girl looked silently up at the ceiling. "Touch it," she said. Rina grinned, slipped her middle finger inside the girl, and slid it up. She repeated this movement over and over again. She had not expected to feel so hot and throbbing down there herself, and she covered her groin with her left hand. Then the sewing factory girl reached out a hand and groped at Rina's left breast.

"Wow, it's crowded up here, let's move the old lady somewhere else," Rina said seriously, and the sewing factory girl laughed. They giggled, and both eventually burst out laughing.

They never did find a good place to put the old woman, so Rina and the sewing factory girl would lock themselves in the shower at night. They would spread towels out on the tiles of the laundry tub and sit facing each other. They hiked their skirts up and pulled their sweaters up to their necks. They kissed and caressed each other until their heads had cooled and the world had quieted. If someone knocked, they would yell, "We're doing laundry!" and hurriedly start stomping on some wet laundry to make the noises to prove it. When they got bored, they would take turns lying on their backs on the floor with their legs spread open and pretend they were giving birth. "Push!" they would urge each other.

If they were still feeling heady after doing the laundry, they went to the shower stall, where they stood, embracing each other under the torrent of water. Ignoring the odor of sewage and the fact that the ceiling looked like it was about to crumble, they rubbed their bodies against each other and kissed until their tongues ached. If the power went out during these moments, they would scream in unison and hold each other so tightly that it felt like mouth was crushed up against mouth, breast against breast, and they touched each other there with their fingers until they reached the height of what was either ticklishness or pain. Strange noises would escape their trembling lips and the lights would flash back on. Afterward, they would exit the showers with their baskets full of laundry, as if nothing had happened. Having solved the problem of the pain and itching, they climbed into bed and slept with the old woman between them, holding hands with their fingers interlaced.

One day, the factory man took Rina to a gambling pit in an arcade building that was five floors tall and had a veranda painted white. There, he introduced Rina to some brokers who were hanging around with nothing to do. They made several familiar proposals.

"Did you know there's a country very close by that takes in people trying to get to the country of P? All you have to do is bring the money, and we'll get you over there. Once you're there, it's easy to get to P. Before winter, even. What do you think? Does it sound great or what?"

Rina chuckled to herself as she listened to them. But she didn't have that much money.

"Do you know what could happen to you if the police came for you while you're busy making up your mind? They'd probably send you back to your country."

This made Rina frown. It wasn't easy to come up with such a sum of money just from doing laundry. And even if she did have the money, she didn't want to go anywhere until she had heard from Pii.

One fine day, Rina and the sewing factory girl walked arm in arm to check out the market. They had to find some medicine for the girl's rash, which showed no signs of abating. They swung their arms back and forth in a large arc and smiled at the sun like two children on a field trip. The market was in a lot by the new highway, and was bustling with locals. There was a barbershop run by a single man with nothing but a pair of scissors and a large cloth with which to cover his customers' shoulders. There were stalls selling shiny fabrics, wild boar meat, fruit, mothballs, plastic buckets, storybooks, earrings, and shoes—the list went on and on. Rina lingered in front of the shoe stall. She noticed the sewing factory girl talking to a man she had never seen before. He had too much oil in his hair, which was slicked back along a side part and thickly matted. *I wonder who that is?* While Rina had been busy watching the shoes, the girl and the man walked away from the market.

"How much are these?" Rina pointed to a pair of black leather flats with red flowers. The next time she looked up, the girl and the man were gone. Then, Rina felt the breath of someone standing quietly behind her and looking down onto her shoulders. It was Pii. He hugged her from behind, as if he'd learned how from the movies, and the people nearby smiled at them. They left the market and sat on a hillock near the one-man barbershop. Both the barber and his customer were old men with white hair.

"The kids are living on their own. That girl went with them, too. She only picked me that day as her groom because she was afraid her mother would get angry with her if she didn't choose anyone. She wants to move to the city and meet a rich man."

Rina opened up a bag of crackers she'd bought for the old woman, poured some into Pii's palm, and listened to him crunch away. The man getting a haircut had been dozing, his head gradually sinking lower and lower, until his chin finally dropped onto this chest. A group of kids who had come to the market with their mothers gathered around a cage of rabbits and laughed, and some lithe young girls gathered to admire lingerie. A chilly breeze blew in from the rear of the lot, and white clouds floated by. Rina had forgotten all about P now, and she no longer felt like an escapee. All she wanted at the moment was enough money to buy some pork or chicken from the stall across the street so that she could feed Pii.

"You've been wanting these, right?" the sewing factory girl appeared in front of them and held out the black shoes.

"Look who's back," Rina answered, without so much as a glance at the shoes. The older girl pouted.

"Yes, I see," she retorted, and turn to Pii. "You're pretty good at finding us, aren't you? And you're not even related."

Rina came to her senses and stood up. She slipped her arm into the girl's.

"Where did you get the money? Did you do it without a condom?"

"Don't worry about it. I got a lot of medicine for my rash, too. Let's get some meat; we haven't had any in a while. Your son's here, after all."

Pii picked up the old woman in his arms and spun her around like a doll until she purred and laughed and told him it made her dizzy. The two of them were overjoyed to be reunited. Pii sat the old woman on his knee, and they chatted away in their language. Meanwhile, Rina and the sewing factory girl spread their ingredients out on the cement floor. As the tiny room filled with the smell of cooking meat, neighbors who had stepped out to empty their chamber pots stopped by to see what was going on. Since there was no table, the three women sat on the bed and Pii perched on the windowsill, and they ate their bowls of meat and stir-fried vegetables.

They poured wine into four small cups and clinked them together. Rina was unable to wipe the smile off her face. They didn't even manage to make a dent in the pot of pork, which they had boiled with lots of onions. The exhilarated old woman sang, and Pii got up to dance. They kept chatting in their own language, and Rina suspected that Pii was talking about the girl from Shi-ling.

"His dick was as small as my finger. That gave me a turn. But what's even funnier is that he had a huge hemorrhoid on his ass," the sewing factory girl told Rina about her encounter with the man at the market, and they both snickered. As they talked, Rina looked around and noticed how quiet it was outside. She opened the window, and a mosquito flew in. Drunk, Rina flopped around, mimicking the mosquito, and sang in a low voice. That's when she noticed several people who didn't appear to be locals loitering in a lot next to the factory and staring up at her. Rina jumped up as if she'd sat on a pin, and turned the lights off. A feeling of foreboding swept over her, and she sobered up in a flash.

A short while later, she felt the regular rhythm of footsteps approaching them from down the hall. With the lights off, their tiny closet was like a dim fishbowl. Orange clouds were floating by in herds above the low roofs. For a second, they were all silent.

"Rina, snacks! I brought snacks."

It was the factory man, who had been gone for days. Rina had been gripping the light switch under the lamp, trying to calm her trembling body. "What's up with that man? We're so full, who needs a snack?" Her anxiety melting away, she turned the light back on, shuffled over to the door in her slippers and opened it onto three men she had never seen before. They were policemen. In front of them stood the factory man, carrying what appeared to be snacks. Everyone stared at the snacks.

"We have got to have the worst luck in the world. We have to go south from here, I'm telling you. We have to go south, where the weather is nice and they'll take us in. We came from the north. Why are you trying to send us back up there? The people up north want nothing more than to send us back to the country that we just fled. I just crossed a border, and now you want me to go back to the mainland? And then, where am I supposed to go? East, or south, or to the sea? This is bullshit. Besides, I don't even really want to go to P. I can live anywhere. Why are you banishing us again? If you just leave us alone, we'll make enough money to leave for the south on our own. All we want is to make enough money to fly to P. Do you really have to bother us like this? You guys are terrible."

Rina plopped down on the floor with her legs stretched out in front of her and yelled at the top of her lungs. She tried to shed a few tears to buy the police's sympathy, but for some reason she was unable to. The policemen stared out the window as they smoked and waited for the wailing to stop. The old woman munched happily away at the dark wheat cakes the factory man had brought; she didn't seem to care whether she lived or died now. The rain began to drizzle outside, and the police waited in the hall for the illegal immigrants to pack their belongings. They looked pleased with themselves. The factory man broke the silence.

"Look, I've been needing to get to the hospital because my liver's damaged, and now I can afford to go. Thank you, very much," he said to the police. It made Rina sick to her stomach. She turned on him.

"Hey mister, you should be thanking *us*. The money my friend and I earned washing those clothes that gave us rashes, they're taking it away and giving it straight back to you. You guys are all freaks. Come on, show some gratitude!"

The man flashed his teeth and grinned, and the old woman wrapped up the scene with a neat statement: "The cakes are delicious. I was feeling a little sick from eating all that meat. You'll all go to heaven for being so good to us. That, I guarantee."

17

THE TRAIN RUNNING UP TO THE NORTHEASTERN PART OF THE continent consisted of a freight car and a passenger car. It ran without stopping, night and day. Early mornings and late nights were cold enough for a thick layer of hoarfrost to form over the windows, making it impossible to see outside. The people that were part of the landscape outside wore thick coats and boots and rode on their bicycles hunched over against the wind, even when it was sunny. Eventually, even those people disappeared.

The train traveled up a hill steep enough that its red soil seemed constantly on the verge of spilling over. Speeding through the shadow of the hill gave Rina a thrill, as if one side of her body was about to be swept off into the ether. The red piles of dirt, which were clearly signs of a landslide, crept over onto the sides of the railway so that wherever the train passed, dirt splattered up the sides of the tracks. When it passed through a long tunnel, the train let out an extended whistle as it huffed and puffed its way back toward the light. At one point, the rails stood at least thirty meters above the ground without any safety system, and looking down made Rina pee her pants a little bit.

There were four bunks in each of the passenger compartments, and Rina, Pii, the sewing factory girl, and old woman lay there, stiff as frozen fish, only whimpering now and then. The vehement spinning of the wheels became increasingly frantic. They were all too busy sleeping to make plans for the future. Pii, who was the only one who could communicate with their broker, lay limply in his cot all day; he didn't seem to care where they were being taken. Whenever the smell of food wafted in from the corridor, Rina went out to look around the other compartments. They were full of men dressed in dark work uniforms, gambling or smoking.

The train chugged persistently along the tracks toward the shadowed center of the mountains. Rina had never felt so bleakly terrified since first crossing the border out of her own country. It seemed like the earth and sky had been flipped, that it would be nighttime forever, that the sun would never rise. When she woke up in the middle of the night she would climb down to the bunk where the sewing factory girl slept and cradle her from behind and try to go back to sleep. The sewing factory girl lay there with her ears covered, shivering. Sometimes, when that wasn't enough to quell her fear, Rina would climb up to Pii's bunk and gently nudge him with her foot. Pii stared quietly and stupidly up at the ceiling, ignoring Rina's constant harassment. Sometimes, Rina would belt out some of the strange songs she had learned from the old woman back on the plains. When she was finished, the men in the other cars would clap and cheer through the cracks, and Pii would go out and see if he could collect any money.

He usually came back with dumplings, wheat cakes, and sunflower seeds. But liquor was by far the most popular product for consumption throughout those murderously relentless days of travel. All four would wait with bated breath for their turn at the bottle, like baby birds waiting to be fed. When Rina raised the bottle to take a swig, the old woman would smack her on the head, snatch the bottle, and gulp away at it. She would only stop when she noticed the others gazing desperately at her, silently begging her not to finish the bottle. Afterward, she would fall into a deep sleep, twitching her lips in a smile as if she were with her old lover again.

Whenever she'd had something to drink, Rina would sit cross-legged on her cot and chatter away without stopping for breath. She needed the liquor to dull the deafening sound of the wheels on the tracks, and to turn the stench of cigarette smoke into a savory fragrance. And whether it was a blessing or a side effect, the alcohol was wholly transformative: her whole body would become light, her chest would open up wide, and her rigid tongue would loosen up until she said everything that was on her mind, and even things that weren't.

"Honestly, Granny and Pii, especially you Pii, you're just going back home. That's nice, right? It's nice to go back to your homeland. She and I, we're the ones being sold, and you two are like bonuses. Why don't you leave us? We're just poor, pathetic escapees. This world is full of weird people. One time, this old auntie that used to live in my neighborhood told me that everyone, even the biggest idiot, gets three chances in life. But what about me? Sure, let's say I've had two chances. No, let's say one. What the hell, what kind of a stupid chance is this? I really hate you, Pii. You like girls with big heads and squinty little eyes. You used to be so handsome. Back when I sang, you were a pretty great guy. And you, Granny. When I think about all the money I've thrown at you to keep you alive. And you, what about you? Do you remember? When we crossed that first border, there were twenty-two of us. That baby died in the woods, and you and I are here. What do you think the other nineteen are doing now? The two of us, we have quite a relationship. Where the hell are my wonderful parents, and my precious little brother? Has anyone heard anything about them? Anyways, you, you're a real bitch. Maybe your husband wanted to ditch you a long time ago. I mean, why would he take *you* all the way to P when he can just find a new woman once he gets there? The way I see it, people only think of themselves, even in the most difficult of situations. They only think of themselves up until the day they die. You, you're like that, especially."

When she deemed it had gone on long enough, the old woman would sit up in her berth and threaten them with retribution if they ever let Rina drink again. This made Pii and the sewing factory girl giggle.

"Granny, don't say that, you don't know anything. Your mind wanders. Pii looks down on me now, he won't even hug me anymore," Rina would continue, unable to stop herself. When the sewing factory girl covered Rina's mouth with her hand, Rina would push it away, and when Pii tried to cover her mouth with his hand, she would push it away, as well. Then her saliva would get caught in her throat so that she couldn't tell what it was that was spilling out of her eyes and her nose, tears or laughter. That's how they passed the time.

The train raced across the endless plains. There were no trees in that landscape; all that decorated the dry grass were the lines of the train tracks. A herd of horses standing in a cluster rubbing their heads together sensed the approaching train from afar and fled deeper into the prairie, their manes whipping. The clouds, moon, and sun also raced across the plains. Rina saw the white clouds, the sunsets that stained the clouds orange, the inky black sky that followed the sunset, and the deep and murky fog that drew itself over the early morning prairie.

When Rina put her face close up against the window and stared into the fog, she could see a giant light rushing toward her on the plains. Rina remembered that light; she'd seen it at the border. Twenty-two escapees stood in a line, faces frozen, watching the train from the prairie flooded with that light. Rina's family and the three other families stood with the children in front, the parents behind them. Next to them stood the sewing factory workers. The newborn baby that had died in the woods was there, too, in her mother's arms. No one knew if she was dead or alive.

The newborn's older brother had grown as tall as the wild grass. The old man who had died in the chemical plant held his brown notebook in his hand, looking straight ahead with a meditative expression on his face. The high-ranking administrator was still spouting her political doctrines, but she was bleeding from having been so brutally raped by the man back at the chemical plant. The newlywed woman was still wearing her white dress and cutting her hair with scissors. The workers of the sewing factory held hoes and scythes, but the hard labor had aged them. And then Rina saw it. Her not-quite-nineteen-year-old self, bulging with child, staring at the passing train. Everyone stared straight ahead as the train passed by except for the young, pregnant Rina, who glared back at herself in the train, for a long time.

One day, Rina began to notice scant traces of humanity on the dreary prairie that had seemed like it would never end—occasional farmhouses, stables, and granaries. Eventually, they passed clusters of kids dressed in bright sweaters who waved at them. They passed tall trees planted in twos and threes, and houses with fences between them. Gradually, the number of houses clustered together increased, as did the number of trees planted together. They began to see more cars and some small markets.

That night, their broker ran his fingers through his grimy hair as he told them that they would be arriving at their final destination at dawn. After being discovered, Rina and the others were taken to the train station by the police, who handed them over to their new broker: the factory man with the bad liver who had turned them in. They were all in it together. Right before they boarded the train, the broker had jerked his head toward them and commented, "Well, this isn't going to make me much money." Onboard, he had warned them, "You'd better behave yourselves, or things will get ugly," and left them to their own devices. Ever since that day, they had all sat cross-legged on their cots, silently watching each other with wide eyes. Sometimes, Rina would mimic the broker's dazed and sullen face and tone of voice to lighten the mood.

The train raced over the narrow tracks all night. The tracks were flanked by darkness, and the sound of the train on the tracks was an angry scratching against tin. They sat around numbly, munching on sunflower seeds and spitting out the shells. No one was moving when Rina saw something white tumble out of the sky and stick to the window. Snow.

"Look, snow!" Rina blurted out. She thought of her hometown near the border, where it snowed so much it made her sick. She remembered someone shoving a small snowball down her pants. She scratched her head angrily, hating her own sentimentality.

The long and narrow tracks connected to the center of the industrial city like intestines. Streetlights shone on the tracks the whole way. Dawn was breaking over an industrial complex that looked like it was contained in a milky glass bottle. A metallic odor hit her nose even before they had reached the center of town. When it had reached the center of the city, the train slowed down, as if musing on the road it had just traveled. The snow came down harder and a polite public announcement came on the loudspeakers. The broker, who had been sleeping in the compartment next door, brusquely stuck his head in the door and told them to stay on the train until morning, and get some sleep.

It took forever for the brakes to kick in and for the train to come to a complete halt. When it finally did, Rina pressed her nose up against the window and looked out at the industrial city that spread out in front of her, too vast to take in all at once. There were no trees, no mountains, no rivers; everything was covered in pitch-black factories. Rina heard the sewing factory girl's shallow breathing next to her.

"I guess we'll all be working at a factory now." Men with giant backpacks streamed out of the train and disappeared among the black factory buildings squeezing in on the train station. The chill that rubbed up against the tip of her nose was freezing, so Rina hurried back into their compartment to gather some warm clothes for the old woman.

18

Rina was plagued by strange dreams ever since arriving at the industrial complex. At times she sprouted wings and flew into the sky, where she could see the whole city at a glance, and then, colliding into a passing bird, plummet for what felt like ages before landing on the ground. She would fall into the wide thicket of reeds that encircled the city and lie on the ground naked, looking up at the white clouds, her eyes twitching. The damp floor of the reed forest was neither cold nor hot, and the small of her back felt like she was lying in lukewarm water. When the bugs in the dirt wormed their way into her crotch and crawled up into her vagina and anus, she wiggled her toes. The reeds swayed in the wind, brushing against her face. When her whole body broke out into goose bumps, she would wake up with a start. Rina thought this dream might be predicting something in her future, but, unable to figure out its significance, she would quickly fall back asleep.

If you could climb to a place up high and look down on this industrial city, what would it look like? Could you even see it all at once? It was something Rina wanted to try. For some reason, and it was impossible to find out how long it had been so, at least half of this immense industrial city was completely ruined beyond repair, as if someone had drawn a line straight down the middle and divided it into two teams—red and blue, industrial and dump. Only the factory district, which was to the right side of that line, was now active. Every once in a while, as if to remind you of its existence, the dilapidated eastern dump would vomit dry dust up over the city.

There was no regular mode of transportation to the ruined side of the city. Among the ruined grounds were giant mounds of old oil drums, cars without tires, and piles of scrap metal. Through the cracks of these heaps, green blades of grass had pushed their heads up in freakish overgrowth. All of the houses were broken down or exposed to the reddish earth while pipes and electric wires spilled out like guts from small windows that had once provided ventilation. Most of the houses were completely destroyed, but here and there were some inhabited ones, from which scowling people would abruptly emerge and disappear back into swathes of drapery. Some residents renovated the carcasses of abandoned buses, while others pitched thick tents and built backyards out of dumps, sunning themselves quite pleasantly on their extensive properties.

The city grounds always squelched with industrial oil thick as tar. The dust, heavy with powdered metal, coated people's hair, then slowly escaped through the gaps between buildings. At the main entrance to the industrial complex fluttered a banner that read "Welcome to the Free Economic Zone," a smaller replica of the giant one Rina had seen at the center of the station the day she'd climbed out of the early morning train. A giant balloon shaped like a person dressed in traditional costume stood smiling next to the banner, its hands folded politely over its belly. A tower crane and a gas separation tower held up the western section of the sky, flaunting the splendor of the industrial city.

According to the local laws, foreign investors coming to the free economic zone received special treatment. They were allowed to employ many more dispatch workers because of the lax labor laws.

Perhaps this was why there were so many strange-looking foreigners in this crippled city. At the end of the workday, at least four different languages could be spoken in the droves of workers heading back to their quarters. Regardless of where they were from, all workers wore the same boots. Their fingernails were caked with a thick layer of grime and their faces, which carried at least a scar or two from work, were somber and dark. They didn't smile often, but when they did, it was to reveal rows of yellowed teeth. Every day, in the dawn before the sunrise, these people would get up and walk to work to heat up cast iron, cool it down, and pile it up into mountains.

After work, the men would line up naked in the hallways to wait for the few showers that were available. It was somehow unreal to see these grown men with their naked pink bodies exposed and bent over at the waist, waiting to wash up. Every time Rina saw the buttocks of these men, she could never be quite sure if they belonged to real live men, or simply her imagination.

Even on their days off, the workers stayed in their identical quarters and ate the same food as they always did. The men usually sat around in their underwear and gambled. When they happened to lose their hard-earned money, they would throw darts at the nipples of the women in the raunchy posters they had stuck to the walls, or mutter curses and incomprehensible foreign exhortations at the photos of the families they'd left behind.

Rina nearly fainted when she found out how close she was to the place where she and the twenty-one others had crossed their first national border. The station they had left long ago to travel for thirty-six hours to get to the southwest of the continent was close to the industrial city. Rina had travelled from the east coast of the continent to the southwest, then crossed another border to get into a third-party nation. Then, from that third-party nation, she had crossed back onto the continent and travelled northeast. When she found out that she'd circled the continent and ended up exactly where she'd left, Rina was too bemused to even cry.

Ever since she had arrived in this industrial city, Rina had become much calmer than she used to be back south. She believed that if she were to be banished from this country, she'd be sent back to the home she had left so long ago, and be killed in the stead of her parents and her brother. Even though this knowledge left her feeling defeated, it also made her feel strangely serene. What plagued Rina more than anything was the food. Whatever they ate, it tasted metallic. So did the water they drank.

The girl who had once vowed she would get to the country of P and buy herself some jeans and high heels and become a college student had somehow ended up in a large industrial plant complex with a gas storage tank system. Rina woke up at dawn every morning, rubbing her sleepy eyes as she set out breakfast for the old woman. Factory buildings lined each side of the main thoroughfare and behind the buildings to the north, a few meters away, were rows and rows of living quarters for the workers. From the very start, it was hard to travel up and down the stairs of these narrow, old four-story buildings. Rina often walked up an extra flight of stairs because all the floors looked the same. The upper levels weren't more comfortable, nor was there much of a view. Behind the industrial zone, a river from the north enveloped the city, but it was so dry that it might as well have been a vacant lot.

Rina's job was to load calcium carbide onto a cart in a corner of the special welding factory, and deliver it as needed to the welder. To hide her identity, she only spoke in the language of this country, as did the girl from the sewing factory, who was on the cleanup crew at the piping construction factory. Pii was learning how to weld, but being a novice, he started off running petty errands.

At night, when they got back home after work, their apartment would be transformed into a patient ward. They would lie down, two to a bed. The sewing factory girl coughed constantly, and when she spat, her yellowish phlegm was mixed with metallic powder. The soles of Rina's feet and her lower back hurt so much that Pii would have to walk up and down all over her back and legs for a long time to loosen her muscles. The old woman, who stayed at home during the day, told them tall tales of the strange-looking birds and insects she had seen through the window during the day.

Then something happened that shocked Rina back to her senses. She didn't know how, but the rumor that she and the sewing factory girl had once been prostitutes spread throughout the industrial complex. There was even a rumor that the old woman had been a prostitute her whole life, and that Pii was her son, a bastard child who had never met his father. One day at work, as Rina shoveled the piles of carbide that had hardened like pieces of gray shit, a man from the south approached Rina.

"Couldn't we make a red-light district here? You could make a lot of money. As you can see, there's a shortage of women. You could live comfortably without having to work in the factories," he said in fluent tones of this country's language.

The smell of the carbide made Rina's throat spasm with nausea, but she didn't want to appear to be caught off-guard.

"I'm very expensive. I'm sorry to say, I'm not one to share my bed with the likes of you workers."

The man grabbed Rina by the collar and shoved her onto a pile of carbide residue.

That night, they called a meeting. Rina's temples were bruised from the incident earlier in the day. They all rubbed her bruises playfully. The old woman was the only one who seemed to have her wits about her.

"From what I've seen, the men here haven't been with a woman for a long time. If we open a brothel here, there's no way you two will get out of it in one piece, let alone make money off of it. And I'm obviously too old to get involved in this."

The old woman's conclusion was this: that Pii and Rina would pretend to be a married refugee couple that had come to make money after being banished from their own country for political reasons. The sewing factory girl would learn how to sing from the old woman and pretend to be a singer. Once you became an entertainer, people thought you were interesting enough that they would treat you with a certain degree of respect. The old woman told them she was planning on making a performance tent somewhere in the industrial city.

"I can't just sit here twiddling my thumbs while you work so hard," she explained of her plan, which seemed rather grandiose for someone who had barely escaped death. The old woman pulled Rina's hair back and tied it up in a bun. Rina started to wear baggy pants that made her look at least ten years older than she was. Rina wished that something in her—her blood, the core of her body— would change into that of a married woman, of a woman married to Pii.

The next morning at work, Pii burned his upper left chest on the sparks of a pipe welder. His clothes were burned in an instant by the sparks and stuck to his flesh. Pii wasn't the only one who welded without any safety gear. The supervisor watched the accident happen as he talked on the phone.

At lunchtime, the welders took two oil drums from a truck and placed a tabletop fashioned by welding together scraps of iron across them. They ladled food into their individual cans and carried them over to a sunny spot. Pii wrapped his burns tightly in dirty rags and sat on a pine board and ate his lunch like all the other men. Even though it was cold, there was no separate cafeteria where they could sit together and eat. All they got were rice, soup, and some pickled radish, and when they were done, they put the cans in an empty oil drum, which they loaded back onto the truck. There was no bathroom, so after lunch, they went behind the factory building to urinate.

Pii was up all night from the pain of his wound on his left chest. They had no medicine for it, and there were no hospitals nearby. All they could do was wet his parched lips and cover him as best they could with a blanket. Rina left the house with a single bill in her hand in the hopes of finding some medicine.

The factory district in the middle of the night was like a deserted castle in a fairy tale, huddled down with its back to the crimson sunset. But even this crippled city of the free economic zone had one street that stayed alive through the night. Outside of the factory district, just before the border of the giant dump was a street not quite five hundred meters long, teeming with restaurants and bars. Those who had worked in the factories for at least three years, or those who were born in the area would come to this place after work to drink at the street stalls that sold roasted bugs of all kinds as side dishes. The alleyways stank of vomit and urine, and small, incomprehensible fliers inundated the streets.

One of the restaurants had a wide glass door draped in red curtains. This was where the supervisors of the factory district had come to eat dinner with their families. Next to the table, their children sat in high chairs, practically strangled by their bibs as they banged on the table with their forks. The wives were too busy taking care of the children to eat. Of the eight supervisors, Rina recognized the man in the black shirt; he was one of the most important supervisors in charge of the entire complex, and he made the factory workers nervous whenever he showed up at work. He dangled a cigarette between his lips as he talked to the man across from him. Two waitresses in red dresses waited closely on him throughout the whole dinner. Rina crouched next to a street stall selling cookies dipped in white sugar and listened to the piercing sounds of some instrument coming from the restaurant. The fragrance of the sweet cookies wafted over on the breeze and pushed its way into her nostrils.

Across from the restaurants, a stall selling roasted tofu and grubs was bustling with customers. The factory workers were delivering impassioned speeches, and although she couldn't understand them very well, she could tell that they were upset about something. One man jumped up and beat his fist on his chest, and another flung an empty bottle at the back wall.

In the upscale restaurant, the food flowed forth freely. The man in the black shirt ate, every once in a while looking over at his wife and young child. When the man loosened his shirt cuffs, one of the waitresses approached him and dabbed at his forehead with a white towel. Rina was admiring his handsome profile when a gunshot pierced the air. Everyone turned toward the food stall, but Rina, who had been watching the restaurant, witnessed the moment in which the man in the black shirt got shot. His head fell into the waitress's lap. The waitress cradled the man's head and screamed. His baby crawled out of its high chair and climbed onto the table, wailing. It was hard to distinguish the blood from the man's face as it mingled with the red of the waitress's dress, but he appeared to be dead. The man's wife clasped her face in both hands and yelled at the top of her lungs for help while the man who had been sitting next to them made a call on his cell phone. When the owner of the cookie stall ran into the restaurant, Rina grabbed a handful of sugar cookies and calmly left the scene.

The weather got colder, and it frequently snowed. Whenever Rina looked up from her work, the sky was thick with flurries. Ever since the middle manager had died, the atmosphere at work was much more brutal. The whole place was thick with rumors that he had been involved in some sort of corruption or drugs. The workers weren't allowed to rest or express the slightest complaint, and if they opened their mouths to do so, they were fired on the spot. Work went on from dawn until late at night, and typically lasting about fifteen hours, and there were no days off. At the beginning of each month, they would ship in new workers on the train and fill the gaps.

During that time, Pii's welding skills improved enough for him to become an official welder, but his entire body was tattooed with burns. Rina, too, had become acclimated to the odor of carbide.

As winter grew colder, there were also more accidents. One of the special welders went blind, while another one, who had been working in high heat without proper protection, burned to death. One chilly day, his wife came to the entrance of the industrial zone to hand out pamphlets that told the full account of the accident. The workers grew angry and assembled at their usual street stall to talk about their rights at work. The meeting went quickly; even the foreign workers spoke the language fluently, and it was abundantly clear what problems needed to be addressed.

"We need safety equipment at work, we need a place to eat that protects us from the rain and the snow, we need changing rooms with mirrors, and showers with hot water, we want our promised raises, time and again, we are not idiots," the people began to yell out these demands like slogans at work, and even Rina would murmur "We are not idiots," while she was doing the laundry or cooking.

A senior government official from a faraway city on the continent was scheduled to visit the next day. They were told that they had to show the rest of the world that this place was the model industrial city, the heart of this country's potential for industrial development. The official, who arrived early in the morning on the train followed by a large retinue, took several photographs and left after ten minutes. Angered, the workers hurled abuse at his back. That night, they all gathered at the stalls again to plan countermeasures. At the same time, the managers themselves congregated in a secret location.

Rina had assumed that it had been too cold for the old woman to give the sewing factory girl her singing lessons. But it turned out that the sewing factory girl had been busy with other things, namely, frequenting the quarters of an Arab worker, a man with dark eyes and purple lips.

"What exactly is your relationship?" was as far Rina got before the girl took Rina's hand and placed it on her already burgeoning belly.

"You're seriously disgusting. How could you want to do it in a place like *this*?"

"I never really wanted to go to P. I just wanted to marry someone from a different country," the girl answered, patting her belly. For a moment, Rina was at a loss for words. Then she snorted.

"Well, that worked out, then. But where the hell are you going to have a baby here? This is insane. How can you be so silly?"

The girl, who had been giggling at Rina's reprimands, made a face. "You know what I'm really craving? Some bananas. He told me that where he comes from, bananas grow outside, indoors, it's bananas everywhere. Now that I think about it, I'm pretty sure I saw bananas in Shi-ling. Those long yellow things."

Time passed, and the working environment in the industrial zone showed no signs of improvement. The workers still ate lunch from cans in a corner of the factory floor, pissed anywhere, and passed out from fatigue at night.

After work, Rina and Pii would bundle up and walk around the industrial zone, arm in arm. The frozen snow crunched under their feet, and from a corner of the quarters, they could hear men coughing.

"Let's run away," Rina said. Pii smiled. The two walked arm in arm for a long time along the river behind the housing complex. They walked right up to the aerated vent tower that looked more than fifty meters high.

"Let's climb it," Rina suggested. The winter wind was freezing.

"You're crazy," Pii stopped her.

"I want to climb it. I want to climb to the top and look down on everything." Pii knew he couldn't stop Rina. The entrance to the tower was much easier to breach than expected.

Rina carefully climbed up the ladder, one rung at a time. She wasn't frightened, because Pii was coming up behind her, but her legs trembled. She kept on thinking about how short the one-hundred-meter dash at school was when she was younger. She tried to remind herself of the forest through which she and the twenty-one other escapees had fled. She climbed the whole tower without looking down. When she was close to the top, she could see the roof of the housing complex, and the tower crane to the northwest was at eye level. Rina convinced her trembling legs to take the last few steps, and finally reached the top of the fifty-meter-high tower, where she could look down at the city. One side of it was flat, the other looked majestic. One side was white, the other black. Rina and Pii were both shivering, but Rina felt as if a burden in the center of her chest had been gloriously punched out. She pointed to the pale area.

"Why is that place broken like that?" Pii hugged her shoulders from behind.

"Seven years ago, there was a gas leak. That's why."

"Really? A lot of people must have died." Instead of answering, Pii took a cigarette from his pocket, and painstakingly lit it. Then he boldly leaned one leg on the ledge of the tower, and looked down into the abyss. Now that she'd fulfilled the prophecy of seeing the other half of the industrial zone, Rina felt anxious, and suddenly noticed a black flock of birds flying from one end of the continent down south.

19

It got so cold that it was warmer inside the factory, lit up by the welders' sparks. The managers pushed the workers, telling them that they couldn't have a single day's rest if they were to meet the construction deadlines, and the workers no longer even bothered to answer. There was still no cafeteria where they could sit and eat, no bathroom, no showers with hot water. Pii could now weld most iron structures on his own. His face was bloodless, at once sallow and sunburned, just like all the other workers here; there was no trace of his old self. Rina now ceased to be startled by the policemen that would drop in from time to time, and no one suspected her of being a foreign escapee.

Banners appeared on walls that advertised the tenth anniversary of the industrial complex. People whispered to each other that that might be the day when the managers would ship in prefabricated bathrooms or shower stalls and install them near the factory, so they bit their tongues and worked on. There was one person who was happy and fulfilled during this worst of times, and that was the sewing factory girl. Luckily, it was winter, so no one had noticed her belly, but when she came back home, she happily played the part of the pregnant woman. The old woman caressed the girl's belly every night, saying, "It's coming soon, it's coming soon." The baby's father, the Arab, followed the girl around everywhere. The girl still craved bananas, and declared that she wouldn't be able to have the baby without bananas.

Pii got a bunch of bananas from some men who worked as cooks at one of the restaurants. The girl ate the entire bunch all by herself, without offering to share with the old woman, Rina, or even the Arab. When she was done, her belly grew even bigger. There was a clock in everyone's head, and each person waited for the day that the alarm would go off and the baby would come.

On the day of the tenth anniversary of the industrial complex, all the workers were giddy with excitement; people smiled for no reason, or stood up from work to look if an unfamiliar car approached. Their hopes that the managers might come to encourage the workers were dashed when the lunch truck came with their lunches chilled by the frosty air, as always. They still had to seek out shelter from the wind to eat. When they were done, they each had a cigarette and went behind the factory to urinate, then returned to their workstations.

The day ended without a single visitor bringing sweets or a bottle of spirits. They were wrapping up when they heard a strange noise at the entrance of the complex. The burly security guards hired by the managers had already blocked the intruders from the west-side dump. They were dressed in rags, and their large eyes peered out of their gaunt, pale faces. They said they were the victims of the gas leak seven years ago. Rina noticed a few deformed children and some very fragile-looking adults with ashen faces. They made no demands, simply stood at the entrance, silently confronting the hired muscle. Rina was told they came every year on this day. She noticed one of the children holding a piece of paper. It read, "Don't forget us!"

That night, the old woman, who had been hiding under her blanket playing with her straggly, loosened hair, suddenly got up and pulled a bundle out from underneath her bed and began to make up her face. She prepared herself as she used to when she was a singer, putting on her white gown with the tight waist, and pulling her hair neatly back. Rina, Pii, and the sewing factory girl's boyfriend followed her out, wondering what she was up to. The old woman directed them to erect a stage in a corner of the square, where people often gathered. Pii and the Arab complained that they were already tired as it was without having to perform strange tasks. There weren't any tools, but they took some bits and pieces from the factory and stretched a canopy up over four poles.

The old woman sent Pii to tell everyone to come watch the show that she was about to put on. For the first time in a long time, Rina struck the small hand drum that she'd brought with her from the plains. As the drumbeat spread, the people walked across the sticky black tar, bundled up in their hats, and gathered under the canopy. The old woman's thickly made-up face was red and blue from the cold. When twenty or so people had gathered, the old woman began her performance. There was no shining halo behind her head like before, and no one in the audience bowed as if in the presence of a deity. Still, the old woman began her routine very calmly. She could no longer captivate her audience with the thick, staccatoed tones she used to belt out. Just as she was coughing and trying to figure a way out of the situation, two men from the audience stepped out to the front with their arms raised, and began to yell out their slogans. *Give us a place to eat out of the rain and the snow, give us safety equipment in the workplace, give us locker rooms with mirrors and showers with hot water, give us the salary you promised us, we are not idiots.* It was the same stuff they were always talking about, but in the dark night, chanted in unison by a large group of people, something was different about it. One of the foreigners wept as he leaned his head against the face of a coworker.

Moments later, the security guards hired by the management rushed the scene. They deftly plucked the old woman off the makeshift stage and placed her on the squelching ground. With the help of some very thick, long sticks, they dispersed the crowd. The terrified people fled toward their apartments, and before long, there was no trace of the special event.

The old woman got called up in front of the managers. Rina looked them straight in the eye as she told them that the old woman had lost her senses ages ago, and had organized everything in her insanity. The managers ignored Rina's explanations; they had their own questions in mind.

"Is it true that you were a prostitute? Are the rumors true? How many men have you slept with?" Rina nearly spat out a rude response in her own language, but managed to bite her tongue.

Pii had a hard time falling asleep that night. On a large piece of paper, he drew the industrial complex, cramming the page with factory buildings. The industrial complex in his drawing was all black and the people were so tiny you could barely see them. Rina lay on her stomach next to him, swinging her legs back and forth as she hummed a tune, and the old woman came back from her severe chastisement and lay down quietly, pretending to be a meek and subservient little lady. Rina couldn't tell what Pii was up to, but he didn't seem to be sleeping. Once in a while, she woke up at the creaking of the bed, and felt Pii's cold feet graze her skin.

When Rina got out of bed at dawn, she found the sewing factory girl heaving and panting on her bed near the window. The girl gripped Rina's arm and looked up at her in pain. Rina woke the old woman, who directed Rina to boil some water and Pii to go fetch the Arab.

"The baby's coming. Don't cry too much. It's much harder for the baby than it is for you. Just imagine how hard it must be to come into the light from a place that's so dark!" the old woman whispered.

The sewing factory girl got very quiet, and the old woman fed her dumplings. It was hard to have a baby the right way on an empty stomach, she said. When the Arab arrived, he started to make a big fuss, rubbing his palms together and praying to Allah. The girl screamed "Mommy!" whenever she was in pain and this prompted the old woman to peer into her crotch, but the baby still wasn't coming out into the light. Rina sat next to the girl on the edge of her bed and felt the baby tense and tighten under her palm whenever the mother's belly contracted.

In the morning, Pii and the Arab had to go to work. The old woman, too, decided that the baby wasn't coming any time soon and took a nap. With the dawn came, as usual, thick flurries of snowflakes. The sky looked gloomy and overcast. Whenever the sewing factory girl came to, she squeezed Rina's hand and thanked her. Rina couldn't help gloating over the girl's labor pains, yet at the same time, she pitied her.

The labor lasted well into the night. Pii brought more bananas, and the Arab brought clean white cloth for swaddling the baby. They were slurping on some noodles for dinner when the girl, who had been lying limply in bed, let out a shriek and thrust her head into the headboard. The old woman stuck her head into the girl's crotch and told the baby to hurry up. As if in time with the old woman's repeated commands, the girl slowly opened up, and the baby's fuzzy black head emerged slowly from the taut, clear flesh of her vagina. The world outside the window was white with snow. The wrinkled red head of the baby exited first, then it rotated slightly, letting its shoulders follow, and the whole thing popped out. Someone in the room belched with astonishment.

The girl fainted as soon as the baby was out. Babies were supposed to cry when they first came into this world, but this one made no noise. It rolled its eyes from one corner of the house to the other as it lay in the arms of the Arab, then shut its eyes as if it were tired from the world.

"Ew, how disgusting," Rina commented, genuinely repulsed by the white discharge covering the newborn baby. At that moment, Rina remembered her mother telling her how she'd had a baby in the dead of the winter in the small border town where they used to live, and how she'd suffered because the baby wouldn't stop crying for a month, "And that's you—you pain in my ass!" Rina walked over to the Arab and looked down at the baby for a while and loosened some of swaddling around its chest. Then, like the baby's mother had once done with her, she drew a little butterfly in the air. The old woman, who had been thumping the sewing factory girl's stomach, tired herself out. Pii took it up, and then the Arab, until eventually, the girl's placenta spilled out. Rina watched it all spill out into the trashcan and suddenly felt cool and relieved down there, as if she was the one who had just given birth. Night had fallen outside the window, and the old woman gathered up her energy to slap the baby on its bottom. The baby pouted as if complaining *why me?* and began to cry softly.

20

THE SNOWFLAKES MELTED AS SOON AS THEY HIT THE PUDDLE-covered, squelchy ground. The smokestacks towering over the factory buildings belched out dark, opaque smoke for days. On humid days, the smoke was too heavy to get very high up, and would instead sink down and spread itself laterally. On those days, the air was too foul to even breathe properly. The nights were punctuated with coughs from all over the housing complex.

It was the beginning of Rina's second winter in the industrial complex. Last summer had been a battle. They entered the middle of the third phase of the plant-building process in a stifling heat of over 100 degrees Fahrenheit. Every day, new raw materials arrived by helicopter and train. But even more important than the materials were giant, rectangular sacks of ice. It was so hot and humid that they simply couldn't work without ice. When mixing aggregate, they had to use ice instead of water, and they had to constantly pour ice on the insulator of the concrete mixer to keep it cool. The raw materials would wilt in the hot weather even before the people did, so it was pointless to start working with concrete during the day; the sun baked the moisture right out of the concrete, causing it to crack. Concrete work had to be carried out in the dead of the night; during the day, they were only able to work on the steel-frame structures or set up machinery.

For the completion of every new cylindrical storage tank, there were always a few injuries. It required a seasoned expert to weld iron pieces into a high-rising steel structure. It was even harder to install the roof of the storage tank, and the managers would often say it simply could not be done without divine help. Inside the tank, it was dark and dusty and too easy to take a wrong step and fall. Workers who were far from seasoned experts were brought in from other countries at cheap prices and inserted into the field with no special instructions. When they were killed, they were dead before they could even realize how it happened.

Rina was now somewhat used to the scorching summers and the bitter cold. Even so, once in a while, she would lose all hope at the idea that she might only get to leave the industrial city once she was an old woman with hair as white as snow.

The sunset slipped through the branches of the trees on the low hill behind the housing complex. The flurries whipping this way and that with the wind disappeared in the dark along with the sun. The sun set quickly, and once it did, it was the darkest time of all. The piles of rebar, the welding station that was heated from the fire, the maze of pipes, the corroded, worn-down trucks that came to pick up the garbage, the dark blue sky at dusk with just the slightest glint of a golden sunset, all these things, from what was visible to what was not, turned darker and darker, each at their own pace. The moment of darkness swallowed up the entire complex in a split second. Then, from the western sky, the tower crane and the aerated gas tower began their nighttime reign of the industrial zone.

The orange sparks from the welding burned their brightest right after the sun had set. As they emerged from the welding rod, the sparks made a *shhhh-fooooo* sound, as if they were catching their breath. They danced in every corner as they cut and reconnected pieces of steel, looking like the fiery eyes of maddened, leaping demons. Rina kept her eyes on the sparks, rotating and changing the part of her body that was exposed to the heat of the fire whenever she got cold. The sparks were orange when they leapt out of the welding rod. Then they grew bigger and turned blue, and finally they turned into a blinding white. Rina felt like she could see a path in the sparks that she could walk into.

Whether the sun was up or down, the industrial plant complex went round and round as it manufactured chemical gas storage tanks. Everyone worked zealously; they had been told that this complex was to become the nation's greatest chemical plant within the next five years. The banner at the entrance of the complex announcing the beginning of the free economic zone still fluttered in the wind, although it was now blackened with grime. The third phase of plant manufacturing was almost over, and it was said that the foreign company that was in charge would pull out once the work was done.

Either way, the workers had it the worst. Several times a day, the ear-splitting sound of sirens reverberated throughout the factory. The sirens were automatically rigged to go off at even the slightest trace of a gas leakage or any other operational problem. Whenever the siren went off, the safety managers would yell, "Six, tank number six!" Of the six gas storage tanks to the right side of the complex, the one in the middle was number six. But no one really knew or cared what exactly happened there. There was too much work and it was far too cold for that.

Even though it was noisy, the sirens seemed at least to prove that the safety system was working properly. But the fact that they wailed constantly throughout the day also meant that there was a serious ongoing problem. The workers joked sarcastically that the managers played cards when they supposedly went off to check tank number six.

When the sun had set, Rina went to Pii's workstation, as always. It was impossible to distinguish him from all the other welders hunkered over, wrestling with the sparks, and it always took her a while to spot him. She could tell him from his long, large feet. As she watched Pii engrossed in his work, his mouth firmly set, she felt sorry for him, but also angry. When he had first started as a welder, Pii would come home with burns every other day. The first burn he had, above the left side of his chest, looked like a dead minnow stuck flat to his skin. But even Rina didn't care about Pii's new scars anymore. As time passed, he came back with more burns, and said less.

Pii held a welding rod in his thick-gloved hands, and he wore safety goggles. Welding was a large part of what went on at the plant. Even the slightest crack in the welding could lead to a large-scale explosion, so the final step in all welding jobs involved x-raying the final product to check for fissures or weak spots. Pii had a perfect record. Rina stood in front of Pii and stomped her feet. It was only natural that he couldn't hear her, but he was so engrossed in his work that he didn't even see her. *Please look at me,* Rina mouthed. After a long time, Pii finally put his welding rod down and took off his safety goggles. Since he began work as a welder, Pii's face had become brown, like all the other men who worked there. His face had lost its usual dumbfounded look, and he had transformed into a strong, muscular man.

When Pii came home from work late at night and lifted his arms to take off his shirt, the muscles on his shoulders and back raised and tightened. Rina always pretended to look at him indifferently, but the truth was, it made her heart pound. Rina was sure that Pii had undergone some sort of magical transformation, or that he was eating iron powder. But Pii never smiled at Rina anymore. Rina believed that this was due to an evil spell cast on them by some jealous malcontent.

After the old woman had told them to pretend to be a couple, Pii became even less fun. "Have you eaten yet?" Rina asked. Pii looked around the work area without answering. "Why won't you open your mouth? Are you saving it for something special? You haven't seen me all day, don't you even want to know how I'm doing?"

Without answering, Pii took a cigarette from his pocket and put it in his mouth. He moved differently now, slowly but more roughly than before. Rina looked at him angrily, but he puffed away in silence. Then someone called his name. Pii's coworkers were often looking for him, so he wasn't free to leave work. Rina turned angrily on her heel and walked away. She felt as if the world were coming to an end, with everything going black. Ignoring her, Pii put on his safety vest and trudged back to work.

"How dare you treat me like this, you bastard! I won't be coming home tonight," Rina snapped. It frustrated her that she was both afraid of and fascinated by him.

When the siren signaling the end of the workday gave a long wail, the people looked about their workstations, then slowly stood up. The sky was already dark. It was so cold that no one dared to shower. Rina shook the giant dust bunnies off her work clothes. It was only at the end of the day, as she whipped the dust off her clothes, that she regained the sensation in her arms and legs. Back in the housing complex, the apartments lit up one by one, and the silvery leaves that had drifted off the naked trees out front shivered in the wind. Shadows paced slowly back and forth past the rusty lattice windows. Rina walked into a storage room near her workstation. Inside, a few elderly women were cleaning up pieces of rubble leftover from the building material and boxes filled with chemicals. Someone had hung a shattered mirror on one of the walls, and under it was a plastic container for washing your hands. The women used the area as a vanity. Rina untied the handkerchief she used to pull back her hair. She carefully wet her hair, shook it out, brushed it, and rinsed her mouth several times with water. She took out the lipstick she always carried with her. It was frozen, and she cradled it in her palm and breathed on it to thaw it. Just as her lips were pursed and taut, ready to expel warm air onto the lipstick,

Rina became strangely angry. Something inside her that had been repressed seemed to bubble up now so that even the blood vessels in her eyes stood to attention. Her throat felt constricted, and she started cursing without realizing. This happened once in a while, and when it did, she would curse and swear to her heart's content.

"Those crazy bastards from the factory should all die. Evil bastards, I hope they all fall over and break their legs." Rina kicked a large can at her feet.

When the lipstick had warmed a bit and was beginning to look shiny again, Rina dabbed some on each cheek and rubbed it in with her fingers. She painted several layers on her lips until they were dark. When she was done, her eyes would well up, and only then would the feeling slowly creep back into her body. It made her want to be someone else, if just for a moment.

She headed toward a walkway that stretched west of the industrial complex. It was crawling with a couple hundred pedestrians, maybe more. Hundreds of men were headed west, their hands in their pockets. They all walked away from the darkened industrial complex without looking back, as if they never wanted to see it again. An upbeat pop song began playing somewhere above their heads, baptizing the road with its rhythm. Rina headed toward the sound. She had been clenching her buttocks all day, and her hips were so sore that it was difficult to walk, yet it was always exciting walking to the downtown area that lay to the west. The bright lights and signs seemed to beckon to her in the darkness like clusters of stars. Rina looked back, and at that moment, the dark industrial complex was slowly pushed into the open sea of darkness, like a giant ship.

As they approached the nightlife district, touts began to solicit the men, grabbing them by the wrist and pulling them into their bars. The men vanished into these establishments in twos and threes, and each time, the loud and exaggerated bellows welcoming them rang throughout the streets. Every night, the men flocked to this area that lay between the factories and the shut-down part of the city—it was the flower of the industrial complex. If they were overlooked at work, here, they were treated like men of elegance, big men who knew how to spend money the right way.

Stuck right between the ruined lot and the industrial zone, the neighborhood looked desolate during the day. The side of the road leading to the shut-down area was literally a dump, strewn with piles of garbage, and the desert began right where the main street ended. The buildings that lined the main stretch were all prefabricated structures with thin roofs and thin walls, and during the day, without the glowing lights emerging from them, they looked flimsy enough to be blown away in the wind.

In the center of downtown was a white building three stories high; it was the best-known bar in the city, and was called The Puzzle. Rina worked at The Puzzle. Here, the factory workers sat drinking side by side until, at the slightest provocation, they broke out into tears or fights. Up a narrow flight of stairs were several small rooms bustling with people who came to gamble away their monthly salaries amid clouds of cigarette smoke. There were several rooms on the third floor that were used as venues for trysts.

Rina had come here because of Misha. Misha was The Puzzle's most popular waitress. She came from a small independent state in the north of the continent, and had been abandoned by her parents during their divorce. She had been wandering the streets when she hitched a ride on a strange bus and was transported across the prairies to this city without even realizing what was happening. She didn't know how many months she'd spent in the car, or what she ate the whole time, but when she got off, here she was. Misha was tall and thin, and there was something foreign about her, like she was a princess from a land of snow and ice. All Misha could remember from her childhood was the odor of cheap super glue, the kind you could find anywhere, and cigarettes as thick and stinky as smokestacks. Misha had been in the audience the day of the old woman's impromptu performance. Afterward, she had approached Rina.

"Do you call this a performance? Come to The Puzzle, we put on real shows there." She spoke the language of this country fluently.

When Rina arrived at The Puzzle, Misha handed her a paper bag, which Rina took to the bathroom. It was a tight black dress with skinny shoulder straps and sequins around the chest. The dress was slightly big on Rina. This was perfect for her, as she would rather have died than forego her long underwear. Rina combed her hair so it fell over one shoulder, sucked her stomach in, and headed out.

The customers drank all night. Rina travelled from the first floor to the third, serving drinks. Opening the upstairs window and sticking her head out at an angle, she could see the industrial complex to the right. Rina liked to stoop down and look out the window this way, shaking her butt from side to side to the music. The men coming to and from the toilets would amicably slap her butt, but she passed it off with a little smile that said, "No big deal." One of the men stopped and turned to stare at Rina. Rina had already noticed him—he worked in her department at the factory—but he didn't recognize her.

"Where have I seen you . . . ?" he mused, and followed Rina around for the rest of the night.

The foreign workers stood up and rubbed their faces, covered in wounds and cuts, on the person next to them and lifted their arms up high and danced. They didn't cry, but their slow and weird movements were steeped with a fatigue and self-loathing like old stains on a blanket. One tall man with dilated pupils climbed onto the tables to dance and refused to come down. He doubled over and whimpered, and told everyone he was a dog. The people around him also got down on all fours and started to bark. Someone who had been drinking nearby yelled, "We're not dogs, *they* are!"

Rina would finish off the leftover liquor in the glasses she cleared while she was bussing tables. Partly because it felt like a waste, but also because she was so cold and hungry. Rina finally felt like she understood the taste of liquor, the feeling she got when it gently scraped her insides as it flowed down her esophagus. She completely understood why the men and women of Misha's cold motherland had to spend their winters soaked in alcohol. Drowsy from her buzz, Rina leaned her chin into her hand and laughed at the customers. The man from her department appeared behind her; having finally figured out who she was.

"I didn't recognize you with all that makeup on. Never knew you were so pretty," the man grinned, smoothing his curly hair back with his fingers.

"Hey, how about some manners? Who do you think I am?" Rina grumbled.

All of a sudden, they heard a scuffle in the stairway leading up to the second floor. A man was being dragged downstairs by his collar as he babbled in a foreign language. He must have been causing a ruckus after losing money playing cards. This was a common sight at The Puzzle, and hardly a cause for surprise. Rina went up to the man and wiped away his green tears and the white cigarette ash on his nose.

"What are you doing here? What are you going to do if she finds out?" It was the husband of the sewing factory girl. Rina walked him and his posse out, her arms around their shoulders.

"Bye, Rina!" the Arab waved, and he headed back toward the industrial complex, his arms around his friends. Rina shook her head as she imagined the girl screaming at her husband when he walked through the door: "I was insane to trust you, you asshole. I can't believe I got knocked up in this godforsaken country. And here I thought an international marriage was going to be something special. I guess I met an international bum!"

Rina stood dumbly at the entrance of the bar after the Arab and his friends had left. It had started to snow again. She could see Misha through the frosted glass of the club, dancing with her arms above her head. The blue eye shadow painted on her ice-cold face looked like the wings of a bird. Misha's movements were smooth and light enough to make her forget where she was, or that it was so cold. Rina was about to head back inside when she turned around and looked toward the factories. The road that the Arab and his friends had taken was deserted, without even a trace of the ubiquitous alley cats. "You rock, Misha," Rina murmured to herself, then pushed open the glass door and went back inside.

When the main room of the first floor had nearly emptied out and the only customers remaining were the card players upstairs, the owner arrived. Everyone called him Big Puzzle. He emptied the register, put the money in a bag, and sat at the bar with a sullen expression, as always. Misha got two bottles of beer and sat at his right, while Rina was at his left with a plateful of snacks. For nearly three hours, they sat and drank without saying a word.

When the remaining customers came down from the second floor, Rina hurried upstairs. She never forgot to check for coins that had been dropped under the table, or bills stashed away and forgotten. Rina took all the money; she never returned it when someone came back looking for it. The booze hit her. She went to the bathroom, stuck her finger down her throat, and vomited. Then she changed out of Misha's dress. She stared at her veiny face and tried to rub the goose bumps off her arms and shoulders.

"Get back down here!" Big Puzzle hollered.

They locked the storage rooms where they kept the liquor, and the kitchen. There were still several drunk customers rolling around on the ground, some foaming at the mouth, others weeping. They left them there to be alone for a while and recover. A white car stood on the road amid the snow flurries, and Rina, Misha, and Big Puzzle got in. As they drove down the main street that was barely 200 meters long, everyone turned to look at them and point. Whenever the car slowed down, they would grin and excitedly knock on the window. Rina stuck her neck out and waved at them.

The traces of the admirers' handprints stayed on the windows long after they had exited the downtown area.

"Where are you taking us?" Misha asked Big Puzzle.

"Somewhere nice," he responded sullenly, and continued to drive.

The car cut across the industrial complex and left via the city's right-side exit. They hit the road that ran parallel to the railroad. Rina opened the window and looked out at the rails. The sound of the train against the rails was so grating it seemed to be tearing away at her ears, which she had covered without even realizing. The car sped freely down the road without any stoplights, lanes, or signs. Suddenly, something big and round fell out of the sky onto the road in front of them.

"A dead polar bear!" Big Puzzle yelled, and stopped the car. But it was hardly a bear, just was a giant ball of snow. Big Puzzle whipped out his cell phone to make a call and beckoned to Misha and Rina to get rid of the snowball.

"He always makes the women do the heavy lifting," grumbled Rina. They weren't able to even budge the snowball, so instead they gathered branches and made a snowman out of it.

"Why didn't you move it out of the way?" grumbled Big Puzzle when he'd hung up the phone.

"We were trying to get it to walk away on its own."

It took the three of them to push the ball off the road and to the top of a hill, where it rolled down of its own accord.

They drove for more than an hour on the dark road, and Misha and Rina dozed off. The car had left the road that ran next to the tracks, and stopped with a jolt on a boulevard in a residential area in a small city. Rina woke up to a hulking man with a strangely tiny head sitting next to her. He was staring at her intently. He told her he was one of Big Puzzle's old friends, and he was the fattest person Rina had ever seen since coming to this country. Rina opened the window and coughed, suddenly feeling suffocated. The four of them drove to a nearby city, parked the car in front of a building, and got out. The giant city was shrouded in smog, and seemed to be swept along in the same direction as the throngs of people that populated it. In the fluorescent light, the city looked like it was slowly melting to the ground. While the big man went to a nearby store to make a phone call, the others leaned on the railing of an old castle gate and waited.

Past the castle gate, lined with sagging willow trees, was a street lined with storefronts. People sat in front of the stores drinking and chatting away noisily. Even though it was cold, they ate and drank with vigor and even recited some poetry. A girl with pigtails came out to meet them, and they followed her to an alley. The alley was narrow and paved with stone. When they got to a small store that sold mundane handmade stationary and little trinkets, the girl pointed up to the second floor. The red tiger painted on the wall leading upstairs was bloodcurdling.

Inside, there was an elderly white woman with the stiff demeanor of an airport control tower worker, a few tall white boys with yellow hair and a lot of peach fuzz on their faces, some nearly-naked young girls, and an old couple sitting side by side with their giant asses mashed together. They were all smoking marijuana. Misha greeted them familiarly in English, as if she knew them well. The four newcomers sat on the sofa and drank tea while they waited.

Soon, the old man who lived there came out and gave them some marijuana. As they smoked, the people in the room debated about world poverty, the endlessness of war, and sustainable development. One of them actually worked at a private development committee that was part of some international organization affiliated with the United Nations, or perhaps it was the United Nations itself.

"I don't think there's a country in the world as irresponsible as this one here about coming up with a plan for pollution," someone remarked, breaking a long silence.

"We really have a lot of complaints about this government—it won't even cough up environmental fees," was the last lucid thing anyone said. After that, the room was filled with mostly groans and the sound of hocking.

Feeling nauseated, Rina ran to the bathroom. The pigtailed girl that had guided them earlier came in, unpeeled a red lollipop, and put it in Rina's mouth. "My name is Rina. My name is Rina!" Rina murmured as she sucked on the lollipop. She lay on her back, unable to get up because the ceiling was spinning. After a while, she became cold and frightened, and crawled out to find Misha. She could see her clearly a few feet away, but when she got close and hugged her around the waist, it wasn't Misha. A young man that she'd met earlier approached her—he was from a country that had a Dead Sea, a country that was to be full of people related to the son of god, who had saved the world—and Rina felt so dizzy that she rubbed her head against what was either his thigh or his backside, and begged, "My God, sir, please save me!"

From that day on, Rina became a lifelong member of the sustainable development committee, and she was to miss her fellow members for as long as she lived. She came to agree with the old western woman that whatever medication or narcotic alleviated disorders of the modern nervous system and helped modern man forget his burdens ultimately contributed to the development of humanity.

The four left the house and walked down the side of the road. The city, which had been moving along with its crowds, had now stopped cold. It was freezing and they were hungry. The streets were as dark as the inside of a wardrobe. Big Puzzle took them to a late-night joint in front of a bike rental store. When he walked in, the owner came out from the back with a cigarette, offered one to Big Puzzle, and went back into the kitchen. A few minutes later he came out with a generous serving of dumplings and meat with rice. Three of them hurriedly shoved the food down their throats.

"Aren't you eating?" Misha asked Big Puzzle, who simply puffed on his cigarette and consumed his beer with a blank look on his face.

Beer consumed at night tasted oddly bland. Rina no longer wanted to think about how much time had passed, how cold it was outside, or what work she had to do at the factory tomorrow. Her plan was simply to eat all the food in front of her until she was full, and then go to sleep. Then Big Puzzle turned to Rina.

"Have you ever slept with a man before?" Rina was floored for moment, but she tried to hide her surprise by eating as nonchalantly as possible.

"What? Don't you know how old I am? Never. Not once."

The fat man and Big Puzzle looked at each other and snickered. Misha looked out the window and yawned.

"I'm a *virgin*. Honest."

And Rina nearly vomited at hilarity of her own words. Of all the English words Rina had recently learned from Misha, the word "virgin" had stayed with her. But she hadn't expected the word to pop out of her mouth as it did. Misha, who had been nodding off, suddenly woke up and started to giggle, and Big Puzzle snickered, as well. They all laughed together at the lie that had edged its way out through Rina's teeth.

The restaurant became silent again, until Big Puzzle opened his mouth with another question.

"I've seen escapees like you. You know what happened to them? They were captured, taken back to their country and killed, or they were never able to leave this country. What are you going to do?" Rina nearly vomited again, but she managed to keep it down. She hadn't told anyone, yet this man knew everything. Rina was trembling inside, but she answered him confidently.

"I guess I'll live here. The air's foul, but it's not a bad place. Hey, pass me some more dumplings, will you?"

They left the store and combed the streets until they found a dance club hidden at the end of the street. Some children with earmuffs sat out front, holding out their hands for some spare change.

The heavy leather door of the club opened onto a whole other world. Girls with short skirts and shiny rings in their ears and noses were dancing barefoot. The boys shook their torsos and blond hair violently. Rina couldn't believe she was near the border of a poor country. Big Puzzle sat at the bar with the same old sullen face and watched the people dance. Misha, who had been swaying ever since she walked in, was already in the center of the dance floor, dancing away. Rina found herself awkwardly gyrating her hips along with Misha.

When Rina got back home, the sky was already tinged with the color of dawn. She opened the door quietly and walked in. The old woman and Pii were sleeping by the window on a steel bed they'd found on the street, and the sewing factory girl and her newborn were sleeping in another bed. The newborn baby was playing by himself and wriggling his little legs. Rina smiled into the baby's black eyes.

"Why don't you yell? The old woman is getting worried."

The baby smiled at Rina, but made no sound. His mother was snoring away.

Pii was curled up like a large shrimp, his face buried in the old woman's fragile arm. A pale green light spilled onto the bed. Rina wedged herself into a small crack between the wall and the bed and crawled in next to Pii. She lay down, her face against his back, which smelled like iron. He didn't wake up, so she ran her fingers through his hair. It hadn't been washed in a long time, and was tangled and matted like a broom. She lay there for a long time, but Pii didn't turn around.

Rina gently lifted the old woman's head and pillow, trying her best not to wake her, and slipped her hand under the pillowcase. She looked around. It was where she kept her container of money. Rina opened the container and took out the carefully folded bills. This secret moment was always her happiest. The slightly fishy smell of the bills, the dampness of the paper, like a frog emerging from the water. At that moment, the sewing factory girl tossed around in her bed and sat up.

"If I didn't have a kid, I'd go out with you. Why won't this baby breastfeed, stupid thing."

She shoved her breast at the baby, even though it gave no milk. She looked undisturbed, which meant the Arab must not have stopped by. Rina swallowed nervously and clutched the money tightly to her chest for a long time. She would have to wait for the sewing factory girl to fall sleep before she could put the money back. She couldn't trust her.

21

ONE MORNING, WHEN EVERYONE WAS AWAKE, THE OLD WOMAN declared that there was something strange about the baby. He was nearly a year old, but he didn't walk, cry, or whine at all.

"I think he's a little dull. Are all children of Arab fathers like this? What do you think?" the old woman asked Rina and the baby's mother as they were about to head out for work. Pii had already left.

"You should know. I've never had a baby before," the sewing factory girl retorted. The old woman cupped her chin in her hands.

"Young ladies, I've never been married, and most certainly never had a child," she answered winsomely. She peered down at the baby. The sewing factory girl worked during the day, so she didn't know how the baby was developing.

"It's because you don't care about the baby. You should pay more attention to him," Rina said.

"What the hell, I don't know. You take care of it, Granny. What am I supposed to do with a baby whose father doesn't care about him?" she snapped at Rina. "Why don't *you* be his mother?"

"We're not the ones who married the Arab!" the old woman spat angrily.

The sewing factory girl ignored her, gave the baby's basket a tap, and left in a huff. Rina went over to the baby and tried to look him in the eyes, but he seemed weak. Perhaps it was just because of what the old woman had said, but something did seem a little off.

There seemed to be a pungent chemical odor floating above the cold morning air. Because the sky was so overcast, the smoke from the smokestacks, instead of rising, had sunk down to the ground. Rina headed to work, her body bloated from the night before. All they received as a bonus for the cold winter months was a box of white masks to cover their mouths. Pressing down on the v-shaped wire that crossed the bridge of the nose, allowed you to cover your nose more effectively. The floors of the factories were littered with these white masks. Now, Rina took hers out of her pocket and slung it over her ears.

They had been served lunch in their cans, and were feeling a little sleepy despite the meagerness of the meal when the accident happened. One of the foreign workers, who usually only did janitorial work and small errands in the workplace had picked up a welding rod and been badly burned. His body, as it was wheeled out on a gurney, was already as stiff as a dried patch of seaweed. It took a long time to get him to a nearby hospital, and he died before he got there.

The dead man's friends gave him a funeral according to their customs, but none of the factory supervisors attended. They said they were too busy. So the next day, the dead man's friends went to the toxic substance management warehouse and protested by grabbing onto a container and refusing to leave. The authorities at the industrial complex quickly called the police and had them thrown in prison. The complex fell silent once again. They all worked hard as they neared the deadline, and the smokestacks burned and burned every day, as if they were about to explode.

Then, friends of the men who had been sent to prison assembled to protest. It was so cold, however, that the protest wasn't much more than a few people gathering with some signs with messages like, *All you do is hire us to work for pennies, and travel the world looking for*

180

people to work for even less. The signs were hard to understand, but the supervisors got the message as soon as they saw them.

"Those anachronistic fools. Cheapest is best whether it's for products or for labor. Those fools are toxic for the plant; we have to get rid of them." This attracted even more protesters.

The next morning, they were all met with a lamentable sight; the protest area was now home to a fifty-foot-high top section of a gas separation tower. Everyone gathered around it, drumming on tin pots. It was a truly multinational protest; each worker had brought a sign written in his or her own language. Throughout the day, people would look up from their work to the top section parked in the lot and click their tongues disapprovingly. In the afternoon, a helicopter flew by, circled the area, then disappeared.

In the middle of the night, Rina noticed lights flashing wildly near one area of the gas separation tower. She ran outside and along the river behind the living quarters. Some people were climbing down the tower. They looked familiar, so she waited at the bottom for them. As she'd expected, it was Pii and some of his friends.

"Are you crazy? Why did you go up there?"

Pii said nothing. It wasn't that he refused to speak, but his nose and ears were red, and his face was frozen. Rina grabbed his head. His fingertips were frozen solid.

"Are you insane? Why don't you say something, you retard!" Rina yelled, prompting some of the nearby men to shake their heads at her.

"Just listen to her speak. Stop being such a brat," they scolded. Pii hit Rina on the side of her head.

"I was getting them something to pee in and some food."

Pii popped a cigarette in his mouth and started walking west with the rest of the men, toward downtown.

"Who the hell do you think you are, treating me like a little sister, huh? How old are you, even?" Rina chattered to herself as she followed them.

The men held a meeting at The Puzzle. The longest national holiday of this country was coming up soon, and they said they couldn't just leave the protesters at the top of the tower like that. Some people refused to even think about this incident; all they wanted was to finish work and get back home as soon as possible. At that moment the door opened and a supervisor, third in charge at the complex, marched in. Misha set a beer in front of him, and he thanked her in English rather than his native language, a gesture that moved everyone present.

"Look, everyone's already worried because it seems like there's some serious miscommunication here, and we don't fully get what the problem is. And then those guys climb up there and are yelling things we can't even understand, now that's a big issue," the supervisor began. Some of the people there agreed with him, and they nodded whenever he finished a sentence.

"Even so, don't you think not going to a man's funeral when he died on the job, working for *you*, is taking it too far?" someone pointed out.

"I understand. But is this really the time to insist so stubbornly on these protests? You should really cooperate with us and try to talk them into coming down. It's not going to bring a dead man back to life, is it?" They all stared questioningly at the supervisor.

"How would we cooperate with you?"

The supervisor downed his beer and slammed the glass down on the counter. "Setting the right tone is key. Don't bring anything up there, not a single pea, not a blanket or a jacket."

Starting the very next day, all aid stopped. The shouts of the people at the top of the tower grew weaker, and their drumming slowed. The construction of the plant was now nearing the end of its third phase. Once every few days, some foreign technicians would come by and look around the facilities. The siren rang several times, but no one seemed to worry too much about safety while the professionals were around.

They also began to conduct experiments with technologies for manufacturing pesticides. First, they would draw the raw materials from a tank and boil them down; once they were done processing the liquid, they would add other chemicals to the raw materials and process the whole concoction again. The ingredients would then be transported elsewhere for the next step of processing. The technological superiority of the onsite processing facilities proved itself in the shininess and complexity of the machinery's silver exterior. It was said the pesticides thus produced were crucial for the country to remain self-sufficient in terms of its food supply.

While everyone was busy not paying attention to the people at the top of the tower, the helicopter returned, with great vigor this time. There was a long cord dangling from it, and at the end of the cord, something resembling a giant claw. The workers were brought back down to the ground, cradled face down in the claw like dead bugs.

Around sunset, Rina went to Pii's workstation. It was empty, and Pii and his coworkers were nowhere to be found. Rina went to his supervisor and asked where Pii was.

"He took a train to work at another factory. He said he didn't want to see you anymore, that he wanted to go far away. You should've been good to him while he was around." The supervisor stuck his tongue out at her from inside the container. He was missing all of his front teeth, so it was impossible not to laugh. Even though she knew he was joking, Rina's heart fell, as if she'd just stepped off a cliff. Luckily, she was done with work for the day, so she could go looking for Pii.

The gas storage tank that spread out from east to west on a diagonal to the right side of the complex was much farther away than it looked. The street lamps, which were positioned several hundred meters apart due to power shortages, made tapping noises as they came on. To the right side of the path was an embankment, and below it flowed the black river. Beyond the walls of the embankment Rina could see the weird cross-pattern of the transmission towers, and beyond those, an endless row of barbed-wire fences, and the dark and distant city.

It got hotter as she approached the complex of tanks, and sweat beaded up on her forehead and under her arms. Even though her shoes kept slipping and she kept on losing her footing, she felt light, as if the white clouds floating in the sky would soon be within her reach.

When she reached the end of the embankment, there was a bridge, and then a gray asphalt road. The right side of the road was the border, so there were no people there, but near the barbed-wire fences, a few people were loading rebar into a truck. The back of the truck was up against the fence, so the rebar that slipped through fell right into the cargo bed. When Rina approached them, they started the truck and drove off in a rush. It was impossible for Rina not to feel some fondness for their efforts to smuggle something out of such a place. The truck drove past the barbed-wire fence and into the darkness, in the same direction as the white clouds. The rest of the men glanced back at Rina as they walked toward the nearest warehouse.

The raw materials were stored in six warehouses set out equidistantly in a line. Behind the tanks was a thickly wooded forest. There were danger zone signs with red lettering practically wallpapered all over the facilities. The tanks were placed in square frames that looked like coffins. The multitude of silver pipes connecting the tanks to each other were installed in such a complex, labyrinthine manner that just looking at them made you dizzy.

Men with helmets were standing on ladders that were propped up against the surface of the gigantic tanks. They were checking each one of the pipes entangled in its complex patterns underneath the tanks to look for potential gas leaks. Pii carried a welding rod and was cautiously examining a steel tube. He leaned over and approached the sparks until it looked like they were about to suck him in. When he was done, he would abruptly straighten himself up, walk over to another area, and bend over, becoming one with the fire again.

The Pii she saw now was no longer the boy Rina had called a dummy and dragged to every corner of the continent. He was now a strong man whose body could handle tough work. At that moment, Rina thought maybe she understood why her father, her mother, and most people in this world insisted on the necessity of having a son. It irked her intolerably.

It seemed impossible to break into the taut atmosphere around the storage tanks, so Rina left without talking to Pii. On her way back, she saw a flock of sparrows sitting on the long wire between the transmission towers. Rina made a gun with her fingers and *bang*, shot at them. The sparrows all flew off but they were so light that the wire didn't even sway.

The authorities of the complex offered overtime for people working during the holiday, but no one seemed to be willing to do it. The customers at The Puzzle got worked up just talking about their upcoming break.

At night, after work was over, Big Puzzle, Fatso, Misha, and Rina went out to the city.

"Today I have some important business to tend to, so we'll skip the pot," Big Puzzle told them sullenly.

"Hmph. Nothing to live for," Rina murmured as she followed the rest.

They entered the alleyway framed by the branches of weeping willows. As the narrow street ascended, it also grew more winding. Misha and Fatso seemed to know where they were going.

"Where the hell are we going?" Rina asked Misha, but Misha was too busy checking out the necklaces and earrings in the street stalls to answer. Big Puzzle stopped in front of a house with a small yard and a little wood chair set out in front. They climbed up a flight of steep and narrow stairs, where Big Puzzle and the owner of the house shared a cigarette in the doorway.

They went up to the second floor, walked to the last door on the left, and knocked. It cracked open. Inside the room were two beds, where six girls and three boys sat huddled together. They all looked down at the floor.

"I see you're from different countries," Fatso observed.

Big Puzzle perched on the bed, and the kids jumped up in surprise. They were from all over Southeast Asia, and looked like they'd been through a lot. They were wearing sweatpants and T-shirts, their faces were brown from the sun, and they all looked terribly nervous.

A moment later, the owner came in to give them some tea. Big Puzzle drank his while he whispered to Fatso. They herded the boys into a corner of the room and told them to turn around and look out the window. Then, Big Puzzle lined the girls up at his feet. Rina and Misha sat behind him, staring at the girls. One of them, in particular, caught Rina's eye; she was short and had a cheap haircut, so Rina was sure they were from the same country.

"Put up your hair, turn around, then turn back around toward me," Big Puzzle directed the girls. His instructions seemed odd to Rina. The orange light from the alley shined through the papered window.

"Well, you all have nice figures," Big Puzzle commented, and Rina found herself admiring the girls' bodies in spite of herself.

"Lift up your bra," Big Puzzle told them. Rina thought this was going too far and slapped him on the shoulder.

"Big, this is ridiculous! Why should they lift their bras? You're taking it too far." Big Puzzle and Fatso glared at Rina. The six girls stood there with their breasts out and their eyes shut tightly.

"Let's just pick two," Big said, as he put a cigarette in his mouth.

"Why do you need to look at their bodies when they're just going to be serving liquor! All they need are strong legs!" Fatso rapped her head with his knuckles.

Rina began to use every single word she had learned since arriving in this country on the train over the river and through the forest to praise the girls' beauty. Big Puzzle and Fatso tilted their heads dubiously, saying the girls weren't pretty, but Misha agreed with Rina that they had faces that the people of this country would find familiar and comforting. One of the girls was from a Buddhist country and her long hair was parted down the center and tied back in a ponytail. She had a black dot in the center of her forehead. As they were about to lead the girls out, one of the boys, a short one, turned around from his corner by the window.

"Hey, big man, can I bum a cigarette from you before you go?"

Big Puzzle glared at him, then handed him a cigarette and some cash. There was some tension over the price of the girls, but the bargaining, too, was over soon. The owner of the house asked for more money, arguing that two of the girls they were taking had eaten a lot of his food. Rina bit her lip, stunned by the fact that she, who had been reduced to human merchandise herself, was now on the side of the men paying for other human bodies.

The whole time they walked down the long alley, Rina was desperate to ask the one girl about her home country. She wanted to find out how the great rulers of the country fared, whether the school lunches at the girls' schools were any better, what hairstyles were fashionable. But she decided to wait until they had arrived at a place that was quieter and more intimate. When they got to the main thoroughfare, Big Puzzle bought some videotapes of movies from a street vendor. Then he gave Fatso some money and left with the plastic bag of tapes swinging in his hand. Fatso took the girls to a clothing store on the main street.

It was very bright in the store. Rina was embarrassed to see herself in the several full-length mirrors installed around the store. Her hair was disheveled and her entire body was covered in black dust. Fatso told the two newly purchased girls to pick out some clothes. The girl who was from the same country as Rina picked out a pink dress and a red sweater, then quietly stood in a corner. The girl who was from the poor, densely populated Buddhist nation blinked her large eyes as she caressed the men's clothes.

"She's married," the girl from Rina's country told her.

"Pick something for yourself, not your husband," Rina told her loudly. The girl blinked her large, brimming eyes, then slowly headed over to the women's section.

Misha, being into fashion trends, picked a short jean skirt and a sweater that showed off her shoulders, and Rina, oddly enough, picked a hat with white yarn bunched about it like white clouds, and a pair of thick pants stuffed with cotton. Misha went over to the Buddhist girl, who was having trouble choosing an outfit. She helped her pick out a knee-length black dress with a green floral pattern that spread out like a bunch of lizards. The girl finally mustered a smile. Misha tried on Rina's hat, and took it off to check the tag.

"It was made near where I was born. Not like I have a home anymore," she said. The hat was made in Eastern Europe.

They met up with Big Puzzle back at the restaurant. He and Fatso had beers, and everyone else stuffed themselves with rice, meatballs, and sautéed greens. After she'd been eating for a while, Rina noticed that the meat was very black and tough. She was about to declare how you just couldn't trust the food in this country, when she decided to bite her tongue. *I guess I'm too spoiled now,* Rina muttered to herself, and giggled.

Big Puzzle asked the two girls how they had ended up here. The girl with the dot on her forehead could hardly speak the language of this country, and it was just as hard for them to understand her as it was for her to speak. The girl from Rina's country spoke quite a bit, and explained to them slowly that she had fled the country through a route similar to the one Rina had taken. The one difference was that she had been captured in a farming town, and was forced to work in the fields every day until she escaped. Big Puzzle sang her praises, saying she was ready to be put to work with the others right away.

While Big Puzzle was making a call on his cell phone, Rina seized the moment to talk to the girl from her country.

"You know, I saved you. If I hadn't encouraged them to take you, who knows where you'd be? You might even be dead. You should be grateful to me for the rest of your life."

Rina waited for her young compatriot, sitting there modestly with her excellent posture, to thank her.

"They say people become corrupt once they've tasted money, and I guess you're living proof. Why the hell should I thank you? I should be someone who goes around buying people who were captured while trying to escape? You're completely crazy."

Rina dismissed the silly girl, and decided that she would neither talk to her, nor become friends with her.

On their way back to the industrial complex, the four girls sat jammed in the backseat, staring out the windows in silence. They could smell each other's bodies and hear the sound of their own breathing, like a sobbing that came from somewhere deep within. They may not have lived very long, but they were overcome with a sense of sadness at the fact that they were crammed into the narrow backseat of a car among strangers. You couldn't hear it, but they were all chanting in unison, *I am being sold, sold.* The memories of their short lives that surged up within them were hard to cope with, and while no one said anything, each felt as if her heart would burst.

Misha was the first to open her mouth. "Please let me out. I'm going to suffocate!"

The car ran a long while before stopping by the road near a lake. The round lake at the foot of the hills was frozen white. It was warmer outside than they had realized. The girls ran down to the ice and glided around on it, yelling, while the men went to relieve themselves in a corner. Rina stood still as she listened to the water course through the thick ice under her feet.

22

WITH THE HOLIDAYS UPON THEM, EVERYONE RUSHED TO THE TRAIN station to get out of the city. Long before the train was scheduled to arrive, people congregated at the station and milled around the narrow platform all day long, staring in the direction from which the train would come. The only ones who stayed behind were the supervisors in charge of the principal facilities and the workers who had no homes to go back to. The heat had been turned down in the housing complex, and it was quiet—no warmth, no sounds. Once in a while, a mouse would creep along the wall in the hallway, or a lone plastic bag would float through the air. What they got for the holidays from the authorities was a carton of cheap cookies, dry in the mouth and wrapped in packaging sticky to the touch. Just like any other day, they ate dumplings or rice and killed time.

Surprisingly enough, it was the old woman and the baby who were the healthiest, both psychologically and physically. The baby was just learning to walk. He toddled around the house holding onto bed and table legs in time to the old woman's chants of "one-two, one-two." It was so crowded and narrow that he would often fall over, and it was a chore to keep him away from the heater.

"Let's hope spring gets here soon, good for you, and good for me, right?" The old woman wanted to let the baby walk around outside as much as he wanted to. She even held the private desire to start performing again in the spring. She sustained her excitement, even though no one thought to agree with or encourage her flights of fancy. Their bodies were soaked with fatigue and the Arab was staying with them for the holidays, making their home exceptionally cramped and unpleasant. Rina was angry that the downtown area was shut down, making it impossible for her to work over the holidays.

Rina waited for Pii, whom she never had time to talk to or even see since he rarely came home. Pii would go to his friend's house in the building next door to play cards. When he came back, he would open his palm-sized notebook with its worn-down corners and draw in it like old times. In the notebook were drawings of the tent where the old woman used to sing, drawings of the large trees being swept away in the flood, drawings of castle gates engraved with special characters. There was the deadly train they had ridden for days on end, and the old woman's adorable old lover. Rina added a drawing to the notebook: the thousand-year-old terrace farms that had become a part of the nature and the red skies above them, all of which had looked like an ancient underground city filled with white light. Most of the drawings were of the industrial complex. The entrance of the industrial complex, which you could see from the station as soon as you got off the train, the dreary landscape of the showers with their worn roofs of galvanized iron. Laundry full of holes, like honeycomb, crowded onto the lines of the housing complex, the vast city swathed in a golden sunset that could be seen from the top of the gas separation towers. Rina searched Pii's drawings for the storage tank of raw materials, and added in the figure of Pii, with his big feet. Next to it, she wrote in *You are my friend* in her language. She wanted to write something much more elegant, but refrained. Whether or not Pii noticed Rina's additions, he said nothing after he'd seen the notebook.

By the fourth day of the holiday, Rina's cabin fever was so bad that she felt she had to leave the house. There was nothing special happening outside either, so she bought some liquor. She stood with the plastic bag, wondering what to do, when she remembered that one of her coworkers had asked her to check on his apartment occasionally while he was away.

The sheets and the curtains hadn't been washed and were dark with stains, the house hadn't been cleaned, and the floors were strewn with empty dishes with old grains of rice stuck to them. Laundry sat in the washbasin, frozen from the cold air. On the walls were faded posters of naked women laughing with their mouths wide open. Their breasts had been marked with X's. Rina couldn't figure out what exactly she was expected to check on. She wondered for a second if she should tidy up the place, but soon she crawled into the bed and lay there, sipping away at a bottle with just her face poking out from under the covers.

Before she even realized how much she'd had, Rina stood up and tripped over the empty bottles rolling around at her feet. She opened the door and stumbled out into the hallway. She staggered around, unable to find her way back to her apartment.

When she finally did get home, it was to find a stranger there. It was an old man she'd never seen, toothless and mostly bald. He was surrounded by the Arab, who wore a grim expression on his face, the old woman, and the sewing factory girl, who was looking down at the baby in the basket. The old man's succinct and clear speech belied his appearance.

"This child and many others from this area are born with defects. As you can see, ever since my accident seven years ago, I cough up blood as regularly as if it were phlegm. Just look at the shut-down area in the west. Hundreds have died and even more will grow up with major health problems. I'm old and weak, but I want to shred those foreigners who have wasted this complex to bits. But that is a task for the young. I hate to say this, but I won't live much longer, and I don't want to cling to the past. I lose my breath just thinking about my death, which is soon to come, and the future that will come after that death." The old man looked about their house.

"What the hell? Who is this old fossil?" Rina demanded as she strode in, her eyes flashing. "What the hell are you yapping on about, you stick in the mud, huh? You threatening this kid who isn't even two years old? Are you a doctor? Are you a doctor, huh?"

The sewing factory girl wept and the Arab prayed to his great god. As he left, the old man turned back toward them.

"It's flowing inside your bodies, too. The gas that swallowed up this entire area seven years ago . . ."

The old woman put some cash in the old man's pocket as he left.

Rina flew at the sewing factory girl's throat and knocked her down. In a second, they were rolling around on the floor, tearing at each other's clothes. The Arab was stunned into silence and the old woman closed her eyes, shaking.

"You crazy bitch, why the *hell* would you have a baby."

"Oh, like you helped me have it, you crazy bitch."

As the two women rolled around the floor, the old woman stood up, still shaking.

"Who gave her liquor? I told you, don't *ever* let her drink!"

This infuriated Rina even further, and she turned on the old woman.

"You got a problem with that? I got the liquor myself, you old hag. Why do you keep on following me wherever I go? Why don't you just die?" She grabbed at the old woman, who had been perched on the bed, and pushed her to the floor singlehandedly. The old woman fell to the floor with a thump. Rina writhed on the floor and wailed, but no one came to comfort her. Eventually, she tired herself out.

"She has a personality disorder, is an alcoholic, suffers from a deprivation of affection, and is homesick on top of all that . . ." the others whispered as Rina cried. When she heard that, Rina began to wail loudly and stamp her feet again.

"I hate the holidays, I *hate* them! They're too long and I can't even go out and earn money."

That's when Pii came home. He looked at everyone and immediately figured out what was going on.

"That bitch is crazy," the sewing factory girl informed him. Pii picked Rina up in one fell swoop and held her up in the air horizontally by her shoulders and butt.

"You idiot, let me down, let me down!" Pii spun Rina around 360 degrees continually, and took her out to the hallway. Rina fell into a deep and sudden sleep.

"That dissipated bitch. Slippery as an eel," the old woman muttered, rubbing her hipbone.

As the sun was setting, Rina heard Pii singing as he dragged his old slippers slowly up and down the hall. She heard him knock on a door and ask, "Is my old lady here?" Rina giggled. Pii continued to joke around. Rina stuck her face out into the hall and beckoned him in. Pii stood there, staring at her, so Rina went out into the hallway in her bare feet and dragged him in by the wrist.

"Let's run away. I have lots of money. The old woman's too old, and the girl and her baby are such a hassle. Let's run away, just the two of us." Rina's eyes became wet with her desperate yearning. She truly wanted to run away with Pii. Yet she wasn't sure, even in that moment, if she really wanted to escape, or whether she was lying to motivate Pii.

Pii continued to sing his song as he smoked a cigarette in the hall. In a mirror that hung next to the bed, Rina could see the small of his back as he smoked, and her own face watching him. This image, she felt, was the perfect reflection of her relationship with Pii, always out of sync. Rina honed in on her emotions like a real actress.

"Please, run away with me. You're my husband."

Moved by her own words, Rina wept. Pii lay indifferently on the bed with his eyes closed, humming his strange song.

At sunset, the darkness veiled the city in layers. Through the latticed windows, Rina could see the storage tanks that stood in a row from east to west, and the black clouds that flocked in the sky. Rina felt that the complex looked beautiful for the first time since she had arrived there. The pure white smoke coming from the smokestacks in a thin line, spreading out like ice cream, then shooting up into the sky; the cold and shining steel; even the chemical odor that always made her gag, she felt a fondness for all of these things. *I'll buy a camera and capture every single sunset in the world. I'll put them in my drawer and take them out to look at them when I'm bored. I can sell them one by one when I need money,* Rina vowed to herself. Pii was sleeping with his face toward the mirror. Rina began to feel pathetic that she had nothing but these depressing landscapes to look at, and burrowed deeper into the mattress.

She was lying with her eyes closed when a familiar voice reached her ears. Ever since she had escaped, Rina had always found herself hoping that what was happening before her eyes wasn't real. But not now. She doubted her ears, but the word "pretty" rang throughout the silent air.

Pii had pushed Rina's shirt up above her breasts and had his lips on her stomach. He was moving slowly down below her stomach. Rina's eyes flew open. In her groggy state, she struggled to find the lipstick in her pocket and apply it to her lips.

"You bastard. I'm going to call the police," she tried to muster in the firmest tone she could. She could see his muscular brown shoulders and his pelvic bones through his frayed and saggy underwear. Her whole body went limp. Pii propped up Rina's waist with his left hand and wrapped his right arm around her shoulder, and nearly fell off the bed. They giggled like a couple that has been married a long time. When she felt Pii touch her deep inside, Rina's mouth went dry. It was different from how he had touched her before. She took one of Pii's hands and brought it up to her eyes. She pressed his hardened knuckles. His fingers, his fingernails, and the thickness of his hands could all only be described as rough. The black grime caught in between his fingers, the leaden stripes crossing his nails. Rina put Pii's finger, with its metallic taste, in her mouth.

For several hours to come, Rina saw Pii's body from all the different angles in the dark. And she wept. Then, embarrassed by her tears, she started to ramble.

"You've slept with other women, haven't you? You're weird. Tell me the truth!" Pii gently slapped Rina's lips as she babbled away. They fell asleep in the empty building, listening to the sound of coughs that seemed like they would never stop. The coughing became worse as the night deepened, but the two slept a deep and sweet sleep. And that's how Rina woke up to the New Year.

The next morning, Rina was too embarrassed to look Pii in the face and wish him a happy new year. Yet she didn't feel afraid, and she didn't feel cold. She felt as if a motor engine had been turned on inside her belly; she felt more alive than ever, she could lift things that she had struggled with before, and she couldn't stop smiling like a fool.

After the long holiday, the industrial complex was a whirlwind of activity. The people paused their work to look up at the sky. They couldn't help feeling that something was terribly different now. Rina, too, couldn't help but notice something was missing—the sound of the sirens. It was silent now.

Finally, the day of the completion of the third phase came. Lively music boomed out of the speakers from early in the morning, and helmeted supervisors strutted up and down the complex. They said that if they were able to light the waste gas from the storage tank on fire, the plant building process would be considered a huge success.

Finally, night came. They all lined up in front of the offices at the center of the industrial complex. There were so many people that Rina was surprised anew at how big everything was. They all stood staring at the flare stack that would ignite with the gas from the storage tank. The flare stack was about a kilometer away from the tank, on a hill to the north. They all waited with bated breath. The fire had to light in order to move on to the fourth phase of the project. The helmeted supervisors standing in front of the crowd looked especially pale. The foreign supervisors talked into their walkie-talkies and prepared to light the sparks.

They all began to count down in unison from ten. They reached zero. But no light came on on top of the hill. The atmosphere in the offices suddenly became one of mourning. Some of the middle-aged supervisors collapsed, weeping. Dozens of technicians were sent to investigate every inch of the complex tank system, and they were soon swarming the tank and gas piping like thousands of ants. Someone tightened a loose valve and sent a signal, which everyone saw in the bright nighttime lighting. The countdown started again. Once they reached zero, there was a silence again. This time, for real, red and blue sparks blossomed at the highest point of the industrial complex. The supervisors yelled out that it was a huge success, and embraced each other as they wept tears of joy.

As soon as work was over, everyone headed downtown. The Puzzle was packed that night. The people could not stop talking about the flame.

Rina and Misha were now the top waitresses, so they stayed upstairs to tend to the card players. The rude young girl from Rina's country and the girl with the black dot on her forehead ran the first floor. The men, who hadn't been able to come to The Puzzle for a while because of having to work overtime, were so intrigued by the new faces that it became a nuisance.

The night deepened. When the first floor was almost emptied out, Big Puzzle and Fatso came by. Wherever they were coming from, they'd already had a drink or two, judging from their ruddy cheeks. Rina and Misha went out with some drinks and joined them at a table. A man with sunken eyes came down from the second floor and greeted them. He offered to tell their fortunes in exchange for money. Big Puzzle gave the man a bill, and the man began to flip his cards showily. Bored, they watched him. Fatso's fate was apparently incomprehensible, and Misha's was the most preposterous.

"You'll die this year," the man told her. Misha and everyone laughed out loud at the absurdity of this. He told Fatso that he would be having a visitor from faraway, and that it was someone he would have to confront at some point. He told Big Puzzle that his business would continue to flourish this year, that he would marry a good woman, and that life would be paradise. Big Puzzle shook his head questioningly at that, but he gladly forked over an extra bill. Now that he had money, the man eagerly ran upstairs to play more cards. After a moment of silence, all four of them suddenly yelled out, "What a fraud! We've been duped! That bastard!"

As she was tidying up the second floor, Rina noticed the younger girl from her country she'd been ignoring. She was perched on a windowsill, crying.

"Why are you crying? Is it cramps? By the way, that's *my* spot," Rina said as kindly as she could, but the girl didn't answer. A few minutes later, Big Puzzle walked by them up to the next floor, and the girl followed him, her head bowed.

On the third floor was a room with red carpeting and a red sofa. Rina was about to open the door without giving it much thought when something made her hesitate. With her hand on the doorknob, she listened to what was happening inside. The young girl was whimpering.

"I'm in pain. It's ignorant and backward to think that you can do whatever you want with me just because I'm an escapee. No matter what you do, I'll never like you." Rina had to admit, she had a way with words; she was as good as a lawyer. Rina stood with her fists clenched, biting on her lower lip, trying to figure out how to break up this situation. The argument continued, and after standing outside for a long while, Rina went down to the second floor.

Moments later, Big Puzzle came down with an irritated look on his face, and went down to the first floor. The young girl followed him, staring at the floor. Rina grabbed her hand.

"What did you do?" she demanded, and the girl abruptly blew her nose.

"What, are you going to act like you don't know? I nearly died up there, and came back to life!" the girl screamed. "You're going to pretend that you don't know what that asshole tried to do to me? He must have done the same to you!" Rina was flustered by the girl's sudden rage.

"So, did you like it?" Not knowing how else to respond, Rina fueled the fire.

"I told you, we didn't do it. If he tries, I'll kill him." The girl had plenty of backbone despite her situation.

"Whatever, stop crying. He's a better guy than you might think. You should try and seduce him. It would be nice to be married to him." Rina pitied the girl's dowdy red skirt and pink sweater. The girl sniffed again.

"Seduce, my ass. It wasn't just me. It happened to Dottie, too." Rina sighed, and held the girl's hand tightly.

On the first floor, Big Puzzle, Fatso, Misha, and Dottie were drinking silently. When Rina went down to get some more alcohol for the upper floors, she glared at them as she walked by. She rinsed out a plastic cup and poured some beer for the young girl. When she got upstairs, the girl was no longer crying.

"How is it over there?" Rina started to ask, but the girl cut her off.

"What do you mean *how*, I told you, we didn't do it."

Rina snickered. "No, not that. I meant the place we both escaped from. Is everyone still starving there?" Finally, Rina had got around to asking about her country. She waited for the girl to say, *Yes, it's still full of starving people. Many people are desperately trying to escape. We're lucky!*

"The kids I escaped with who got into the country of P are in college now. Shit, what the hell am I doing!" The girl blew her nose violently. The country of P! By now, it sounded like a place from a fairy tale. Rina patted the girl's shoulders.

Rina watched the white tail end of the car as it disappeared into the dark. The two new girls, Misha, Big Puzzle, and Fatso were headed into the city without her. Her young compatriot turned around to look at her, but Rina waved at her to have a good time, and went back into the club alone. The door creaked ominously.

"I guess there's nothing like the disadvantage of being a married woman," she murmured to herself. The sound of drumming rang in her ears as it had once, a long time ago. She went to the box where Misha kept her clothes, and took out a dress covered in spangles and ribbons that still smelled like Misha's sweat. She changed into it and went out onto the stage and danced awkwardly by herself.

It was a long while before she realized that the pitter-pattering was the sound of raindrops hitting the windows. Pitter-patter. The sound of the streaks of rain avoiding the wind. Rina was drinking by herself when she heard a car squeal to a halt outside and Big Puzzle opened the door roughly. He had Rina's young compatriot by the throat, and he flung her onto the floor. Misha gazed out the window with a chilly look of indifference on her face, and Dottie was trembling.

"Bring me some liquor!" Big Puzzle yelled. They all looked wretched, their faces drenched in rain. While Big Puzzle drank, Fatso nudged the girl's buttocks with his foot.

"Who the fuck told you you were allowed to fight back? You're nothing but an escapee." The girl glared up at him from the floor, huffing with anger.

"Escapees have rights too." Rina prayed the girl would never lose her spirit.

"Follow me," Big Puzzle took the young girl up to the third floor. The sound of his heavy tramping mingled with the pitter-patter of the rain was terrifying. Dottie was crouched near the doorway weeping, and Rina was sitting in a chair, working her brain as she'd never done before. She went upstairs without even realizing that she held a liquor bottle in one hand.

Through the cracked open door, she could see the girl lying on the sofa. Her eyes were shut and her lips were quivering, and between her legs Rina could see her labia like raw, pink fish flesh. Just as Fatso was about to climb on top of the girl, Rina realized this was a reality she had to confront. The sofa sagged as if it were about to rip. *Now's the time. I have to save her before he puts it in her. That is what I must do.* Rina looked at the rain outside the window and rushed into the room and smashed the bottle on Big Puzzle's head, who had just let out a big fart. Frightened by herself, she let out a shriek before he had time to react or turn around. Fatso floundered and tripped over a table in front of the sofa, falling backward. The girl, who had jumped up, smashed a decorative pot over Fatso's head. *I'm dead.* Rina stood still, smelling the alcohol in the room, waiting for what was to come to her. Surprisingly, neither of the men got up. "Crap. I wasn't planning on murdering again." Rina put her hand on her hip and tried to catch her breath.

They dragged Big Puzzle downstairs, the young girl holding him by the legs, and Rina holding his shoulders. Every time his head hit a stair, it stained the floor with blood. When they got to the first floor, Misha and Dottie screamed. Big Puzzle seemed to have lost consciousness. Rina calmly walked over to the door and locked it. Misha approached Rina.

"Did you kill him? Why are you wearing my clothes?" Rina looked down and saw that the red blood on Misha's black dress had created a mysterious new hue.

"I'll take off your clothes," Rina said, "And this happened because—" She was interrupted by Misha, who began screaming and dancing.

"*Nam evo zagrobit*?" she asked, in a language no one understood, then suddenly bent over at the waist and fainted, the way princesses are bound to do. Dottie had whacked her on the back of the head with a long iron bar. She'd learned one thing at least since she'd been in this country, and that was how to say "bitch," which she repeated over and over again in a low voice.

"Are you insane?" Rina demanded. "What did she just say?" No one knew.

They simply couldn't drag Fatso down on their own, so they took a laundry line, tied one end to a built-in closet on the first floor, the other around Fatso, and dragged him down by pulling on the line. Even as they were sweating, they couldn't help giggling when they looked at each other. It was still drizzling gently outside. The three girls looked at each other and came to a silent agreement.

The young girl took the car keys out of Big Puzzle's pocket, and Rina took his wallet. They opened the front door of the car and shoved him in the backseat. His legs stuck out of the door, so they had to bend them. They put Misha in the trunk. She was slender, and fit perfectly, but it pained Rina to see her cold and beautiful face rub against the floor of the trunk. Fatso was still breathing heavily. When they put him into the car as well, the tires sank and the car looked like it was about to collapse. Rina told Dottie to get a shovel from the back of the store. Once they were ready, Rina started the car. Although she'd never driven before, she felt comfortable in the driver's seat. When they started to move, however, she nearly ran into the building next door.

The car crawled slowly toward the industrial complex to the east. The pitter-pattering had by now turned into a light sprinkling. Rina parked the car near the embankment that she'd seen on her way to the gas tank complex. It was so late that even the streetlamps were out. Rina ordered the girls to start digging in one of the lots below the embankment road. She kept the headlights and ignition on.

The girls shook as they dug. To bury all three bodies, they had to dig wide and deep. They got excited when they hit some earth that was soft from the rain. The sky slowly grew brighter and the rain sprinkled on. They found plastic bags and other sorts of trash during their excavation. Dottie took off her long dress, saying it was a nuisance, and dug in her underpants. Even though she was so out of breath that the air around her head was surrounded by little clouds, Rina's young compatriot smiled at Dottie.

From the embankment, the hole looked fairly wide and deep. Rina and her young compatriot got Fatso out of the car first. They counted one, two, three in unison and shoved him off the top of the embankment. His weight rolled nicely down the slope and landed perfectly in the hole. Next, it was Big Puzzle's turn. When Rina put her hand on his waist, he frowned and shook his head violently, as if he was coming to. Dottie, who had been waiting in front of the hole, smacked him with the handle of her shovel, and he fell silent. Misha was last. Rina held her in her arms.

"We didn't actually have to kill her. Princess Misha from the country of ice. Farewell." When Misha rolled down into the hole, the hem of her white coat flopped over the two men's faces. Big Puzzle was still moaning faintly.

Rina and the young girl turned the headlights off and walked down to the hole. With two shovels and a pair of hands, they began to fill the hole back up with dirt. They made strange noises as they worked, as if they were beasts. Rina saw Misha's pale, thin fingers white in the dawn light.

When they got back to the club, they mopped the entire place from top to bottom. There were more bloodstains than they had expected. The blood had frozen in the cold weather, so they had to attack it with rags soaked in hot water. The floor of the main hall had been soaked in blood, and would not wash easily, so they flooded the place with water as the morning sun spread itself on the wet floor. Even when they were done, something felt amiss.

They poured some coarse salt in a bowl and sprinkled it out by the entrance to chase away evil spirits.

From the next day on, the three girls, now the new owners of the club, decided to change up the dreary atmosphere. The floor was already clean from the night of the murder, so they started with the cobwebs in the corners and ceilings. They took some brightly colored cloth and hung it up in color-coordinated swathes. Together, the strips of cloth formed a rainbow. Whenever the door opened, they fluttered in the wind, and when it was overcast, they gave off a smell of dye. Every time she looked at the bright cloths, Rina felt like she could forget that she was a murderer. It made her feel like she had softened a bit, and that her wounds were healing. *All I need to do now is make some money. I need to make some money and get the hell out of here, then I can forget everything.* Rina waited for night to come.

Misha had performed a flashy, acrobatically challenging dance that no one could emulate. The plump girl with the dot on her forehead did a belly dance where she would just twist her hips ever so gently, and this was much more appealing. As the work at the factories got harder, more people came to drink. And with more people working overtime, the place stayed busy all throughout the night. No one asked where the two big, sullen men were. Rina handed out marijuana to the people she knew well; that's what the third floor of The Puzzle was for. Rina recalled the words of an ancient auntie who had died in a famine back at home: "Even the biggest idiot will face three challenges in her lifetime for which she will stake her life." Rina felt certain that her time had come.

One day, Rina took the girls out in Big Puzzle's car for a drive to the city. It was too hard to drive all the way out there herself, so she hired a young boy who was a good driver. She rifled through her memory to find the house with the pot. When she got there, she knocked and knocked, but they didn't open the door for her. So she waited outside all day. She told the old man it was an errand for Big Puzzle, but he refused to sell her any.

"I can't sell this to the people who work so hard at the factory!" he insisted. Rina didn't approve of the old man's stubbornness. She returned again the next day but he still would not sell.

She had to go to a foreign dealer and pay twice as much. On their way back, the girls stopped by the club that Rina had once visited with Big Puzzle. All three of the girls in the group had dressed in jean jackets and skirts and tank tops, just like Misha. The girls would dance awkwardly around, then suddenly yell in unison: "We all pretend to be Misha!" They bounced around like cheerleaders, they screamed at the top of their lungs, and they wept. They baffled the other customers, who eventually sat down to watch their antics. Someone approached Dottie and told her her dancing was very moving. They asked the girls if they were part of the Third-World Performing Troupe of Tears. That night, the three girls screamed and sobbed at the club as if they'd made a bet about who could be louder.

"Granny, it's spring now, wouldn't you like to come perform at our club?"

The old woman was happy as a child at this proposal. As she ran around the apartment adorning herself, Rina dressed the baby and they all drove off to the club.

"This is really the perfect place for my performance!" The idea of performing seemed to bring color back into the old woman's cheeks. It was true that the club had been geared toward a younger crowd, and that the older folk had had nowhere to go for a long time. Rina wanted to use the old woman to attract an older clientele. Rina put the baby down on the floor of the club, and he spun around and around until he collapsed. At night, the club thronged with people. Rina was now literally sitting on a pile of money; since she trusted no one, the only way she felt at ease was to sit awkwardly on top of her red money box, slightly hunched over.

Young local girls began showing up at The Puzzle asking for work. They told Rina that they wanted to make enough money to get out of this industrial complex that belched out white smoke. They wanted to move to the city. They were all pretty, lithe, and leggy. They all called her ma'am. This annoyed Rina, since she wasn't much older than they were. But when she saw her reflection in the mirror, she could see why. *I can't believe how pretty those girls are, and how their dreams amount to nothing more than working at a bar like this.* At first, the thought depressed Rina so much that she turned them all away, but she eventually gave them all jobs, regardless of where they were from or how old they were. The Puzzle was now a utopia for working women. It began to attract people from outside the industrial complex, as well.

The Puzzle had two performances every day. The old woman revived her tent act in a show for the older customers, who went to bed early. She wasn't able to dress up like before, but this made her more endearing, more at ease. When she sang songs of her youth, the old men at the bar, with bent backs and voices as husky as rusted iron, thumped happily on the tables.

The old woman's biggest helper throughout her performance was the baby. Every time the old woman's voice warbled up and down, the baby would totter around the stage in time with the beat, lifting his legs up and down, peering into people's faces and winking. When the performance was over, the old men would spout a few aphorisms before leaving.

The problem was getting the old woman, completely drained from the performance, back home. The only time Pii came to the club was to take the old woman and the baby home. He said hello to the people in the bar, but never glanced over at Rina.

Dottie wore a dress made of thin white lace for her dance. Before every performance, she turned to the wall with her hands clasped and her eyes closed, and muttered a long prayer. The club went wild when the Indian girl came out in her pretty lace dress and danced to the brisk music. The rainbow cloths fluttered along with the girl's movements, and the customers spun around with her.

One day, amid the din, the front door suddenly opened, and Rina nearly dropped the bottle of alcohol she was holding at what she saw: Big Puzzle and Fatso stood in the doorway. All the strength seeped out of Rina's spine at the thought that Misha was the only victim of all their trouble that night. She was glad the other girls hadn't seen the two men yet. The men marched across the main hall straight toward Rina. Rina realized that this was the greatest crisis since her escape. She gave them a little smile, expecting a fist to come flying at her. Big Puzzle opened his mouth.

"We're looking for our brothers."

Rina's sphincter loosened and she let out a deep sigh in spite of herself. One of them was Big Puzzle's older brother and the other was Fatso's younger brother. Rina contracted her abdomen.

"I can't say, they haven't been around in a long time. They must be somewhere playing cards or doing drugs. With that girl from Russia, what's her name, oh, Misha. They left with Misha." The two men looked at each other in confusion. Dottie came downstairs and was so startled that her hair, which had been pulled back in a bun, came undone. She ran into the bathroom.

Rina brought out beers and snacks for the two men and turned on the music as if everything was fine. The men drank their beers, sitting in the same places as the two dead men once had. *Hey, why don't we take charge of this place? But we don't have a Russian girl! I bet we could find one.* After a lengthy business discussion, they approached Rina and proposed to split the profits The Puzzle equally. She couldn't refuse them. As soon as they left, Rina went out and sprinkled the entrance with coarse salt.

The official moneymaking had begun. There were so many customers that there wasn't enough room for everyone. Men waited in line outside, blowing on their chilled hands while they waited for a spot to open up. Rina had the idea to draw a plastic canopy out by the entrance. They put a heater inside the canopy and sold drinks there, too. They even spiked the drinks with a secret ingredient so that the weak workers got drunk faster, and went home earlier. Rina talked with the old woman about quitting her work at the factory altogether. Rina had no qualms about acting as if she'd always owned the club. She had no problem with Puzzle and Fatso's brothers and their strange-looking white-skinned female companions coming to sit and drink at the bar. Their presence made it easier to forget the crime, and it put Rina and the girls at ease.

Spring came even to the industrial complex, which had seemed like it might stay frozen forever. If you lifted your eyes to look into the distance once in a while, there seemed to be a bright yellow energy piercing through the gray of the industrial complex. The ground was as squelchy as always, but there was something warm in the air. Still, it was far from perfect. Dust flew in from the west, and the baby's diapers and poop were always gray.

From time to time, Rina would walk to the place where they had buried Misha, Big Puzzle, and Fatso. The road along the embankment was still mostly deserted except for the occasional smugglers. Rina stood at the top of the embankment and looked for the spot where they'd dug the hole. She went down to it and stomped or peed on it. If she had one wish, it was to ask the gambler who had prophesied Misha death's what her own fate was.

23

Pii and the other welding technicians were called in to headquarters by the supervisors. The technicians, the supervisors, and all of the equipment, were loaded onto a truck that ran at a moderate pace. The workers sat with their hands over their ears. Someone began to sing.

"Be quiet. We're driving," someone yelled, but the singing didn't stop.

The truck drove down the road to the right of the industrial complex and through the gates. Just as they were slowly turning the corner to drive by the housing complex, they passed the baby and the old woman playing on a bench out front. The old woman squinted in the sun. The baby was sliding off the bench, and he was babbling to himself. Even though he saw them every day, Pii got so excited that he yelled out, but the truck sped up, and the old woman and the baby didn't hear him.

The special equipment awaited the workers. The supervisors reminded them of the gas leak that had occurred seven years ago in the west, and asked them to be extra careful. That's when Pii learned something shocking: the sirens hadn't been going off lately because the management had cut the sound system altogether. They argued that since they hadn't been able to find a good reason for the alarms going off in the past, it was necessary to turn the sirens off to avoid negative publicity. The supervisors had made a risky decision for fear of disrupting the completion of the third phase of the plant construction.

"Come on, nothing's happened yet, has it?" the supervisors said, perhaps buying their own logic.

The flare stack towering in the north, with its complicated network of crisscrossing pipes, spewed out flames as usual. It was true, as the supervisors had said, that as long as the flare stack steadily emitted its flames, nothing would go wrong. The problematic giant chemical storage tanks stood silently in a row, as if they were dead. Tank #6, the patchy one that everyone was always talking about, was third from the right.

The workers dispersed and gathered around the tanks. The large ladder they had brought with them on the truck was placed on top of the tank, which was about thirty meters high. The welders who had to climb on this ladder were afraid, but pretended to be calm.

"Well, we made it, so I guess we should fix it."

"Isn't it amazing what man can do?"

They all tried to say something brave and casual. Pii looked down at the vast industrial complex. It made him dizzy and he had to look away. For the first time, the workers came together to cheer themselves on.

"OK guys, let's figure this out. In the name of the unlimited development of the national chemical plant business."

They never found any problem. Neither did those who were in charge of examining the tank bodies. Which meant that the waste gas must be flowing back into the tank without being properly ejected. It was most likely a problem of the connections between piping or a problem with the facility itself. But it wasn't easy to figure out what was going on in such a tight, sealed-off space. At least, if there was an explosion due to some sort of chemical reaction inside the tank, they would be able to see what was going on.

All they could hear was the *piiing* of the sensors. They didn't really have the time to sit back and sentimentalize, but they were so tired that they took their safety helmets off and went over to a corner for a cigarette break. It soon became dusk. Dividing the complex along a diagonal line, the right side of the complex still had a bit of sunshine left in it, while to the left, the sun was setting. White smoke was spurting out of the smokestacks, and above them, the sky was just turning gold. Suddenly, the gold sky ripped itself open horizontally, surged up above the smokestacks, and sucked the opaque white smoke curls into its belly. Then it shut its mouth again.

It was now time for the last inspection. In separate teams, they went down under a pipe that looked like a water tank. One team checked for proper valve connection while the other used sensors to check for traces of gas. They welded certain sections over again, but from where they were, it was impossible to see what was happening on the inside. The sun set, and the workers scattered despondently and returned to the truck like defeated troops.

On their way back home, they took the road that passed by the western ruins. Pii looked out at the industrial complex, sunk deep into the dark. The west had long since been destroyed in the gas leak, but there were still campfires scattered throughout the terrain. Pii could hear people singing, and smell meat cooking. It seemed like a dream that people would still live in such a place.

The truck stopped downtown. The supervisors took them all to The Puzzle and treated them to several rounds. The liquor tasted strangely bland, so Pii marched into the kitchen, where he found Rina watering down the barrels of liquor. From time to time, she would stick her finger in the barrel and taste the alcohol, smacking her lips as she often did. When she saw Pii, Rina hid the water jug behind her back. It occurred to Pii that while Rina might be a bitch, she was very pretty. He wanted to say something nice to her, but couldn't think of anything. For the first time, he hated the fact that he wasn't good with words.

KANG YOUNG-SOOK

"You'll definitely never go hungry, no matter where you end up," was what he came up with. Rina stuck her tongue out at him and went back to pouring water into the barrels.

Rina came home late that night, opened a pot on the kitchen counter, and ate some of the dumplings out of it. She was always so hungry these days that her stomach felt like it was burning. If it had been winter, she would have walked down to the baths with layers of clothing to keep herself warm, but now, the energy in the halls was hot and cramped, and made her feel like she was suffocating. Wearing nothing but a thin sweater, Rina shuffled down the hall in her slippers. As she brushed her teeth and washed her face, her eyes stung so badly that she had to rinse them several times.

Back in the apartment, Rina was humming as she applied lotion to her face, when she suddenly noticed how plump her face had become.

"I really have to quit drinking so much. My face looks as round as a tea tray," she mused. She jumped up and took out her container of money, which she had stashed in a bundle of the clothing she'd used to wear when she sang. The red nickel box was as big as a wide drawer. Rina counted the bills one by one. Then she wrapped the bundles of money back up in the paper, held them close her chest for a second, and put them all neatly back in the box. She wrapped the box up several times in red silk. She prayed for the money to keep flowing in. If that happened, she would be fine buying a three-story house and living with everyone who was with her now. She smiled at the thought.

The sewing factory girl coughed violently, but Rina paid no attention. Whenever she was done counting her money, a wave of melancholy would wash over Rina, and she would find herself thinking about her family. She thought of her father, her mother, and her younger brother sitting in the churchyard filled with gently swaying tree blossoms, and it made her sad. But she shook it off quickly. *I have this money*, Rina she snickered to herself, and rubbed her eyes again.

The baby began to cough, and Pii joined in. Rina looked back at them. She walked to the window and opened the curtain. The entire industrial complex was covered in a thick white fog, and she couldn't see anything through it. Her eyes began to feel like they were about to fall out of their sockets. They weren't the only ones—the entire building was suddenly filled with the sound of coughs. By now Pii and the sewing factory girl had woken up and were looking around wildly.

Pii wrapped his face in a towel and tried to go outside, but as soon as he opened the door, white smoke came rushing in. He slammed the door back shut, put on his welder's mask and ventured out again, instinctively lowering his body. The hallway was so full of smoke that he could barely keep his eyes open. It was then that the sound of sirens came through on the speakers.

"It's been a real long time since I heard you!" Pii glared at the hallway speakers. They soon fell silent. It was impossible to figure out where the white smoke was coming from. The speakers let out a series of strident screeches, and then came the voices of the flustered supervisors.

"Look at the computer. Isn't the dashboard coming on? Where is it, where is it?" Then, a hasty click, and the speakers were silent, forever.

Pii went back inside the apartment. The sight of the terrified women forced him to stay calm.

"I think there's been an accident. Stay together, and don't leave the house under any circumstances." Rina and the sewing factory girl glanced at each other with frightened looks. Rina spread out a sheet over one of the beds, and they all crawled under it. Both of the women were shaking.

The halls of the apartment building were littered with people rushing about or passed out on the floor. From close up, Pii could see that their faces were the color of lead and that they were vomiting and having trouble breathing. A man in his underwear suddenly grabbed hold of Pii's pants and started yelling that he felt like he was going to die. He refused to let go. But soon enough, a trickle of saliva flowed out of his mouth and down his contorted chin, and he did let go.

Pii barely made it outside. The fog made it impossible for him to figure out what where he should go. A pale green smog had blanketed the entire world. The smell of burning cloth stabbed his nostrils. If he covered his nose with his hands, his eyes stung, and if he covered his eyes, he couldn't breathe. Everything around him was shattering, breaking, crying. He lowered his body and covered his eyes and nose.

Somehow, he managed to crawl to the containers. He felt like he was on the verge of asphyxiating. The supervisors were running around with gas masks on. Pii hurled a blow at one of the pairs of legs he saw rushing about near him and took the man's gas mask as he lay collapsed on the ground. He found the door to the main office that housed the super computer. The office was also inundated with smoke, and he couldn't see the dashboard, the computer, or the supervisors.

After a few minutes, powerful vibrations from somewhere up north began to reach Pii belatedly. Then, he heard an explosion, and mammoth sparks pierced through the fog. Like a volcano erupting in a mountain of white ice, the sparks flew up into the sky and fell back down. The explosions continued. Pii watched, tears flowing inside his gas mask. It was the storage tank to the east. It was tank #6.

Back inside their apartment, Rina, too, felt the vibrations like an earthquake. They made the entire building tremble. After several booms, the windows began to shatter on their own. Rina noticed the old woman's shriveled belly puff up like a balloon. The old woman was so weak that she could barely breathe; and she lay limply like a frog, her eyes wide open. If she was going to die, it would probably be today. Rina gripped her hand. The baby's face was blue as lump of lead. Rina and the sewing factory girl began to sob uncontrollably.

The blasts and explosions came consistently now, loud and small. When they stopped crying for a moment, it was to stare into each other's red eyes.

"If I'd known this was going to happen, I would have shown the Arab his baby one more time," the girl sobbed, putting her cheek on her baby's. Rina stroked her face.

Soon, they heard violent sirens, not just from the industrial complex, but from all over the city, approaching the site. The sounds enveloped the complex, closed in on it. By now, they were all close to passing out from the smell of burnt cloth. The old woman's stomach had flattened out again. Rina cried and pinched the old woman, but she didn't open her eyes.

Then, there was a series of blasts louder than any so far. They curled up under the bed until the blasts had stopped. Then, the building began to crumble. Cement dust splattered down from the ceilings and the floors began to sway from side to side, as if they were made of putty. Rina wriggled out past their thin sheet tent, recovered her money box wrapped in red cloth, and crawled back to the fort. At that moment, something above her head let out a terrific crack. She threw herself on top of the old woman, over the sewing factory girl, and the baby. She told herself everything would be all right as long as she didn't lose the red money box.

24

ONCE IN A WHILE, A HOLE WOULD OPEN UP IN THE ASH-COLORED veil that filled the sky and a ray of sun would pierce through, like the edge of a razor. At other times, each day felt like it was the last of this world. The thick lead-colored air seemed to lock the sky in. The damage caused by the explosions was incalculable. Orange flames blazed up from the quagmire that once been an industrial complex, and only giant clumps of cement covered in blankets of ashy dust like bodies in bags, seemed to squirm once in a while like sea sponges.

It took a while for things to settle. For a few days after the accident, it was just heat, everywhere. For several hours after the first explosion, the atmosphere was filled with a suffocating red force in which it was impossible to distinguish how many had died or had survived, or even whether it was night or day. But now, the industrial complex was as silent as the scene of a marine accident from which the last lifeboat had left.

Rina, who had been stuck indoors in a small, dark space, penned in by the debris from the crumbled building, abruptly came to one day. Her lower back, on which she'd been lying for the past few days, was numb. It was so dark, and she was covered in so much dust that it was hard to move. She caught her breath several times and slowly looked around. The first thing she was able to see clearly was that the old woman was alive. *That her face at death's door is the first thing I would see after nearly dying myself is great fortune for her. Terrible fortune for me.* Rina looked away.

The old woman had plunged to the floor below, along with the bed. Aside from the fact that two of its legs were broken, the bed and the old woman both seemed fine. She had always been calm and bold, but even the old woman now wept, and blinking her wrinkled eyes. All Rina could do was to reach out a hand and wipe away the old woman's tears before they trickled down into her ears. Then, Rina started to lose her breath. Everything was different now. The sewing factory girl and the baby and Pii were gone. Even though she refused to believe it, the gruesome truth hit her whenever she opened her eyes.

One day, a bright light invaded the narrow space.

"Is anyone there?" The rescue workers' voices came and went in shards, echoing throughout the debris. It wasn't that Rina didn't want to be saved, but she didn't answer. Instead, she clutched her red money box tightly against her chest. The rescue workers banged on the floors with metal pipes for a while, but soon grew tired. "No one's here. Let's go, what's the point in saving them anyways, they're all cripples now." They were about to leave when the old woman yelled out, as loudly as one might expect from a former singer.

"Hey! We're in here! Help!" And then, she passed out. It was the last time Rina would hear her voice.

It took a long time for the rescue workers to clear all of the debris from the building and lift away all of the obstructions piled up over Rina's head like the lid of a coffin. When she first caught sight of a patch of open air, it was a rhombus of ash-colored sky. Men dressed in white with masks reached down toward Rina, their backs to the sky. Rina's eyes widened, but she didn't want to thank them for saving her, or even stretch out her hand to be saved. Her left shoulder was dislocated and she couldn't move it, but neither did she want to be

saved in such a wretched physical state. And she definitely did not
want to step out into a world ruled by that ashen sky, meting out
cruel punishment to people who had done nothing bad.

The men poured water into Rina's and the old woman's mouths,
and gave them shots. While Rina was lying in a daze, neglecting to
bask in the glory of being saved, the rescue workers evaluated her
condition and exchanged furtive looks with each other. Moments
later, she was pinned down, and her dislocated shoulder reset in
a flash. An unimaginable pain swept over her body that had been
as stiff as a board. She wanted to sob out loud; her tonsils itched
with the desire to cry, but she was unable to, and all that came out
of her throat was a frustrating, raspy whisper. The rescue workers
praised her for her strength. They said ridiculous things about how
her patience had kept her alive in this hellhole for so long.

She was moved to the rescue camp, where she lay for several
days in the tent that made up most of the camp. A fairly kind nurse
and several rescue workers looked after the patients, who were
constantly moaning. Rina looked out at the lead-colored industrial
complex through the flap of the tent that fluttered in the wind.
Without even realizing it, she sat up resolutely. And then, she stood
up, as if it were the most natural thing to do. But she couldn't force
any energy into her thighs and ankles. After shuffling around for
a long time, she was finally able to stand on her own with her two
feet firmly on the ground. Like a toddler learning to walk, Rina fell
down and stood up, fell down and stood up again.

She was leaning on a pole, staring dumbly into space, when
someone approached her from behind and grabbed her shoulder.
Rina's lips began to tremble, and she called out Pii's name. She
slowly turned around, her eyes filling with tears. But it wasn't Pii.

"Why don't you go take a shower? The showers are over there, I'll
help you." It was a woman, her face covered in freckles, smiling at
Rina. She was smiling, but her face looked terribly cold. Disappointed,
Rina calmly wiped her tears and runny nose, and smiled politely.

The prefabricated shower building was the finest Rina had ever seen in her life. It was even cozy, like an incubator being pumped with warm air and light. When she turned the faucet, hot water came pouring out. Her body moved toward the stream of water. She was looking down at the muddy water that flowed off her body and about her feet when the woman approached her.

"It'll feel better once you're clean, just bear with it." The woman sat Rina in a small chair, and washed her hair and soaped her body with her large hands. She left the water running so the hot stream trickled down Rina's back all the while. The woman's words and gestures were as soft as bread. Rina's eyes closed on their own when the smell of soap tickled her nostrils, and when the woman pressed down on her scalp with her fingers her whole body felt like it was being tickled.

After the shower, Rina's body was enveloped in a large, thick towel. It had been so long since she'd felt such a soft sensation that it tickled, and she had to stifle her laughter. The woman took Rina to a small room next to the showers. She sat her down and clipped her nails and toenails, and picked the grime out of them with a file. There was a lot of it. She slowly brushed Rina's hair, which was tangled like the straws of a broom. She disinfected all her little wounds. Rina flinched every time the hydrogen peroxide touched her skin. When all the basics had been taken care of, the woman brought out a large mirror and held it in front of Rina's face.

"Look at yourself now. Congratulations on surviving." The woman stood behind Rina, gazing into the mirror with her. Rina could not figure out why everyone was being so nice all of a sudden. *Have they collectively gone insane? Are they on drugs that make them nice?* The more her doubts grew, the more Rina became confused about what had happened to her.

All of the survivors waddled around the tent in the white tracksuits that were given to them. Dressed like everyone else, Rina went and stood in a line. She could see the industrial complex through the flap of the tent, which fluttered open occasionally, like a secret door.

"Sit here, please."

Rina didn't notice the man in front of her. She silently stared at the flap. What she wanted to do was boldly lift it up and look out, but she was scared.

"What's your name?" the man asked. He had a shiny forehead and thick lips. She didn't answer. He asked again.

"What did you do here? How long have you been living here?"

Rina moved her lips, but like a person paralyzed in a dream, was unable to speak. Then, a skinny man with wild hair marched out to the front of the room.

"Our weak bodies have already been exposed to tons and tons of toxic substances! You'll never find specimens like us anywhere else. Take a good look while you have the chance. We're going to cough and hack our whole lives, then go mad like rabid dogs. We'll die in the streets, or contract some terrible disease and disappear silently. So leave us alone, you bastards!" he yelled. No one batted an eye at his outburst.

"If you remember anything, please let us know. It needs to go on record." Rina backed out of the line without being able to add her name to the list of survivors.

Two large men were carrying the old woman on a gurney to the washrooms. Rina followed. The old woman lay like a wounded fish on the bamboo bed full of holes. One of the men propped up the woman's head with a small piece of wood. The woman who helped with the baths looked at the old woman contemplatively for a long while, then headed off somewhere. She came back with a pair of rusty scissors.

"Why? What are you going to cut with those?" Rina demanded. The woman didn't answer. Armed with plastic gloves, she cut away at the old woman's dust-caked rags. She started in the middle, then moved up and down. The old woman's body, covered in feces and wrinkled in every nook and cranny, was exposed to the world. It was impossible to decide where to start—her ears filled with dust and grime, her face lined with cuts from barbed wire and pieces of cement, her hair that had hardened into clumps of mud. They started off by cutting her hair, which would never untangle, no matter how much they washed it. The old woman looked younger and almost edgy without her hair. But what was the point, when her body was covered in filth? Her skin had turned muddy; every nook, every wrinkle was caked with dirt, and her armpits, her belly button, and all her orifices was packed with filth.

When it came time to wash the lower half of her body, the woman, as kind as she was, made a face ever so briefly. Nothing this, Rina handed her the showerhead and took over the washing. Rina rolled up her sleeves. With two fingers, she lifted the sagging skin around the old woman's vagina and cleaned out the pieces of dirt and leaves that were stuck between her labia like bugs. She stuck her finger in the woman's anus and the old woman shuddered. Luckily, she didn't seem to have sustained any serious injuries.

Together, the two women lay the old woman on her side. A patch of moss was flourishing on the old woman's lower back. Rina gently rubbed it away with a thin towel. The green clumps of moss fell off easily, and there was pink skin underneath. She kept on rubbing at the clear patch of protruding skin at the center of her back. All of a sudden, the friction wore away at a thin layer of skin, and the little protrusion wriggled on its own. Several small white moths flew out of the spot. They seemed to emit a low buzzing as they flew around the shower, which was suddenly brimming with the tiny white creatures. Rina looked at them, and turned to the woman next to her.

"This old woman is really something. Just look at how she's been breeding these strange creatures in her body."

Immediately after the explosion, the industrial complex had seemed to be at the center of the world. There was a steady influx of drinking water and food from relief organizations that came in boxes marked with indecipherable stickers. Cans of dry, lean meat; cans of vegetables that were too overcooked to really be called fresh—mushy corn and beans in strange-smelling sauces. The cans smelled so bad you had to hold your nose once you opened them. Even though they gave you diarrhea and made you vomit if you ate too much, there was something wonderful about the energy they provided.

A big fuss was made, as though they were about to lift up the industrial complex and move it up to a paradise where everyone would eat well and live forever. Young medical staff in white coats lived on-site and cared for the sick. It was a series of fascinating events for the workers who were used to fighting for a single decent shower stall. The medical staff had to listen to the fairly similar life stories of the victims and pretend to be interested. Under their protection, the old woman slept and slept. Had she really been alive, she would have been terrifically rambunctious. As it was, Rina thought it very strange she should lie in a bed in a corner without saying a word. *The world will become a much quieter place when she dies,* Rina thought. And the old woman did not live much longer after that.

Some of the victims believed they were lucky to have been around for the explosion. "This is the perfect chance to make some money, maybe even worth the pain and suffering." They argued that this was a once-in-a-formerly-miserable-lifetime-chance.

Once they brought in forklifts and some other large pieces of equipment to move the debris of the collapsed buildings, the source of the accident became a bit clearer. In the beginning, it looked as though the recovery would move quickly once the professionals were brought in, but gradually, the yellow machinery stopped working. No one knew what to do when this colossal mess remained after a few days of digging. Without clear signs that there were survivors still alive in the rubble, the rescue workers were reluctant to crawl into the debris to pull out dead corpses. All they did was hope that the survivors would walk out of the rubble on their own. The heavy machinery became a playground for the bored children, who jumped up on the long claws of the forklifts and screamed with pleasure as they hugged the ash-colored skies.

The victims looked at the industrial complex, which was now nothing more than a pile of ashes, and wept every single day. But as time passed, their tears dried up. Whether it was a good thing or a bad thing, their instinct to survive was aroused, partly by the mysterious canned food from the relief organizations. But what aroused that instinct more directly were the corpses. The sight of the dead bodies, twisted and burnt and broken, aroused in the living the desire to live. They all wanted to draw a clear line between themselves and those dead bodies, and show the world that they had survived. To do so, they needed a well-timed ritual, and the ritual they settled on was a memorial service.

The flare stack, which had once stood proudly at the center of the industrial complex and spewed out smoke to let everyone know that all was running smoothly, was now burnt down to an ugly skeleton. The earth around it had also been discolored; it was no longer red. All that remained intact was the section north of the flare stack and the mountain ridge that faced it.

There were barely two hundred people in good enough shape to walk. First came sloppy funeral banners made from torn bed sheets, followed by attendants carrying bottles of liquor and cans of food, trudging up the hill with their heads bowed as if they'd done something wrong without knowing what it was. From the top of the mountain ridge, they could look down on the wasted industrial complex and the city beyond it at a single glance. The silver train tracks leading up to the industrial complex that had been designated a free trade zone, the pungent metallic stench and the fishy water vapor, the giant buildings that overflowed with chemical odors, the wires that had wound themselves around the skies—all of these things were now gone. A crimson sunset enveloped the wasted industrial complex. From the westerly skies, sand, redder and murkier than the sunset, blew in without cease. The people tried to shelter themselves from the wind with their clothes.

They held small, palm-sized photographs of those who had disappeared, and wept. They burned the clothes of the dead and waved them about. Some people had managed to get flowers or incense, which they stuck into the soil along the ridge. Even the incense smelled like chemicals. They placed the photographs, opened cans of food, glasses of liquor, a lone sweet or a cookie, in the reopened wound that was the ground. They all turned in different directions, looking off at various parts of the industrial complex. They bowed down on their hands and knees to the dead, sadness in their mouths, buttocks pointed up toward the sky.

"We're ruined, ruined, ruined, ruined, ruined, ruined; how did we become ruined?" they chanted.

After crying for a long time, some of the people brought their palms together to pray, while others wept tears of rage as they dug away at the ash-colored earth like moles. Some of them were tipsy from drinking on an empty stomach and spun around in circles. The people used all of their senses to express as much sadness as they could. Then came the finale. They picked up the empty bottles of liquor and the leftover food and flung them all off the mountain ridge. Rina faced a dilemma. *Should I pray for the old woman to get better? I really want to pray for Pii to come back, but what if I only get one prayer? Which should I choose?* They all stayed long after the sun had set. They sat and cried until their noses turned red. At night, they stood up and marked the end of the memorial with a moment of silence.

Spring came inconspicuously. There were no flowers, no pale green buds, but they could feel a sort of pale green vitality blow in with the breeze from the west. Once in a while, it seemed like the outlines of the ash-colored sky cleared a little, showing a hazy patch of something brighter. But it wasn't enough to open up the clogged-up sky. Then, one day, the smokestacks began to crumble, letting loose pieces of stone, piercing through the gray. When they stopped, the people went on with their sluggish days. Neither the people nor nature could handle the energy that spring brought with it. The people had nowhere to direct their anger, so they shook their fists at the ash-colored skies.

They hoped the spring would bring something good, but things got worse. The multinational corporations that ran the industrial complex began negotiations for compensation from the national government rather than with individual victims. Together, the government and the corporations decided to give up on rebuilding the industrial complex, because it wasn't worth the time or the money. This made all of the survivors hopping mad—why would they choose to neglect this land, when it was all that was left? But the corporations and government agreed that the best thing to do was to shut down the complex and let it fade away on its own. Time would do the rest.

The people who stayed until the very end were the environmentalists from several nations who prided themselves on their progressive politics. Their signs, which read, "Rise from the ashes of your despair. Don't lose courage," were so bruised by the dusty air that the writing was practically illegible. When things took a turn for the worse, even the environmentalists could do nothing but smoke and stare off into space. They couldn't deal with the despondency of having lost their opponent. Like the elite, they stuck by their pragmatic beliefs that activism and principles were useless if they yielded no profit. When they ran out of cigarettes, they left for the other side of the globe, in search of an issue even trendier than the plight of the industrial complex. Of course, it wasn't like they left irresponsibly; they left everything to an international religious organization to tie up the loose ends. The industrial complex, which had been slated to be the cornerstone of the nation's northeastern regional prosperity, was turned into a giant heap of garbage overnight, and left to fall by the wayside.

The cracked walls, which had lost the pillars and cornerstones on which they leaned, continued to fall and crumble without warning. Soon after, people, their faces sallow with fear, would emerge from the rubble. As more and more buildings collapsed, the industrial complex got lower and lower and wider and wider as it expanded its ash-colored territory. The survivors walked around numbly, sniffing, squeezing their bodies into the crevices of half-demolished buildings or rubble when they could. They all started to look like shit again. Things got so bad that they were unable to focus on anything other than their hunger. Rina could hardly hear the old woman breathing anymore, and as an extreme measure, she pressed her lips up against the old woman's and wet them with her own saliva.

One day, Rina popped out of a collapsed building with a quilt wrapped around her shoulders like a poncho and holding a burnt pot. Her face was as plump as a fat caterpillar and she looked worried. Her eyelids drooped over her pupils, and yet she was looking upward, making her look a little insane. Rina looked back and forth between the ash-colored sky and the bowl of porridge she had made with a handful of rice. She blew on the porridge to cool it down, then went back into the collapsed building.

The old woman slept all day and ate nothing. Rina would gently slap her cheeks and pinch her thighs, but she got no reaction. Rina suddenly became afraid. *What will I do if the old woman also dies, if I don't get to hear her voice?* She put the spoon in old woman's mouth, but she did not eat.

"Grandma, if you keep acting this way, you'll die real soon," Rina told the old woman, blinking nervously at her. Without even realizing what she was doing, she began to spoon the porridge into the old woman's nostrils, her ears, even her belly button. The truck that brought them drinking water three times a week now came twice. The workers of the international religious organization began their days with an elaborate ceremony. They wore long robes, and whenever they moved to a new location, they had to bless all of the walls there, which took a lot of time away from relief work. Soon, the drinking water truck came once a week, and the food aid from the relief organizations also stopped coming. Children and adults alike began to dig through trash heaps as if it were the only natural thing to do. Everyone lingered outside of the buildings, anxious and unsure of what to do.

Rina spent most of her time sitting and staring dully off into space. Whether it was a good thing or a bad thing, she could no longer feel her own weight, that unpleasant weight of being alive. She saw hallucinations if she turned her head too quickly. The industrial complex would come alive again with the fresh fragrance of metal. The welders' orange flames would spark up here and there and the blue skies would twist and squirm after swallowing up the white smoke from the factories. The collapsed buildings would rebuild themselves, stronger than ever. The workers would go to the clubs to drink after work. Misha would dance in her sequined dress that sparkled like fish scales, and blow kisses to men. The drunks would roll around the floor of the club. The old woman and the baby would walk around in a warm patch of sun in front of the housing complex. Rina and Pii would giggle and fool around in their creaky bed. But the second she turned her head the other way, those pictures crumbled and disappeared into the ashen ground, and she was consumed by a wave of dizziness. The industrial complex that reconstructed itself in Rina's head always deteriorated on its own.

25

RINA WAS WATCHING THE BUSES TAKE PEOPLE AWAY FROM THE industrial complex. Many of the survivors had gone, and more were planning to leave in the summer. *Where do they go when they leave this place? Where are they going that they won't even say goodbye?* Before she even realized what she was doing, Rina had climbed onto a bus with her box of money.

The bus slowly ran parallel to the train tracks. It gradually drove further and further away from the industrial complex. *I finally get to leave this hell hole.* Yet, even though she was truly happy, Rina was filled with a sense of dread the farther they drove from the ash-colored skies of the industrial complex. As soon as the bus had left the city, it dumped its cargo on the side of the road, people and bundles alike, and drove off, farting out black smoke. The nearest city was at least seventy kilometers away. They would have to hitch a ride on a truck or catch another bus. From here on out, it was every man for himself.

The cars whizzed by, leaving a stinging wind in their wake. The people in their cars were munching on sunflower seeds, smoking, and looking out the window, but no one stopped. It was only natural, since all the people walking down the newly constructed highway looked like hobos. To the people who hadn't eaten in a long time, the tall trees that grew in groups of two or three with paddies and fields as their backdrop looked as if they were stretching and shrinking. The gaps between the different clusters of people grew wider and wider. Those who were too hungry to walk eventually crouched over and lay down on the road like abandoned dogs.

Rina sat, crouched over, looking at the heat shimmer in front of her eyes like a mass of insects. She felt pathetic that she couldn't even take care of her own tiny body.

"I'm sorry," Rina apologized to her inner organs. Then, as if an idea had suddenly come to her, she jumped up. She knew that if she didn't get her act together, she would never eat again, let alone get a ride. She untied her ponytail and ran her fingers through her hair. She pulled her pants up to her knees and started to murmur to herself: "You are pretty, you are pretty, you are definitely pretty enough to hitch a ride." Filled with a burst of energy, she jumped up and down, waving her arms. She noticed a blue truck and managed to make eye contact with the driver. The truck slowed down and stopped a little bit ahead of her. Fearful that others might follow her, Rina ran to the truck and got in.

The truck driver was playing loud music and smoking. It had been a long while since Rina had been exposed to the smell of cigarette smoke and the sound of music; her nose sniffed and her lips twitched in spite of herself.

"Where are you coming from?" the driver asked her, turning the volume down.

"From nearby," Rina said, her lips twitching still.

"Nearby? Nearby where?"

"What business is it of yours?" Rina retorted sullenly.

"They said this whole area was razed to the ground by that accident over in the industrial complex. Nearby where?"

Rina looked at the driver's profile, her lips still twitching.

"I'm from that industrial complex that was razed to the ground, okay? You got a problem with that?" The driver looked Rina up and down several times, as if he were staring at an odd creature. Rina stopped her twitching and looked out the window.

Rina's eyes opened with a flash when her head banged against the window. The truck had stopped by the side of the road. The driver was sleeping in his seat. Rina's eyes instinctively went to the man's wallet, which hung from his waist like a belt. She calmly wiped the drool from her lips and approached the driver. His face was covered in a network of fine wrinkles and there were dried flakes of food stuck to the corners of his mouth. A few moments passed. Rina made her decision.

She would have to unclasp the wallet from the belt in one move. She boldly and gently put both hands around the driver's waist and pressed the plastic buckle on his belt. The wallet fell to the floor with a plop. Rina grabbed the belt, which had fallen between her seat and her waist, with her left hand. She twisted around and looked out the window to make sure that no cars were coming from the direction in which she planned to run. As she plucked the wallet off the belt, the driver grabbed her by the hair.

"Let me go! I'll do what you want!" Rina tried to squeeze her arm to reach down to the man's groin, but the man came at her with such a frenzy that she couldn't figure out where it was. She surrendered to his physical force.

The man pushed Rina so that her head was in the driver's seat and opened the door to the passenger's seat so that her legs stuck out. He quickly moved over to the passenger's seat and pulled down his pants, and Rina saw it, brownish red like clotted pig's blood and shaped like a cluster of small berries. The driver pulled Rina's white sweatpants down and jumped on top of her. But the next second, he backed off in shock.

"Ugh, what is that smell?" He leapt up. Rina could smell it too, the toxic stink of chemicals.

By now, Rina was sick of escaping; she'd done it in so many different ways. She bit down on the driver's hand, grabbed his wallet, and jumped out of the truck. She wiped the saliva off her hands and mouth with some leaves from a tree by the side of the road and ran at full speed away from the truck. After a long while, she managed to hitch a ride on a pig manure truck. It smelled just fantastic. Rina flared her nostrils, as if the stench was a hallucinogen.

Rina limped into the city. She finally felt like she had landed in a world with actual humans. She realized that she had hurt her leg badly enough that it hurt to walk. She limped through the city, pushed aimlessly by the crowds of people. It was a city full of tall buildings, and she came to the plaza of a train station that was right in the center of the city. The people gave her strange looks as she limped among them. Her dirty white sweat suit stood out in a crowd. Whenever she caught someone staring at her, Rina glowered back. People covering their faces with masks or towels were swept into the station with their large suitcases and children. The atmosphere was so murky that it was impossible to guess what time it was.

Out of nowhere, it began to rain; it was a dirt rainstorm. The smell of dirt was a shock. Rina thought of the truck driver's stunned expression as he caught wind of her chemical odor. The crowds in front of the station evaporated. Drops rain splattered mud everywhere. The restaurants near the station were empty, yet lit up as bright as operating rooms. *Where could I get something to eat? I need to go somewhere where there are a lot of people,* Rina thought to herself as she stood under an awning in front of a restaurant, trying to stay dry. She had completely forgotten about her money. Not realizing that all she had to do was to walk into a restaurant and pay for a meal, Rina looked down at the rain falling violently on the dirt in front of her. She was too tired.

In the morning, Rina woke up in a homeless shelter in a park in the center of the city. The mud that had rained over the city overnight weighed on the landscape. She watched a giant yellow shadow loom over the city, with its old trees and houses roofed in dignified black ceramic tile. The river that ran through the center of the city was now muddy brown, and people and all of their livestock were leaving the city to get away from the chemical gases that were blowing in from the industrial complex. A crazy homeless person circled the corner of an alleyway now that the streets were emptied.

"Can I have a cigarette? Please, just one cigarette, sir," he asked loudly. Rina trudged through the city in her slippers, looking for something to eat.

She saw four boys kneeling in front of a restaurant, waiting for hand-outs. Out of habit, Rina joined them, bowing her head. But time passed, and no food came.

"We have nothing for you," the owner told them coldly. The boys clung to the trousers of the customers leaving the restaurant. That's when Rina remembered her money.

Rina took the boys into the restaurant. They went up to the second floor, picked a round table on the terrace, and called the owner.

"I'd like a menu, please," Rina told him. The owner demanded to see their money first. Rina showed him her cash. The food was slow to come. On the side of the building next door, the thigh of a model advertising cell phones flashed in neon lights. They all stared at the model as they waited for the food. The waiters were rude and the food took forever. The boys didn't notice because they were too busy stuffing their faces.

They were sprawled out on their seats after they had eaten their fill when the owner approached them and asked them why they were still there, cursing. Rina took her money out of her underwear and paid for the food with pride and contempt. The boys whistled in admiration.

"You're the best, Rina! A fine-looking woman!" they yelled.

The four boys had nowhere to go, so they followed Rina around. The first thing she did was to take them to an outdoor sink and have them wash their faces. Then they went back out in to the street and sat in a row under the awning of a building and watched the sandstorm. People passed on their bicycles, followed by the sandstorm. One of the boys, who had gone inside to use the bathroom, came back out and announced that the building was empty. Rina and the boys went in.

The elevator wasn't working, so they used the stairs. All of the doors leading to each floor of the building from the stairwell were unlocked. The kids went into some offices on the fifth floor. One boy sat at the front desk and pretended to take calls, while another perched on a chair at the end of the hallway and pretended to be the CEO. The offices looked as though everything were in place; only the people were missing. The boys sat around the desks and laughed at each other.

In the inner part of the offices was a large room. There was a round table at the center surrounded by high-backed chairs. The kids sat at the tables and horsed around and looked out the windows. Rina was taken over by a wave of sleepiness, and she lay down on the floor. But she couldn't fall asleep, so she went to the bathroom. There were towels, soap, and warm water. Her reflection in the mirror was covered in soot and her clothes were splotchy with grime. Rina took her clothes off and stared at herself from the waist up. The smell of chemicals diffused throughout the bathroom. Rina tried to think of a way to get rid of the smell, but came up with nothing, only tears.

When they got bored of the empty building, they went out into the street again. The boys scattered to go pick pockets, and Rina lost track of them. But when they had gathered enough money, they all returned and sat behind some trucks, shivering but still giggling. Rina realized, *it's the same everywhere in the world— boring and messy.* She suddenly felt the need to return to the industrial complex. The boys said they had nowhere to go, so she decided to take them all back to the dilapidated complex. It took them two days.

The industrial complex had naturally become isolated from everything. The ultra-progressive environmentalists from abroad, who had paid out of pocket to visit the area, had left. Some fifty people who had been living in the west gradually began to expand their territory. The survivors who had stayed until the end lived around the old rescue camp.

Even when they had lived among others, the old woman had slept the whole time, so it took Rina a while to realize that the old woman had died. The people called Rina an ungrateful bitch. They said that in this country, you would only be let into heaven if you took good care of your parents, and that heartless sons and daughters would be dropped into hell without any ado. They told her the story of a devoted man who had never left home until his dying mother expressed an interest in traveling, at which point he attached a portable cot to his bicycle and rode around the entire country.

"I'm not from this country," Rina told them. But the elders chastised her even more for not taking responsibility. Why would you want to see new things when you're about to die? And what could be so beautiful about a world that you see from your bed? Rina thanked god she didn't have such demanding parents. What was truly surprising was that that devoted son had been seventy years old when he decided to travel with his mother.

The old woman had died without leaving so much as a will, and they spent several days trying to figure out where to bury her. It was a woman from the west side that suggested burying her under a tree, explaining that she'd done the same with her own husband.

"The nutrients from the corpse help the tree to grow. If it doesn't help the tree, at least the ants will have a feast! Don't worry about the dead."

What nutrients could possibly be in the body of this old woman who had suffered so long? Rina wondered. But the old woman from the west persisted: "If we can become one with the trees when we die, that's a wonderful thing." Rina was so tired of the nagging that she agreed to have the burial under a tree.

The boys from the city each carried one corner of the old woman's bed. There was an abandoned lot thick with yellowing weeds by the border along the western region of the industrial complex, where less damage had been done from the explosions. They found a small tree there and buried the old woman under it. Before the burial, Rina sang one of the songs the old woman had enjoyed performing when she was a tent singer. It was in memory of their friendship. Then she lay down on the cot next to the old woman, with her arm underneath her head, and they looked up at the sky together.

That night, Rina dreamt that she turned into a flowering tree. Buds and leaves came bursting out of her skin. Unable to sleep all night, Rina went to the tree where the old woman was buried. She thought she could hear the songs from the old woman's country that she used to sing in staccato. The old woman's sturdy back, the five-minute intermission back in the days of the tent, the sticky sweat that trickled down your neck, the persistent mosquitos, the repulsively hot hours that were eventually swallowed up by the moon that rose beyond the tent, the strange desert snake chimera that had poked its head into their tent after traveling all night across the desert.

The long, boring summer rolled by. Rina spent most of her time cutting hair for the elderly and the children. They didn't get much to eat, but their hair grew quickly. She could never understand what the people from the west side were saying, but it gave them nothing to argue or fight about, and it wasn't a problem for when they were interacting or having a good time. People asked Rina if she had a family. Whenever they asked her that, Rina would say the old woman was sleeping under a tree. Then they would look for the old woman.

The people from the west stayed up all night eating hunks of meat and jerky and drinking the strong liquor they said they kept stored underground. They shared their food equally, regardless of age, and prayed to the heavens before eating, although who knew what they had to be so thankful for. On hot nights, they slept without blankets, shielding just their faces under a canopy. The mosquitos that used to bother them were now nowhere to be seen. It hardly seemed like a midsummer's night.

During the monsoon, they would all gather in the tents and laugh and play cards, and when the rain stopped, they would make porridge and eat it together. When they were bored, they would bring over broken bicycles or even the empty husks of cars with only the steering wheel left, and horse around with them. Rina's boys could spend an entire day playing around in an old car.

Once in a while, Rina would go around to where The Puzzle, the road with the gas storage tanks, and the embankment used to be. When she found a very familiar-looking brick in the southeast region of the complex, where the housing units used to stand, her heart skipped a beat. A torn red curtain covered in dirt, stuck in the rubble, fluttered. It gave her a lump in her throat. She and the sewing factory girl had once concocted the silly plan to open up a small brothel in their apartment. They had planned on drawing a red curtain in the window to attract the men. She could hear the sewing factory girl's voice ringing in her ears. She missed her. If she were to see her ever again, she would tell her she loved her, and they would rub each other down there, slowly and warmly. Rina believed that the sewing factory girl and the Arab had gone back to his country with their baby. *They'll be in a house painted white, with lots of small flowerpots out front. The baby will just be learning how to talk, and they'll pat him on the bum. But maybe he still can't talk. I wonder what language he'll speak. She might be cheating on the Arab with her neighbor. That's definitely something she would do. They say there are loads and loads of bananas over there, so at least she'll get to eat as many of those as she wants.* Rina fondled the curtain with her thick, rough fingers, but she felt nothing.

The wind became cooler, and curiously enough, the ashen veil over the sky was drawn away bit by bit, revealing patches of blue here and there. Rina could not believe her eyes when she looked back and forth between the clear autumn sky coming and going in swift patches, and the gray of the industrial complex's usual skies. The colossal industrial complex that had once shot out orange flames was now nothing more than a big, ash-colored quagmire. *What more am I to do here?* Rina would often ask the skies. But she never got an answer.

Once in a while, Rina would braid her long hair into pigtails on each side of her head and head out to the city with her four boys. The five of them would pile onto a motorcycle and move slowly toward the city in a big clump. The population of the city was decreasing due to a citywide relocation plan, and more and more areas were now uninhabited. Rina praised the boys whenever they came back with stolen goods, and whenever they came back with something good to eat, they all shared.

Flocks of crows moved into the abandoned houses and flies took over the main halls of empty restaurants. There were cars parked in the streets covered in sand whose tires would spontaneously explode, causing the cars to plunk down onto themselves. Clocks without second hands rolled into the river and were washed out to sea. Old shoes that had lost their soles took over the city. These shoes, abandoned in front of stores, on curbs, and near bus stops, were the only ones to keep watch over the city.

They often watched the news on TV at a store in the center of the city. The borders of several nations in the region were suffering since the turn into the new century, and the lines to get into the country of P were detailed on the news. It showed a bus parked in front of a hotel at the center of a large city in the country of P. The curtains of the bus were all tightly drawn, and it was raining. The entrance to the hotel was crowded with reporters, cameramen, and government officials in suits. A girl opened the curtain to look out onto the city and frowned. Rina stared at the girl, who looked about her age. *So, they say this isn't a bad place to live, huh?* The girl seemed to be thinking as she chewed her gum. The camera flashes started to go off in her face, and the girl quickly drew the curtain shut. When Rina turned away from the television to see what was going on, she saw one of the boys walking behind a man dressed in a suit. She wished him success.

Rina had once given some thought to the questions they might ask her when she tried to enter P. *I want to go to college and study hard, I want to become someone who protects the rights of other escapees like myself, I want to make a lot of money and be rich.* She had once stayed up nights coming up with all the grandiose answers she would give to such questions. Now, Rina kicked at a can on the ground. The can stopped in front of a handicapped woman who had a locket with a photograph in it. The woman caressed the smiling face of the man in the photo and called out to the passersby.

"Have you seen this man? Please take a look, and tell me if you've seen him. Please, just once." Rina crouched down and peered at the photograph. It was a man smiling in front of a flowerbed. Rina leaned over and whispered into the woman's ear.

"I know this man. We worked at the industrial complex together. He's in good health, and he's fine. He told me to tell you not to worry." The woman didn't seem to understand; she crawled around on her knees, repeating her pleas. Of course, Rina didn't know the man.

She noticed a shoe stall in the center of the market. The owner held a cigarette in one hand and dusted a pair of colorful beaded slippers with the other. Rina approached the stall and examined the shoes. Rina's heart always skipped a beat when it came to shoes. She picked up a pair, put them on the ground, and tried one on. She put them back on the display table. She had to have those dowdy-looking beaded slippers. They were shoddy little things that would surely fall apart in less than an hour had she worn them during one of her escapes. But Rina knew that one day, when she had stopped to look at a sunset during one of her escapes, or when she was done escaping and was old, or at peace, she would want to wear those shoes on her bare feet and feel the wind and the air of wherever she was. So, it didn't matter whether or not they fit her, or whether or not they were sturdy.

She approached a group of men standing in a corner of the market, smoking. She held her hand out, asking for a cigarette.

"She's crazy," said the men. "They say if you sleep with a crazy woman, it'll change your luck." They laughed, and each insisted on giving her a cigarette. One of the men handed Rina a cigarette he'd tucked behind his ear, and another lit it for her. They all stared at her lips, waiting for the cigarette smoke to blow out of it. Rina coughed violently.

"My body's been completely contaminated by chemical gases. They say that any kids I have will be handicapped, retarded, or sterile. And their kids, too. For generations to come." The men looked Rina up and down.

"Hey, I'm fine, pal, why don't you take her," the men passed her back and forth among each other, then left. Rina sat on a tree stump and stared at the man selling shoes.

It started raining mud again. The sky was soon taken over by a big clump of ash-colored clouds. The shoe-stall owner grabbed the four corners of the cloth on which his shoes were displayed, rolled up the shoes, and took shelter in a broken-down truck. The people in the lot scattered, and a tired old horse walked in circles after its own tail. Only lost dogs and hungry cats roamed the lot, eyeing each other.

Rina took shelter from the rain in a minivan without tires. The air inside the bus was muggy from everyone's breath and body odor. She saw a little boy, feverish from the heat, sitting in his grandmother's lap. He was so heated he couldn't even cry; he just breathed warm air out through his mouth. The boy's grandmother sang in a thin, high voice to console him. *The summer day your mother was born, a lovely flower blossomed in front of the house, a slender horse came prancing into our yard, and a group of dancers walked by our house with green streamers. Oh, it was all at three o'clock. Don't die, don't die. You and your mother, don't die.*

The mud rain stopped. The man selling shoes quickly set up his stall again, and the people began to gather around the market. Rina made a fuss over the shoes as if she were seeing them for the first time. She held the dowdy slippers with their pink beads close to her face. *How long have I walked? Do my thighs know that?* Suddenly, she heard the sound of pistols going off nearby. She heard the footsteps of the twenty-two walking toward the border, and the sound of gunshots amid the footsteps.

"Hey lady, buy them or stop touching them."

Rina considered the words of the dark-skinned stall owner.

All the money she had right now was in the red box. She walked over behind the minivan to take her money out where no one could see it. With one hand, she grabbed the bottom of the tin, and with the other, she pried open the lid. It was an epic moment, the first time she'd opened it in ages, and the lid stuck. Rina braced her whole body and pulled. With a crack, the hinge cracked off. White ash tumbled all over Rina's knees and her feet; it was all that was left in the box. Unable to withstand the heat of the explosions, the bills had burned in their tin. Rina collapsed, the wind knocked out of her. There she was, floating in an ocean, with no boat, no oars, no telephone. She began to cry like a baby.

She cried for a long time, with her legs stretched out in front of her. She dipped a finger in some of the white ash that had fluttered onto her knee, and licked it. She couldn't believe what had happened. She was in a rage. She wished Pii were there so that she could to hold the tin upside down and show him how that thing she'd protected so carefully for so long was now empty. Rina flung the can, but it didn't go very far. A couple of dogs ran gleefully after it.

RINA

When Rina turned back to look at the market, every single person there looked like Pii. She rubbed her eyes like she'd seen an apparition. She felt like someone had approached her and told her in a low voice near her ear, "You've really aged." She stood there, imagining Pii's voice gently cradling her head. A yellow dog came up to her with the tin in its mouth, and dropped it by her feet. Rina wandered around the lot, looking for the broken-off lid.

That night, Rina dreamt that she saw Pii welding. Back in the industrial complex, with its colossal buildings and its white smoke that smelled of metal, Pii was hard at work. His head was very close to the welding flames, as if he were bewitched by the fire, ready to dive into it. The flames grew, as did the sound of welding, and the entire welding station lit up a brilliant orange. All of a sudden, Pii was peering into one of the pretty shoes Rina had been admiring at the market. He tried to weld the shoes. They caught on fire, and Rina ran over to stop him, but no matter how far she ran, she couldn't reach him. The fire from the shoe did not go out. It got bigger and caught on to Pii's body. Rina sometimes thought that maybe Pii's dream had been to go into the flames while he was welding and die there.

When Rina woke up, she was so sure that she'd be holding the beaded slippers in her hands, but they weren't there. Her head hurt and her body trembled so that she couldn't sleep the rest of the night. Instead, she buried her face in her arm and wept silently. She wanted to fall asleep peacefully to the metallic smell emanating from Pii's body. When she was able to tell herself that she had to accept the fact that she would never own the pretty beaded slippers, or see Pii ever again, she quietly closed her eyes.

KANG YOUNG-SOOK

26

THEY HAD TO PREPARE FOR WINTER. THE PEOPLE FROM THE WEST side set up partitions in buildings that had even the smallest habitable corner. They joined together pieces of wood stuck on to wooden boards or pieces of Styrofoam that might serve as insulation, and covered those with pieces of cloth to serve as insulation. They pulled broken iron bed frames and chairs together and thought about how they might create a decent home. But no matter how hard they tried, it was hard to hide the fact that they had little more than rags, and the industrial complex would always be under construction.

Late autumn was very short. The days were short, the evenings rushed in, and the skies fled from the earth as fast as they could. As it got chillier, Rina coughed more. Her skin became spotty and she lost weight. She often had problems digesting her food, and she constantly felt constricted and heavy, like a blunt stick had been shoved down her throat. She often hallucinated the wail of sirens. She became very irritable, and killed time by cursing at her four boys and throwing things at them.

Winter brought constant blizzards that turned the ashen landscape into a dreamlike winter wonderland. When the snow was particularly heavy, they couldn't even leave their houses, as their front doors would vanish. The people with pulmonary problems had it the worst during these winters. Mornings were spent shoveling snow and clearing roads. If they stopped to take a rest for even a moment, the snow would catch up with them. The world became lighter and brighter and the people became more insane.

"I love the industrial complex forever. I'll bury my bones here!" they would yell as they floundered in the snow. There was so much snow that some people started to show serious signs of oxygen deficiency. It was then that Rina received two gifts that would haunt her for the rest of her life: acute sensitivity to sunlight in both her skin and eyes. Nowhere outdoors was safe for her, so she would sit at home and curse like a sailor, tears streaming from her eyes.

Winter seemed like it would never end. They were isolated time and again by the snow. No one was able to leave the industrial complex during the winter. Everyone slept in, except for a single old man who woke up early every morning to quietly clear away the snow that had piled up overnight. He seemed to be the only sane and living one among them. But sometimes even he looked like a corpse. The roads were blocked by the snow and the people from the west side had no way of bringing food over. Without any money to bet, and nothing besides money to bet, they staked their sick, diseased lives. They dealt cards and sat quietly, each person looking down at his or her own hand. It would get so quiet that even the mice that had accidentally crept in would tiptoe along the walls. No one said it out loud, but they were all secretly waiting for the phone to ring—the phone with the broken cord that someone had brought to use as decoration—and they hoped that help would be on the other end of the line.

One day, like a miracle, a helicopter flew over the industrial complex. In a quiet so deep you could even hear the snow falling, the helicopter was deafening. They all ran outside, yipping for joy at the thought of eating as many canned goods as they wanted. The helicopter dropped off a few sacks and flew off. Everyone ran over to look. The sacks were chock full of black electronic chips—no soft bread, no canned meat. The first ones to rush up to the sacks felt like their pride had been wounded. They tried eating the chips, but ending up spitting them out.

The kids made a snowman in front of the houses. They made the snowman's eyes, nose, and mouth out of the black chips, so that Rina woke up in the morning to a snowman covered in electronic chips guarding her. The kids built more snowmen every day. As long as there were chips, and as long as it kept on snowing, they made more and more replicas each day.

After that day, the helicopters came regularly. They followed them around the first few times, but the sacks never held anything useful, and the people gave up after a while. It was always mysterious-looking machine parts. The industrial complex had become a dump for trash that was difficult to dispose of elsewhere. The people shook their fists and cursed at the helicopters.

"If you keep mocking us like this, we'll get you!"

Trapped inside her half-destroyed house, Rina spent her days singing to herself in a low voice. The four boys had by now turned into surly looking teenagers with pimply foreheads. They sat around reading books or looking at fliers they had found in the city. The dilapidated industrial complex was so boring that these hot-blooded young men were on the verge of insanity. Sometimes, Rina would entertain them with stories of her own boredom back in the days when she'd worked at the youth vocational training center.

"At night, when I got out of work, I'd be terrified to walk back home because of a rumor that there was a man who kidnapped the smart girls and ate them. One day he appeared and he did try to eat me. I told him to hurry up, before I got cold."

At the punch line, the boys, who had been pretending not to pay attention, would clutch their heads and yell, "Stop lying Rina! God, that's the most boring story ever!" Rina made the boys stay indoors to listen to her. So the boys began going to the bathroom indoors.

"Rina, your stories are boring as shit. I think my head's gonna explode. Please stop. Jesus, I hate this fucking shithole dump." When Rina ignored them and continued with her stories, they began to fight with each other. Rina would throw whatever was in her reach at them.

"OK, fine, I was making that one up. I'm really sorry, guys." But no matter how Rina tried to apologize and console them, they would punch each other until they'd punched all the anger and frustration out.

There was one kid who sucked his thumb. He would whimper in his sleep, especially after he'd been in a fight, making sucking noises. Rina crawled up to him and tried to take his thumb out of his mouth. He was a big kid who acted like a baby sometimes. No matter how much she scolded him for it, his hand would always instinctively move toward his mouth. One night, Rina lay down next to him and put her nipple in his mouth. He seemed to relax for a second, then woke up and got very angry.

It began to snow even more often. The helicopters kept on coming, but everyone had distrusted them now, so no one bothered to open the sacks. Then, one day, they heard shouts from outside.

"Come out, everyone, come on out! It's food!"

It was indeed—sacks full of cookies, candies, sausages, and cheese. Everything looked fresh. The people tied rope around the sacks and dragged them into their half-destroyed houses. They put all of the food on their tables, one by one, evaluated the quality of each item, sampled them all, ate until they were full, then ate more. Rina sat on her bed and ate what the boys fed her. She couldn't taste the sweetness, and her tears refused to stop flowing. The canned fruit salad was the most popular item. Fruit, and what's more, fruit that looked like actual fruit. The gratitude expressed by the people that day would have moved even the most indifferent of gods. Perhaps that was why the snow finally stopped that night.

KANG YOUNG-SOOK

Rina was ill for a few days. It would have been nice if they'd saved her some food, but despite their promises, everyone else ate until you could see the bottoms of the sacks. Then they suffered because they couldn't go to the bathroom. Rina didn't want to open her eyes or lift a finger. Everyone asked her if she was sick. She didn't feel like answering, so she shot back, "Who the hell isn't sick around here?" and turned around to face the wall.

She woke up in the middle of the night from the noise of wailing sirens. Her clothes were drenched in sweat and chills ran down her spine. She wrapped herself in a quilt and went outside. The snow had been packed so tightly that she slipped on it several times. The entire industrial complex was covered in white snow. The snowmen with their electronic chipped faces were walking somewhere. Rina followed them. She wandered the grounds in pursuit of the sirens ringing in her ears and it was only around dawn, her body blue from the cold, that she returned to her sleeping, half-destroyed house.

Then, something special happened: a group of world-renowned artists decided to visit the industrial complex in the dead of the winter to put on a performance for the victims. They said that the performance would focus the world's attention on the forgotten place and on the accident, and that the government would be forced to confront the problem. The performers were dancers and actors. First came cars with cameras and filming equipment. The artists, dressed magnificently in bright colors, came to solemnly survey the land for a good place to stage the performance. They spent the next day installing and lighting candles around the complex. It was to be a so-called candlelight performance. The following afternoon, the crowds began to gather. Everything looked magnificent in candlelight. But there was something strange about it; Rina and her neighbors had never met the people who claimed to be survivors of the accident. Even so, everyone cooperated as best they could, figuring that the accident was so big that perhaps they hadn't met all the victims, and that the most important thing anyways was to get word out about the accident.

Rina was standing among the crowd when a man came up to her and said, "Well, look who it is, the cutie from The Puzzle." It was one of the men who had worked in the same workstation as Pii at the factory. He was neatly dressed, and seemed to have come with his wife and children.

"I went to a different industrial complex. They say it's much safer there, but who knows. I think about this place sometimes. I heard about it and came to see." Rina was speechless.

"If he were still alive, he'd be a great technician today. He was really talented. Even on that day . . ." Rina covered his mouth with her hand.

"Don't even mention that asshole," she told him.

Decorated with banners, the industrial complex looked magnificent in the candlelight. Camera crews sent by the television networks captured the whole performance and interviewed the victims. The candles burned through the night as the performers consoled the suffering of the victims and asked for forgiveness— we are all sinners, they said. A man danced naked on the white snow. The actual victims in their half-demolished homes were excluded from the event, and they quietly played cards inside. When the performances were over, the artists threw on their thick, weatherproof parkas, lit up their cigarettes, and left. They probably hadn't expected anyone to touch their belongings while they were there, but Rina and her posse had gone through the celebrities' pockets and taken all of their dollars.

The real performance began once everyone had left. The inhabitants of the ruins came out and lit what candles were left. They wore straw mats to keep warm and danced all over the complex. Over and over again, hundreds of times, Rina sang the song that she'd learned from the old woman before her death. She sang, too, the party doctrine songs she'd learned at school. She sang and sang, wandering around the industrial complex until her lips turned blue. The people weren't healed—they were acting more and more outlandish. They insisted on settling down among the ruins, they said they would never leave. They yelled at invisible antagonists: "Clean up this mess and leave us alone so we can live in peace!"

Rina sank to the ground. Her legs hurt. She saw a patch of land over which the ice had frozen blue. She bent down and swept at it with her arms. She wiped and wiped. After a long time, a clear blue sheet of ice appeared. She could see bodies lying under the ice. They had their arms around each other in what seemed like a friendly manner, and they were smiling. She could see Misha in her sequined dress. The contrast between Misha's red lips and the blue ice was bracing. Rina waved at her. Looking at Misha had always compelled Rina to ask herself, *Where do I come from?* Misha had once been a princess who had traveled from east to west and back, back in the days when the land of this nation was nothing but desert. And now, the princess smiled from her grave in the ice. Rina wanted to lie down in the ice with her, but she couldn't break the ice, no matter how hard she stomped on it with her feet.

One day, it had snowed so much that Rina couldn't reach the tops of the mounds of snow even when she held her arms straight up above her head. The barometer had fallen, and the wind was like a thousand knives. The people were cooped up inside, craving fresh air. Like a miracle, the phone rang for the first time ever. They were all so stunned that they just stared at each other. Finally, an old man answered the phone, and eventually said into the receiver: "We need good food and thick blankets, and hundreds of trucks to get rid of all this garbage. Send them now." But they never found out who had called, or how long it would take for the things the old man had requested to arrive; as they all wondered at the old man's blank stare when he had hung up, a giant claw came crashing through the barricade of white snow. The last remaining houses in the industrial complex were being torn down. They all jumped up like grasshoppers, some of them still holding cards in their hands. They kissed the industrial complex goodbye. Their time had come to leave, and they vowed that they would do so voluntarily, without leaving a trace.

KANG YOUNG-SOOK

27

Rina remained in the industrial complex by herself in a partially destroyed building. The forklift went away after making sure all the houses had been demolished, and the people were left in confusion. A faint, brown wind blew. Everything else stood still.

Helicopters still came by from time to time to drop off enormous quantities of rubbish, vast showers of electronic chips and parts, cans of chemicals and film negatives—Rina wondered what they would reveal if developed—as well as heaps of capsules of all different colors, videotapes with serial numbers, and boxes of bullets.

All the cats and dogs had fled. They didn't return, even after night fell. Rina began to draw the destroyed industrial complexes one by one on pieces of paper spread out on her desk, as Pii used to do. Each night, she gave birth to achromatic cities without a trace of human beings or movement. All that illuminated the dark were the candles left behind by artists. Rina no longer asked why things happened. She just chased aimlessly after the white pollen that drifted in from afar on the back of the hot nocturnal wind. When she felt like talking, she yelled at the ground that crumbled away under her: "Stop it! Doesn't it hurt? Stop!"

After several days, another helicopter came by and showered down little scraps of paper. They were small fliers announcing a large-scale disinfection in the area.

"Who for?" Rina yelled at the ground. "Do you need disinfecting? I don't!" She lay down in the warm sunlight and listened to her own breathing. Hidden beneath it was another noise, something deeper and lower, battered by fear and despair. She didn't eat or sleep. She stayed wide-awake for twenty-four hours, then thirty-six, then forty-eight. Her wrists and ankles were so thin now that they looked as if they might snap at the slightest pressure. Her face was small, her hair long, and her eyes sunken.

The temperature kept rising. Green grass shot up from cracks in the destroyed building and squirmed in the ruins like sea creatures. Some birds flew into this polluted place by accident. Rina crouched down next to them and shooed them off. She told them not to come back ever again if they could help it. It got quiet again.

Drip, drip, drip. Raindrops started to fall onto her head. She set buckets outside to catch the rain, and went back in to the partially destroyed house. It was time to enjoy the falling raindrops! Rain came pouring into the house. Rina closed her eyes and listened to the rain. The sound passed right through her small, skinny frame, and ascended above the roofless house. As long as there was no thunder, she would be fine. Boom! came the first crack of thunder. Rina covered herself with a piece of straw mat—leaving only her eyes peeping out—and gritted her teeth, trying to shut out the thunder.

The next day, Rina was startled awake by the chirping of birds. It was a miracle. Birds with mysterious calls had suddenly appeared at the dilapidated industrial complex. The day after the rainstorm, the sun was bright and heat waves shimmered in the air. Rina's eyes watered. Waves of heat rose up softly from the ground and she swayed along with them. When she found herself thinking too much, she grabbed a pair of scissors and cut her hair. Then she climbed up on a forklift and played the way the kids used to.

She liked it when it rained, but there was always a terrible stench afterward. She finally realized that it was the same smell that came from her body. It made her want to drain her body of all unpleasantness and transform herself into a lump of protein.

She took off all her clothes, which were rags by now, and put on sweatpants and a T-shirt. When she felt that even her clothes were too much, she took everything off and lay down to bask in the sun. The warm rays poured down on her, making every joint of her body feel loose and soft. But it was no use; the tears kept coming. To enjoy the sunlight longer, she rummaged through the piles of trash for some sunglasses. She was greeted by corpses, who waved their bones at her. Some shook their hair; others were left only with a clamped jaw. To her surprise, she found a pair of sunglasses on the mirror near the driver's seat of the forklift. She put them on and glanced around the destroyed industrial complex with a satisfied look on her face. Now she wouldn't get dehydrated from all that crying.

When the rainwater warmed, she climbed inside a big bucket and took a bath. Wearing the sunglasses, her body immersed in the warm water, she looked up at the sky. As time passed, the wounds in her skin, her veins, her blood, and her bones floated up to the surface, bubbling like amoebas. Looking down at the debris in the water calmed her down.

Early the next morning, a helicopter flew by. Rina came out of her partially destroyed house and looked up at the streams of white powder falling from the sky like rays of sunlight. The helicopters were spraying disinfectant powder all around the complex, starting at its outer edges and circling toward the center. Rina, who had been looking up at the sky with her hands on her waist, began to walk around with the sunglasses on and a bag in her hand. She hadn't been to the city in a while, so she figured she would go there and return when the disinfection was over and everything was clean again. She slowly made her way across the industrial complex and headed south, where she could see the railroad. The helicopters were circling toward the center of the complex.

There were people standing in a square in the middle of the nearly empty city. Those who had stayed behind were faced with days of nothing to do and no one to see. They were all slight, with dark faces and large blinking eyes.

Here, there were two groups of people. The first group wanted to go find jobs in an industrial complex in another city that was being built nearby. The other group wanted to move to a land of nomads in the north, where it was so cold and remote that there was no place for industrial complexes. Rina stared vacantly at the people quarreling over where to go.

Rina lived with her four boys, guarding the square as it gradually filled with spring sunlight. She now used the steel money box to prop her feet up. She stared down at the gray shadow hovering over the square, and waited for night, which always came suddenly, once things grew still.

One day at high noon, a man wearing a hat with earmuffs—as though he didn't realize what season it was—walked by Rina. When she saw his profile, she didn't recognize him right away, but instinctively knew that he was one of those people who lived off of escapees like her.

"Rina, it's you!" he exclaimed. She hadn't heard her own language in a long time. It made her feel odd, as though the words were stuck on her tongue like fish scales that she couldn't shake off. It sickened her, and the nausea in turn flustered her. It didn't matter who the man was; she was bowled over by the fact that she was hearing her own language, which she had almost forgotten.

"It is you, isn't it?" the man asked. Rina could only manage to say hello, and stood there staring at the ground, her heart thumping.

"You do remember. I was wondering what had happened to you. So, how have you been?" he asked. She felt disgusted all of a sudden. *Shouldn't you know how I've been? You sold me off, after all,* she wanted to ask.

The man took Rina's arm and led her to a place where they could sit. The boys started to follow her, and she tried to stop them, but they insisted, so she let them come along. The man acted so friendly that she wondered whether he was in fact the same man she'd met while pretending to be a singer. She regretted letting on that she had recognized him. Encounters with such people always led to betrayal and lies, while plunging into the unknown. He still feigned thoughtfulness; the only difference was that now his face was a bit darker. He reached into his bulky pack, took out a bundle of letters, and flipped through them one by one. Each letter he flipped through seemed bursting with the desire to let loose its stream of tearful stories.

"Here, this one's for you. I've been carrying it around with me—I just knew that I'd run into you one day. I'm very good at following up. Whatever you pay me for, I make sure I render the full range of services."

Rina took the letter from the man in the bright sunlight. Without her sunglasses, she was momentarily blinded, and she thought the envelope was on fire.

"How can I trust this is for me? It could be for someone else," she said crossly.

"You haven't changed at all, have you? Despite everything you must have gone through," he said, clucking his tongue and looking her up and down.

It took her less than a minute to read the letter. The paper was stained yellow. With a little more time, and a little more rain seeping into the man's bag, the pages would have stuck together. Rina read the letter in silence, then folded it up and put it back in the envelope. Then she rubbed her cheeks with her hands.

"My dear little Show-off," the letter began. In spite of his diffidence, her father seemed to have gone to great lengths to make it safely into the country of P with her mother and brother. It was difficult to tell from the handwriting who had written the letter. The letter told of the political training process that new escapees had to undergo, the entry process that had wounded their pride, and the disappointing settlement funds, which had hardly been as substantial as they had hoped. Her father rode his bicycle to his job as a security guard, and her little brother studied English at a school for young escapees. Then there was the part that said, "You have a room here, we hope you get here soon!" Rina pronounced the word "room" several times, but it didn't mean anything to her, since she'd never had one of her own.

Rina knew that she should show some appreciation, but she didn't know what to say to the man. For some reason, words that expressed gratitude or regret no longer came easily to her. In fact, she was furious.

"Hey, Mr. Missionary, I have no money. Everyone at the factory died in an explosion, and I'm the only one left. And I don't know how you came across this letter, but I don't trust people like you," she said, opening her eyes wide.

"See, this is your problem. This why you're still wandering to this day, without having made your way into P."

There was another silence. Rina was so angry that she felt like biting off her own arm.

"Shit, what would I do there, anyways?!"

Hearing her swear, the man flushed, and grabbed Rina by the shoulders. She shoved him back hard up against the wall. She had no idea where she got the strength.

After parting with the missionary, Rina roamed the streets all night and all day, dragging her heels through the empty city. The building that had once been a hospital now served as a center for the homeless. Rina walked up and down the hospital stairwell talking to herself, and poked her head through what used to be the reception window. The cafeteria, which used to be stacked high with dishes that always slipped and crashed, was empty as well. Rina climbed into a huge nickel dishwashing tub and fell asleep, scrunched up in a ball.

She kept coughing violently, even out in the warm sunlight. She believed that her whole body was rotting away, so she wandered around the city, her eyes welling up with tears. The thumb-sucker followed her around, worried. Rina crossed roads recklessly and stole bicycles that people had parked on the street, and then pushed them off bridges. She went into one of the only fast-food restaurants left, rammed the head of a girl who was eating a hamburger into her tray, and was dragged outside by the employees. The thumb-sucker chased after Rina as she was walking through a dark alleyway in her white sweatsuit. When she fainted, he caught her in his arms.

Rina knew that the letter had actually come from her parents. Only her family knew her child nickname, Show-off, given to her because she hated to lose, and told a lot of tall tales. Rina had always been as good as any boy in academics and athletics. She knew that lying was necessary for a more exciting and fun life. So when she was a child, she lied all the time. She wanted to be an actress on television or on the stage. She hadn't known that life would turn out to be one struggle after another.

Some people were playing soccer in the square. They played at all times of the day. Sometimes they played in yellow dust, and sometimes in muddy rain. But they were also able to enjoy, from time to time, a shower of white pollen on balmy spring nights. Rina would rest her head in the laps of the boys who had been ordered off the field for fouls, boys who sat down with their hearts still thumping from the exertion, and she would think that everything was beautiful in its own way.

While the men played soccer, the women cooked. They would put some meat that had been dried underground into a sack. They would dry steamed rice into little lumps, which they would wrap in plastic, and pour strong liquor into bottles. Wandering had always been a part of their lives, so they travelled with as few belongings as possible, flattened into a bundle. They told Rina that they wore as many layers of clothing as possible, to lighten their loads. When the ball rolled off the field and toward the women, the women would kick the ball back, and sometimes end up joining the game.

Whenever Rina sat staring blankly into the space without talking, the boys told her, "You can speak the language here, and you're so pretty. You should stay. Look at you. You look more like a local than the actual locals." For some reason, this infuriated Rina. She would take off one of her shoes and fling it at the boys.

"So, you're saying I look cheap! I have dreams, too. Don't wake a sleeping lion!" she shouted, laughing.

After reading the letter from her family, she entered the country of P dozens of times in her mind. She was determined to find brokers who helped people get there, but she didn't take any concrete steps.

People sat in the square and drank. The older ones went to sleep early, and the younger ones stayed up late into the night. It had been a while, but Rina had a drink as well. It rushed to her head and she kissed the four boys on their cheeks, put her arms around them, and sang.

"Guys, call me Mom from now on," she told them. The boys laughed at her, saying she was acting silly. Rina, now actually drunk, walked in zigzags, grabbing at people she didn't really know and picking fights with them. The boys hoisted her up onto their shoulders and took her home.

Back at home, Rina felt wide awake. She took out all the money she had and rearranged it, put it in a bundle, and then into an envelope, then tied it up with string. She put the rest of her belongings into a bag. When everything was done, she felt at peace.

The next morning, she wandered around the city in search of Jang, the missionary. She found him at a restaurant. He didn't seem too happy to see her, probably because of what had happened the day before. Rina sat down in front of him and handed him the rectangular bundle of money. The missionary had been eating noodles. He looked pleased.

"You've made your decision. Yes, you should go where your parents are, and get an education, a job, get married." Rina coughed.

"This is in dollars, not the currency of this country. Please get it to my family in P. I know you won't send them all of it. I know what kind of a person you are. You're going to take your cut. That's fine. We'll run into each other someday again, just like we did a while ago. Keep that in mind, and get a letter from my family saying that they got the money. If you don't, I'll kill you. You remember yesterday, don't you? I'm much stronger than you."

The missionary took his chopsticks from the bowl of noodles and set them on the table. He grabbed Rina's hands, pulled them toward him, and began to pray. He asked god to watch over the weary souls of escapees wandering the borderlands of the world, and to protect their rights. He prayed for at least ten minutes, going on and on and about how good shepherds like him staked their lives to care for poor little souls wandering around borders, only to be mistaken for brokers. Rina, too, prayed for the first time in her life, to whoever was up in heaven.

Like a blessing, the yellow dust had lifted, and the sky remained relatively clear for three days. The men played soccer in the square, and the women breastfed their babies. Rina watched the players. When it grew warm, the people began to stretch out and move. One of the four boys read novels all day. Another did nothing but chase girls. The other two played soccer until their faces turned red.

The sun grew more and more intense. Rina could barely keep her eyes open. She thought she would need a new pair of sunglasses to survive the approaching summer, which was sure to be long and hot. She thought of the huge goggles Pii used to wear when he did his welding. She felt she would be able to endure anything if she only had a pair of orange goggles.

RINA

The thumb-sucker made a kick toward the goal and collapsed. People started to yell. His leg had cramped up. Rina snatched a paring knife from one of the women who was packing up next to her, and ran over to the boy. He was kicking and struggling, his face contorted. Rina tried to make a cut in his thigh with the tip of the knife.

"Don't! I don't want it to hurt!" the boy yelled.

"It's all right, it won't hurt. It'll make you feel better soon," Rina said, and plunged the knife into his leg. Dark red blood dripped down from his taut thigh down his leg and into the ground. Rina stared at the blood for a minute without speaking, then walked away.

She walked north. Then she got on a bus to the borderland up north. The bus had a maximum capacity of thirty people, but there were fifty passengers crammed on board. There was a country of nomads to the north of this country. It looked like a slightly crazed rhinoceros on a map, and had once hoped to swallow up the European continent whole. Everyone had told Rina that she wouldn't regret going there; just seeing the proud spirit and vast extent of the land would help her breathe more freely. They told her she'd be able to eat as much mutton as she wanted there. It would give her strength, and she would never get sick.

Apart from everything else, Rina didn't like these escapees who seemed to have set out on their journey as if they were tourists going out to enjoy flowers. Old or young, they all had the same innocence in their faces. As far as Rina could tell, they were reckless people who had never before attempted an escape. Far off in the distance, she saw a herd of sheep with fresh, curly wool headed toward them. Sometimes it rained, after which the pink sun shone through again. It grew increasingly humid, and the flowers and trees on both sides of the road became brighter and more vivid. The people in the bus slept the whole time.

The bus traveled for two days. The scenery outside gradually changed. Sand blew over a meadow on which little children in colorful clothes ran after passing buses until they were out of breath. A man in the group stood in the aisle of the bus and began to talk with a serious expression on his face. He said it would take two more days to reach the border region that led to the country up north. It seemed, up to that point, that he was being serious, but then he said, "Above all, I beg of you, please don't fart on the bus." Everybody laughed.

Fog, rain, and fierce wind came barreling down the road. Rina looked out the hazy window. The bus was entering the highlands, and the road was very crooked. One moment they were on a rainy mountain, and the next, on a sunny plain. The girl sitting next to Rina turned to her.

"Why does everyone here look the same?" she asked. Rina stared blankly at the girl, who looked a little younger than her.

"Why do they all look so expressionless?" the girl asked.

"Think about it," Rina said, cupping the girl's chin in one of her hands. "All of us are either suffering from, or about to contract, fatal diseases that would horrify most doctors. We're very unlucky. Would you look happy?"

After a long while, the bus stopped in front of a group of people in uniforms with guns. They climbed onto the bus. No one understood what they wanted. They seemed to be a minority tribe that lived in the border area. They made a big fuss and got angry when no one reacted. One of them fired his gun into the air. Still, no one reacted, and the men stared meaningfully at the people on the bus, tilting their heads. Soon after, they told everyone on the bus to take all of their belongings outside. To Rina's surprise, they all threw their bundles out the windows, not even bothering to get off the bus.

"Hey, are you all insane? Do you even know how hard it is to cross a border?" Rina tried to reason with them, but no one listened. The armed men took the food, leaving the clothes and everything else by the side of the road, and disappeared into the fog, firing their guns. The people on the bus didn't even look very upset.

They traveled for another whole day. The bus ran up the gentle slope toward the top of the highlands. About halfway up, the driver stopped the bus. People got out to pee, smoke cigarettes, and take in the scenery. The vast city below looked as far off as a strange world they had never visited. Rina picked little flowers growing low to the ground and smelled them. She picked some peculiar-looking plants, put them in her mouth, and chewed on them.

That night, the people built a fire in a corner of the cozy plain and sat around it, taking turns talking about their past lives. They said that they were sick and tired of living, and sick and tired of the yellow dust as well. They all wanted to cross the border and build a country of their own.

All night, they drank and danced and laughed loudly. Their mouths were laughing, but their eyes were full of tears. They kissed and comforted one another with awkward gestures. Rina sat in a tent, wrapped in a blanket, and watched them frolic. The blue sky crept higher and higher, as if trying to run far away, and white stars fell from the sky. Rina looked up at the sky and the white stars, then down at the people. She grew tired, and sleep washed over her. When she opened her eyes, she noticed that the ground on which people were dancing had cracked wide open. She came to her senses and looked up at the sky, then back at the people. It seemed that the cracked part was going to split off from the rest of the ground, carrying the people away.

The next afternoon, Rina managed to hitch a ride on a truck transporting a heap of wire netting. It let her off in the northern border area. There were no buses, no people, not even any smells; it was as unfamiliar as a place that existed only in pictures. A wind as soft as cotton swabs came blowing in from somewhere on the dry

261

plain. It carried no yellow dust, no chilly draft, and was as gentle as could be.

Standing before the border was a watchhouse the size of a matchbox, and in front of the checkpoint, a little desk. The dark shadows stretched out, enveloping half of the border area. Rina's heart began to thump, and she had trouble breathing. She pressed her left chest with one hand, and dropped to the ground. Then she re-tied her shoelaces, and walked forward.

When she arrived at the checkpoint, she opened her mouth wide and heaved a deep breath toward the half-darkened plain. A soldier carrying a gun came slowly out of the watchhouse and sat down at the desk, crossing his legs. He and Rina looked at each other for a long time. The soldier's sunburned face was so smooth that she couldn't discern his features. Before she realized what she was doing, Rina bowed. He raised a hand and gestured for her to approach him.

Rina hastily took out her money. The soldier opened the desk drawer and took out a faded piece of paper and a pen. He wrote something that looked like hieroglyphs on Rina's false documents.

"What country are you from?" he asked. Rina rubbed her toes against the ground. She felt sixteen all over again.

"Why are you swaying? Stop moving, and speak up, where are you from?" the soldier asked again. He didn't, however, talk down to her, or make her get down on her knees and sing, like others had in the past.

I was born in a little country to the east of this border. I tried to get into the nation of P, which was known as a land of prosperity completely different from ours, though the people there speak the same language as we do back at home. I crossed the border into this country. At first I went west, then southeast, then northeast, which was where I had started. How far did I walk? How old do I look? The industrial complex was destroyed, but the people there still built houses, raised walls, and brought telephones with broken

Rina

cords. They wanted to stay until the day they died. I want to get to the northern country beyond this border.

Rina moved her lips, but she couldn't get the words out. Several minutes passed, and the soldier took a map out of the desk drawer and spread it out before him. With her finger, Rina traced on the tattered map the paths she had taken so far. The soldier followed the trail with his eyes as she drew a circle around the large continent.

"You sure took the long way around," the soldier said, and stamped the fake ID. He handed Rina her money back. A confused look came over her face, as if she wasn't sure if she should cry.

"Are you hungry?" the soldier asked. Rina just stood there, fingering her money.

"You're thirsty, aren't you?" He went into the watchhouse and came out with a large bottle and a glass. He poured the contents of the bottle into the glass, then went back inside and brought out a small wooden chair.

"Have a drink. This place will be swarming with escapees any minute now, so you won't have a chance. It's dangerous to go it alone, so you should wait for the others to get here. Timing is the most important thing. This is the perfect time for a drink. This is the best time of the day. I've got a good job here. It's quiet."

She took a sip and rocked back and forth in the wooden chair. The wind that blew against her face was chilly. Hungry, Rina emptied the rest of the glass in one gulp. Fatigue washed over her whole body. The shadows stretched out over the plain in the distance. It looked as though the border beyond was about to come rushing toward her, like an unbroken levee. Rina rubbed her eyes and look again. It was nothing more than a plain old horizon.

Rina untied her shoelaces, took her shoes off, and walked barefoot out onto the middle of the plain. She took off her clothes as she walked. Only the birds flying across the border watched her, who was naked save for her orange safety goggles. As Rina walked to the middle of the plain, the birds followed, flying low.

She lay down in the overgrown grass. She felt the roughness of the dry grass and the dampness of the red soil in her hair and on her buttocks. Luckily, the thick grass wasn't prickly. A big black bird perched next to Rina and looked out onto the plain, as though to protect her.

"I always worried, what if I die on the border, naked like this? Who will take care of my body if I die on the border without a name, without a nationality?" she asked the bird tenderly. The bird nodded, but this had nothing to do with what Rina had just said.

The world was so still that Rina noticed a white ring around the moon. The sky moved farther and farther away, and Rina's body seemed to be sinking deeper and deeper into the ground. She hid in her grassy spot, tears streaming out of her eyes, but she opened her mouth wide and laughed, feeling refreshed, as though a huge weight had been lifted from her mind.

Night came. The escapees, their faces worn from exhaustion, but with sparkling eyes, came flocking to the border. The truck that delivered food to the border checkpoint arrived. The night shift soldiers came to relieve their colleagues and changed into their uniforms, joking around and laughing easily.

Savage beasts roamed the border, their eyes sparkling like diamonds in the dark. The soldiers shot at them from time to time. The sound of gunfire pierced the hearts of the escapees, not the skulls of the beasts, and the border area grew darker. All of the escapees were busy getting their IDs stamped. Rina glanced furtively at the people over the soldiers' heads. Everyone had a story to tell. But no matter what she heard, it seemed that no one had been as unfortunate as she, who had been to every corner of the country.

Rina tightened her shoelaces. The others didn't seem nervous or afraid. They just waited quietly until they were told to get up and go. The soldiers came out and signaled to them. They had to walk briskly until they could no longer see the light from the checkpoint behind them.

"My thighs will get thick again. Well, all I've got are my strong legs," Rina mumbled to herself, and finally, the wide border, rushing toward them like waves past the darkness in the distance, came into view. When she stood on the border again, everything became clear.

When she'd walked for quite some time, Rina turned around and looked back at the path she'd come along. She saw twenty-two escapees in a single file on the plain, walking toward the border. The three families and the sewing factory workers were all alive and well. The baby who had died in the woods was alive; and the girl from the factory and the old man who had died in the chemical plant were all still alive, too. At the end of the line were the sewing factory girl, her baby, and her Arab husband. Rina waved at them.

After a moment, she turned around and looked again. The twenty-two escapees were no longer there. Once again, Rina began to run toward the border, spread out like a blue levee before her.

CRITICAL COMMENTARY: A POSTMODERN EPIC

Open paragraph   It was the first day   period   She had come from a far   period   tonight at dinner   comma   the families would ask comma   open quotation marks   How was the first day interrogation mark   close quotation marks   at least to say the least of it possible comma   the answer would be   open quotation marks   there is but one thing   period   There is someone   period   From a far   period close quotation marks

—Theresa Hak Kyung Cha, *Dictee*

NEVER-ENDING EPISODES BETWEEN "BORDER" AND "BORDER"

When I opened my eyes I was lying in front of a human trafficker. He said to me, how did you end up here? Can you tell me? That's the only way I can set you free. He said he liked fairy tales. So I told him stories every night. Stories of crossing the border, of splitting

my shoes open. He enjoyed them. I asked him to let
me see that man. That I hadn't even spent the night
with him. And then he said if you tell me lots of good
stories, I'll let you see him. And so I lied every day. So
I could get my first night with the man I loved.

Thus confesses Rina, who has become a singer in a tent in a city
of drugs and tourism—that only "lies" will free her, that she has to
tell these "lies" in order to find the person she loves, no, rather, the
person who sold her. Faced with a human trafficker, Rina becomes a
Scheherazade who must, and does, tell fairy tales every night. Since
these are stories and lies, the story of Rina's escape is constantly being
changed or distorted for the sake of a neat ending. More specifically,
these fairy tales are constituted of Rina's journey toward the border.
Must Rina's adventures continue in order for her to cross borders?
Or are the borders dragged into the narrative so that Rina can tell
her stories? The narrative singularity of *Rina* as a whole is that it can
be condensed as "a story or a lie that can be modified or distorted."

Still, Rina had no doubt that the border, which
hovered before her like a vast blue levee, would open
itself up for her. The blue levee would flow toward
her like a colossal wave and open up like a stairway
to heaven. She believed that an invisible hand would
gather up the escapees safely in a net and magically
usher them across the border. [. . .]

After a moment, she turned around and looked again.
The twenty-two escapees were no longer there. Once
again, Rina began to run toward the border, spread
out like a blue levee before her. (264)

Kang Young-sook's first full-length novel *Rina* begins and ends
before a "border, spread out like a blue levee." In ending in front

of the very border at which it opened, *Rina* is a profoundly tragic novel that alludes to an ultimately inescapable existential bleakness. Interestingly, however, the work itself never wallows in a sense of grief, nor does it attempt to suppress a sense of life's overwhelming tragedy. What we do get between the endless stretches between border and border are incidents that unfurl at a breathless pace, unexpected twists, and human throngs that appear and vanish without ceremony. The novel is filled with so-called unethical and amoral scenes that involve theft and pickpocketing, prostitution and rape, murder and the criminal disposal of dead bodies, and human trafficking, yet *Rina* is not a cruel or heartless work.

What is unique about the countless episodes that make up *Rina* is the lack of continuity between them. If we were to compare *Rina* to a "full-time" dramatic performance, during which thousands of episodes occur onstage for the duration of the performance, this work leaves no lingering imagery that speaks to what episode might follow. *Rina* is made up of episodes that begin with transitional opening words that mark a sense of coincidence, such as "And then," or "Suddenly," and it refuses to be reduced to a single significance outside of the myriad unavoidable incidents and calamities.

It is, however, in this mountain of never-ending episodes that are connected only by "And then" and "Suddenly," that we can locate the author's unique style of managing narrative, which involves the integration of disparate narrative layers in such a way that distorts a conventional sense of lateral chronological progression and vertical plot development. The leitmotif of "crossing the border" may be the narrative force that permeates the work as a whole, but *Rina* has little to do with the nuances, scenes, and moods that we typically associate with the border escape genre. Fully predictable episodes—prostitution for survival, murder, rape—are unpredictably intertwined, and "poor" countries are portrayed through an indiscriminate amalgam of distinctive scenes and well-known conventions.

The diegetic world of *Rina* revolves around the latter terms that make up the binaries of urban/rural, civilized/primitive, central/peripheral, man-made/natural; and builds itself up through the accumulation of these various worlds—it is a world concretized through the layering and overlapping of these heterogeneous images. According to the internal escape route of the novel, Rina's party traverses several nations that act as third parties to the first third-party nation that they must travel through to eventually get to the country of P. Yet the novel does not end with the closure of the escape route. The specific places, sights, and sounds that make up the diegetic world naturally conjure up real-life counterparts in the reader's mind—people trying to escape to a neighboring country that shares the same language as their own while operating on completely different political ideals, rural villages with vast fields and paddies and black cows wandering among houses, cities that can be summarized in the descriptions of the vast fleets of bicycles with which they are overrun, villages where people only drink bitter tea and eat so much rice per meal that the grains seem like they could be blown away with the slightest puff of air, free economic zones filled with giant industrial complexes, whores that are beaten to death by migrant workers.

The contours of reality become increasingly confused and blurred as the novel's realistic language offers up a tangled mass of images describing the escape route, the country that everyone is fleeing, and the countries they must travel through—all of which can be reconstituted on an abstract level. The process through which the world of *Rina* is constructed relies on the relationship of the distinction between "~ and ~", to the time it takes for the reader to question the lucidity of that distinction, or the slash (/). By penetrating the gap between banality and originality as a method of transformation and distortion, Kang Young-sook creates a peculiar territory for scenes that are unfamiliar yet familiar, neither unfamiliar nor familiar. The incidents that befall the characters of

Rina are terrifying yet cheerful nomadic adventure tales, escape narratives that are not really escape narratives, but rather a bundle of episodes. The bundle of never-ending lies or stories told by Rina/Scheherazade is what constitutes *Rina*.

A POSTMODERN EPIC, A NARRATIVE OF EXCESSIVE RELEASE

From Kang Young-sook's perspective, life is nothing but a trifle, made up of banal details. What does make moments of life interesting from time to time are its small, unpredictable chance events. It makes sense, then, that *Rina*, a collection of banal and petty episodes, becomes a novel this way. This is also why the escape or adventure genre specifics of *Rina*—i.e., "what happened on these adventures"—are not particularly important. *Rina* is a novel filled with a superfluity of narrative and detail that is unnecessary to the world of fiction that we have come to expect, the world of the "colossal maybe."

> If Kang's novel sometimes comes off as impenetrable and incomprehensible, it may be due to the abundance of seemingly unnecessary details and items, and this is perhaps an unexpected framework in which to locate the second of the author's operational tricks. Kang has stated that she "wanted to portray a person faced with the whole of life, and to use a style of writing that would cool down the violent and heated narrative" (*Every Day is a Celebration*, 2004), which gives us some insight into how she captures a sense of our present reality. More specifically, the author latches onto reality so closely that the lack of distance compels

us to perceive the familiar from a novel angle. This technique invokes the present in unfamiliar forms and thereby confuses our sense of the novelistic plot. Even though we live in a postmodern era in which it is impossible to experience anything wholly new or confront reality as a whole, it is thus that we bizarrely encounter the scene in which the narrative impulse is restored.

The very experience of encountering the narrative impulse, which is in itself old and worn, is a rare and valuable experience, and we must pay attention to the reality that has been captured by that narrative impulse, which is out of harmony with our time. As the irony of the realistic details implies, the persistent narrative impulse that is present in *Rina* actually makes all situations of reality opaque and ambiguous. The more we try to draw out a consistent escape narrative, the more powerfully *Rina* confirms the simple fact that nothing is fixed and unchanging. The border is no exception. Even though *Rina* begins and ends at the border, the border remains just another symbol that slides through signification. The border—or perhaps the life that lies beyond the border (or the promise of it)—may have the power to transform an otherwise contemptible life in the blink of an eye, but in actuality, the border is just "part of a hilly path, blocked from all sides without an escape route." It may be the border that spreads itself out like a hallucination in the rapturous moment that Rina and Pii make love—albeit through the channels of prostitution—but, as the close of the novel confirms, the border is still a blue hope spread out in the distance, as well as a mirage-like disillusionment that cannot be crossed even after the most roundabout of detours.

Rina tumbled down the steep embankment and joined one of the older girls from the sewing factory who was squatting with her bare buttocks exposed. Both of the girls were pitifully bony, but neither was ashamed. Rina pinched the girl's butt cheek and they both giggled. As she shook herself off after peeing, a blade of grass grazed Rina down below. It felt like the tickling of raindrops on her face, and a shiver coursed through her entire body.

If the only aspect of the border we can pinpoint is that it has no rules or regulations, or that the rules and regulations change each time, *Rina* ultimately snatches up—regardless of authorial intention—precisely that postmodern reality that resists signification and analysis. As we can see in the above quotation, *Rina* captures the girlish playfulness and the heterogeneity of the physical senses that surface even in moments when the characters are without a guide and being transported along a precarious escape route by a driver who doesn't speak their language. Of course, these passages may not smoothly correspond to the urgency of the situations in which the fugitives find themselves, and they are perhaps simply not necessary to the narrative. Regardless, one thing we can be sure of is that *Rina* remains completely free of value judgments regarding which is more important—the anxiety of an escape tale, or a tone of girlish playfulness. By breaking free of the epistemological boundaries of meaningful and un-meaningful to strip away meaning itself, this deferral of judgment is tantamount to a Derridean encapsulation of textual reality, and it contains a postmodern destructuralizing move that annihilates the value hierarchy between inside and outside.

Between border and border lies either nothing or the universe itself, and there is no hierarchy established among the escape narrative and its offshoots. *Rina* is simply a point of intersection of heterogeneous values, or a collection of their successive occurrences. This is why, when we attempt to analyze *Rina* based on a consistent narrative, we find ourselves simply repeating the adventure stories. It is because *Rina* rejects conclusive meaning or a clear plot, and through its "releasing" of excessive narrative demands an alternative kind of reading. What Kang Young-sook is telling us through *Rina* is that everything flows by without being signified. Nothing remains of reality except for this fact. Because the world of the novel is not particularly different from the real world, the space of the novel allows for an entanglement of inside and outside the novel. This is precisely the true nature of reality in the postmodern era.

RINA—EMPTY, PUSHED OUT, AND WANDERING

Rina is most certainly a novel about and for Rina. But *Rina* is also a novel that has nothing to do with the specific character named Rina. In the same way that the border is a symbol that rejects signification, Rina is a symbol that points to the quintessence of opaque ambiguity. In order for *Rina* to be summarized as a coming-of-age narrative, for the Rina standing in front of the border to become a starting point for bringing up diasporic problems, Rina's adventures must be integrated into questions of her identity. When the uncertain and vague spaces and times that have "already left/yet to settle" return to Rina herself in the form of questions of identity that are filled with confusion and also the foundation of a baseless existence, the network of innumerable offshoot episodes form a patent network centered on Rina. However, the profile of Rina that we are given at the beginning of the novel—"She was short, and had a thin face with yellow pimples on her forehead. Rina was sixteen years old, and her parents had been coalminers back home"—is simply an example of the impoverished and wretched (young girls) who are unable "to decide which was worse: spending the rest of her life in a cramped house in a mining town pockmarked with graying linens drying on laundry lines, or getting a taste of life abroad, even if it meant becoming a whore," rather than a specific description of this character called "Rina."

It is impossible to find any kind of contemplation of Rina's identity in the novel that is named for her. This is, of course, because of the uncertainty of the border, which remains inconsistent and unfixed, and the irrelevance of the infinite episodes that fill *Rina*. But at a more fundamental level, this has to do with the fact that Rina is a being who is crowded out and broken off, and left wandering. As Julia Kristeva elaborates through the term "abjection"—the name she gave to that which is forcefully expelled in the process of suturing together self-identity—it is not the space filled with disaster, the space that has been divided and folded over, that renders uneasy the expelled and the excluded, but rather the homogenous space that has been unified and combined. This is why the abject entity, rather than being self-aware, desirous, or belonging, is pushed aside or broken off and left wandering.[2]

Rina is an empty cypher, and more than anything, a character that does not develop over the course of the episodes she undergoes. In spite of her innumerable adventures, Rina does not accumulate experience. There are no instances in the novel in which the extracts of previous experiences are used to resolve later issues. Through her experiences of escaping, being driven out, sold and re-sold, Rina experiences, down to the very depths of her actual person, the properties of multinational and a-national capital, but as she passes through these experiences, all that happens to her is that she

---

2 Julia Kristeva, *Powers of Horror*, trans. Min Won Seo (Seoul: Changbi Press, 2001), 23-30.

becomes, slowly and little by little, hardened. This is because Rina, as a wandering entity that is pushed about by forces she does not control, is forced to ask "Where am I?" rather than "Who am I?" Frankly speaking, Rina's own parents wouldn't miss her if she was abducted or executed by firing squad while crossing the border. At least, this is how Rina understands her situation.

Then, why Rina? More specifically, why is it that the entity that is pushed out and around must be a girl? Why must *Rina* unfold around a skinny, diminutive girl? Why must the girl continue her journey/adventure toward the border?

> I wanted to be in the middle, belonging neither on this side nor that, neither man nor woman.[32]

Kang Young-sook's writing, including her autobiographical "The Era of the Giant," which treats the matter more directly, has always shown a tendency to do away with stereotypes and traverse the binaries they set up. It is clear this impulse is at the root of her selection of a girl for the protagonist of *Rina*.[43] This is not entirely unrelated to the interest in sisterhood or female camaraderie that Kang Young-sook's body of work has displayed from the beginning of her career, and this is where we find Kang Young-sook's last trick. That which impels Rina to "escape/move" is made up of at least three layers, and it is through these overlapping impetuses that *Rina* pushes the reader to extremes where it is impossible to rely on the dichotomous structures of good/evil and right/wrong.

On the surface, Rina is the one who is buffeted about from place to place, wandering or "escaping/moving" all throughout *Rina*, while

---

3 Young-sook Kang, "The Era of the Giant." *Black in Red* (Seoul: Munhankdongnae, 2009), 246.

4 In this sense, Rina slips in between orders, acts, ages, and sexes, thereby evoking the image of an entity that exists "in-between" or as an interlude that acts as a creative bloc, much in the Deleuzian sense of the term "girl" (524-526). Gilles Deleuze and Felix Guattari, A *Thousand Plateaus*, trans. Jae In Kim (Seoul: Saemulgyul, 2001).

the space and time of the novel moves in direct correspondence to Rina and her party. But what makes Rina and her party's movement possible, that is to say, the foundation of what makes them move, is paradoxically money, or a logic of exchange that is represented by money. "Like everyone else, the first thing [the brokers] demanded was money," and it is this logic of money that reveals its suggestiveness at its most extreme in scenes of human trafficking, themselves consolidated moments of the process of commodification. As Claude Lévi-Strauss has pointed out, the exchange of women stemming from the incest taboo was the first form of trade in which women were commercialized and objectified, and the first exchange logic that substituted a woman with an object. The guides that facilitate the escapes, the soldiers/policemen that prevent the escapes, Producer Kim and Missionary Jang—all conspire not out of personal greed or cruelty, but because they move according to the logic of capital that uses currency to quantify and make interchangeable.

Of course, this is not the outermost layer of logic surrounding the "escape/move" of Rina and her party. The logic of capital as the potential for exchange and the potential for measurement has been closely examined in many modern novels, and is not a particularly new idea.

> "Everyone, even the biggest idiot, will face three challenges in her lifetime for which she will stake her life. When those three challenges are over, so is your life."

And here we have what one of Rina's ancient aunties said, a trite quotation that shakes up, on a different level, the world in which everything is interchangeable through money. As the single layers of single logics shore up *Rina* on various different levels, the power that supports reality becomes diffused across innumerable layers that cannot be consolidated, then released into a void of meaning.

Rina's character does not belong to the several layers, but neither is she captured in her entirety through a multilayered complex logic. Rina does not show a sense of belonging at any point of her journey. Therefore, in *Rina*, strictly speaking, there are no escapes for which people put their lives on the line. Rina's escape is a realization of her own free will in that she voluntarily gives up the opportunity to reunite with her family and travel to the country of P, but she is also "an entity that is sold" by the betrayal and deception of those (men) in her life, perhaps, even, sold of her own volition. The only foundation that remains consistent throughout this journey is her readiness to accept everything that happens to her.

Thus, the individual factors that constitute Rina reveal the instability of reality and the transience of its nature. What we discover in *Rina*, which is a result of the postmodern narrative impulse, is not just the female protagonist Rina, but also our unsummarized reality today, a world evoked by Rina's adventures. I would like to emphasize that *Rina* doesn't exist because of Rina, but it is rather because of the countless episodes and offshoots that *Rina* is *Rina*. Of course, the same goes for the character Rina. Is it problematic, then, that Rina denies the patriarchal world represented by the title of father-mother to bond with the old woman, who is of an older generation, thereby skipping over the sequence of the steps of becoming-woman, or that she is not naively ignorant of the steps of becoming-woman or the secrets of sex, but rather cuts across borders and logics of prohibition?

A NOVEL OF THE BODY—CRUMBLING BOUNDARIES

Rina is a novel of the body. Strictly speaking, it is not a story about the body, but a story through the body. In *Rina*, the passage of time or the itinerary of a journey is perceived through the body in the passage of seasons, or changes in the weather that are felt by the flesh, in moments like those "When Rina's bottom had become so numb that it no longer seemed to be a part of her own body." "The pain she experienced on the field of salt" stays vividly with Rina far longer than the memory of the long and arduous escape itself, and the never-ending journey leaves its mark on Rina's "thighs, which had become as solid as rock."

> With his lips and his fingers, Pii drew all over Rina's body the things he had wanted to tell her but didn't know how to in her language. Through her body, Rina heard his story, from his birth to how he ended up at the chemical plant, and she understood. It became light inside her head and the cramped walls of the room fell away so that the blue border stretched out at the other end of the sky rushed up toward her. When that blue levee rushed toward Rina like a tidal wave, her pelvis opened up infinitely and a strange voice that she'd never heard came spilling out of Pii's mouth. [. . .]

> On their way back to the industrial complex, the four girls sat jammed in the backseat, staring out the windows in silence. They could smell each other's bodies and hear the sound of their own breathing, like a sobbing that came from somewhere deep within. They may not have lived very long, but they were overcome with a sense of sadness at the fact that they were crammed into the narrow backseat of a car among strangers. You couldn't hear it, but they were all chanting in unison *I am being sold, sold.* The memories of their short lives that surged up within them were hard to cope with, and while no one said anything, each felt as if her heart would burst.

These girls from different countries, who cannot communicate verbally with each other, can hear each other's stories through their bodies. Likewise, the gloom of crossing borders, the grisliness of the gas leak, the trials of being sold as merchandise, the acute pain of hunger—all of these experiences are gathered up and released through the sounds of weeping or the odors emanating from bodies. The comment *"I guess I'm too spoiled now"* is Rina tempering herself, and is not unrelated to the fact that the hunger that cannot be filled by transforming The Puzzle into a women's utopia and turning huge profits is expressed as the unbearable aching of an empty stomach.

To sum up, the characters' interiorities, emotional changes, and their ways of forging relationships with others is revealed and communicated through their physical senses. The body is not only a way to experience reality but a starting point from which to understand humanity. Because the novel focuses on the hidden expressions of the body in its treatment of social or artificial relationships, even the soldiers, whose job it is to ferret out the escapees, are neither threatening nor antagonistic; even as they level their guns at the escapees, "they too had hunger written all over their faces," and these delicate observations capture this undeniable connection. How else would we explain the fact that Rina sometimes misses Missionary Jang, who conspired with Producer Kim to deceive and sell her? After all, "he looked just as hungry as everyone else."

The men in *Rina* exploit women for labor and sexually abuse them. Because the perpetrators of human trafficking are typically young men, there is a strong tendency toward sisterhood or female solidarity in *Rina*. As we can see in the moments when Rina commits unplanned murders (that of the neatly square man, or of the owners of The Puzzle, for example), male defamations of women, especially on the level of "the violation of chastity" are dealt fairly thorough punishments. In this sense, there is a clearly hostile and irreconcilable oppositional structure defined by a gender division. But this oppositional structure is not borne out through the end of the novel. Even the issues surrounding sexual identity cannot be reduced to the oppositional structure of man versus woman. From a perspective of bodily senses, that boundary is a fluid one that can be collapsed at any time.

The pain of others that can be detected through the bodily senses is ironically the sole link connecting individuals to each other. While they may not be able to share their pain, they can share the bodily perception of each other's pain. Although the method of sharing can be very individual, disparate, and therefore temporary, the body is the sole path to gaining comfort and consolation for the author and for the young female characters who live in a world without hope. Bodily senses like hunger or odor breakdown the hostile dichotomy between exploiter and victim in the blink of an eye and shake the foundations of our common-sense understanding. In *Rina*, sharing the bodily senses is a powerful enough experience to annihilate the distinction between the self and the other or the enemy.

"BEDLAM" IN A PLACE THAT IS NOT A "BAD RED-LIGHT DISTRICT" BUT A "WHORE-TOWN NONETHELESS"

Nevertheless, according to *Rina*, "life meant looking at the neatly square man her whole life, listening to his two-syllable word her whole life, having a baby on a festival day and killing it with her own hands." The reality in which we live is perhaps, like Shi-ling, not (considered) a "bad red-light district" but "a whore-town nonetheless," a hell of lesser evils. Even though Rina can share of moments of happiness with Pii, who has left his family behind, the reality is that she cannot travel back against the current of time, in the same way that her feet can never "go back to not being covered in scars." What Rina has learned from her detours in many countries is the tragic lesson that no matter how far she travels, the place she has left behind is not very different from the place that awaits her—this is a cross section of the author's cold assessment of the hopelessness of both the present and the future.

The first victims of the onslaught of catastrophes are always the weak—children, girls, women, workers. The chemical plant workers who ignore Rina's cries of "'You're all free now. Get up! Get out of here!'" only to hunker deeper down in their sleep do so because they know that, wherever they are, they will inevitably fall victim to some sort of catastrophe or another. They must bear even the most wretched scenes with which they are faced. The question "'And where would it be safe for you?'" that the guide asks Rina and her twenty-one initial companions is a question not just for Rina, but for all of the disenfranchised, and it is one that forces us to look into and confront those entities that live a sad and inescapable life without the hope of settlement, without even the hope of hopelessness.

The virtue of *Rina* is that, while it displays a levelheaded awareness of the cold reality, it refuses to simply be disheartened or to embrace an escapist optimism. Rather, the author is interested in constantly cutting across the line of demarcation and the fundamental prohibitions that come with the structure of dichotomy, each time creating a "bedlam," and in doing so, peeping—with great difficulty—at a possibility of hope that is so minute and subtle that it is invisible to the naked eye. The detours that Rina must take to get to the country of P are therefore not just detours, but rather ends in themselves, the author's presentation of hope as a "festival every day" that can be obtained solely in wandering, in remaining un-settled.

Along with the fact that the space and time as experienced through the body in Kang Young-sook's novel frequently takes the form of "festival," the old woman formerly a singer who accompanies Rina on her escape journey—or rather, whom Rina wished to have with her until the end of her journey—puts on performances of a highly festive nature.

> The people gradually got excited and stood up. Someone lit a stick of incense and placed it in front of the singer, and someone else played an erratic song on a two-stringed homemade instrument. A woman got up and wandered around the audience, waving her hands in the air. The singer's voice fluctuated with the audience's reactions. Her voice was as unsteady as the wind that wandered across the plains, and at times, it seemed like her throat might start to bleed. As the fluctuations in her voice became greater, the white makeup on her singer's face became splotchy with sweat. The atmosphere in the tent ripened. A man with a crew cut came out and clasped the singer's knees and wept. Others followed suit, murmuring about all of the unjust things that had happened to them. As the singer's voice rose, the people began to sway aimlessly or droop to the ground, clinging to their neighbors' sleeves.

As we can tell from this scene that depicts the tent performance as simultaneously an elegiac exorcism and a religious catharsis, the old woman's and Rina's performances act as loci of purification where both the performers and the spectators can regurgitate their sadness, their pain, and their remorse. So, when Rina takes on the old singer's work, she also inherits a foresight with which she detects a new world, and expresses it through the low voice and the moderate tempo with which she consoles her fans' souls. These performances, or the various festivals that Rina experiences are often proposals of marriage, births or funerals, or requiems—

events that open up a new world by traversing the divided paths of life and death.

What Kang Young-sook wants to emphasize through Rina is then perhaps a faithfulness to the "now" and the value of living the moment as a way of taking brief respite from an endless wandering without settling. The motif of shoes, which crops up often throughout the novel, illustrates this. It may be more important to detect the bodily perception of what may only amount to a "moment" in our lives, rather than to brood on the possibilities of a dark future or ruminate on past time. For example, let us consider a pair of dowdy and coarse handmade slippers with beads on them, and how useless they are in an escape situation. If we step out of the practical logic of questioning whether or not the shoes fit or are sturdy enough, these shoes may be absolutely necessary in those moments when Rina is taking a moment somewhere to watch a sunset, or wishing to feel the wind and the air in a moment when she has become old and peaceful. Even if mankind is fated to struggle to escape an inescapable destiny, or rather, even if there are no other paths to take than that of never-ending escape, as long as we don't forget that escape is a way of life on the border, wouldn't a few such pairs of shoes be necessary for the moment of repose that may one day arrive, or for this very moment in which we dream of the arrival of that day?

Of course, the writer is not arguing that such moments are unrivaled spaces into which we must settle. Nevertheless, by traversing countless lines of demarcation marked off by common sense and frameworks of prohibition, Kang Young-sook realizes the construction of her world and thereby seeks to emphasize through Rina's escape journey the importance of moments of "brief respite" and the value of "feeling" those moments through one's body. When the Rinas of the world stand in front of the border without a fear of change or the ambition to settle down, Kang Young-sook is arguing that the most important thing is "timing" and the "now." The value of this observation comes from the author's deliberate attempt to delve into a complex and deep reality in a complex and deep way. If a general and epic recognition of the world is still possible in a postmodern era, it would probably look something like this.

So Young Hyun

KANG YOUNG-SOOK is the author of four novels, including the award-winning Rina, and five short story collections. She often writes about the female grotesque, delving into varying genres as urban noir, fantasy, and ecofiction. Since her debut in 1998, she has received numerous awards, such as the Hanguk Ilbo Literature Prize, Kim Yujeong Literary Award, and Lee Hyo-seok Literature Award, among others. She was most recently a resident at the National Centre for Writing, and currently teaches creative writing at Ewha Womans University and Korea National University of Arts.

BORAM CLAIRE KIM is a translator and writer based in San Diego and Seoul. She studied at Johns Hopkins University and Seoul National University before receiving her PhD in English literature from UCLA. Her work has been recognized by the Literature Translation Institute of Korea and published in the *LA Revicw of Books*.

Printed in the USA
CPSIA information can be obtained
at www.ICGtesting.com
JSHW022335030624
64248JS00003B/3

9 781960 385086